Enchanted by Love

A Blossom Hills Romance, Volume 3

Kate Alexander

Published by A Blossom Hills Romance, 2021.

ENCHANTED BY LOVE

First edition. April 11, 2021.

Written by Kate Alexander.

This book is dedicated to those who still believe in fairy tales and true love. You all inspire me.

Prologue

Ariel was sitting under a pine tree in the woods just a few blocks from her house, hoping someone would find her. Her pretty white pants were ripped with a hole in the knee and her pale-pink, ruffled top was covered in mud. She had gotten into a fight with her brother, Derek. He wouldn't let her play with him and his new friend, Kyle, so she took off on her bike, not wanting them to see her cry. Now, she was sitting under this pine tree with her bicycle on the ground beside her and the chain dangling on one gear.

She was crying so hard when she pedaled away, and she just wanted to hide at her favorite spot in the woods. Normally, she would have left her bike at the edge of the woods and walked to the clearing, but she didn't want anyone to find her. What she didn't realize was that her fancy pink bike wasn't meant for rough terrain. She hit a hole, causing her and the bike to flip; and she landed on her arm with a loud cracking sound. Now here she was, hurt, her bike was broken, and it was starting to rain.

Ariel called out to the empty forest for help, but no one was answering. Knots formed in her stomach since she wasn't even sure if her mom and dad knew she'd left the house, and they may not even look for her until dinnertime.

Pain shot through her arm as she tried to pull herself up and the world started spinning. Looking at her arm, she started to cry. Stupid brother. It was all his fault. She wouldn't have run away if he just would have let her hang out with them. Sure, she was only nine and he was twelve, but she was just as smart as he was... maybe even smarter. He was just a dumb boy who liked to play sports, but he was really good at them.

Derek's new friend wasn't like the other boys their age. He was nice to Ariel and never seemed to mind when she wanted to hang out with them. He even talked to her at school, unlike most of the kids in her class. They always made fun of how she liked to dress in pretty clothes, and that her name was the same as a cartoon mermaid. She hated her name. It wasn't her parent's fault, though. They named her Ariel a couple of years before the movie was released; it was just her dumb luck is all. The kids in her class loved to call her Princess and didn't want to play with her. Her mom said that it would get better, and things would change. Maybe they would change, but not soon enough for Ariel. Kyle was different. She'd first met him when he came over to play basketball with Derek. He didn't ignore her and even took time to show her how to dribble the ball better. Her stupid brother only showed her once, and got mad when she took too long to learn.

Ariel gazed down at her arm and realized that she wouldn't get to play with the boys now for sure. She couldn't move it at all. Crying out for help again, she still got no reply. She wasn't sure how long she was sitting against the tree, but she knew it had to be at least a couple hours, because it was getting dark and cold. Finally, she thought that she heard her name being called, but it was pretty far away.

"Hello? Can you hear me?"

Nothing. No more echoing cries for her name. She thought that she must have been hearing things, but then a beam of light flashed between the trees.

"Ariel!"

"Hello! I'm down here!" As footsteps rushed towards her, she cried out a happy little squeaking gasp.

"Ariel. I'm coming!"

Ariel couldn't see the person behind the flashlight, but she knew it wasn't an adult. After a few steps, she saw Kyle's relieved face as he dropped the flashlight beam to the ground.

"Kyle! You found me."

Kyle leaned down and appeared to be looking at her now bloodied knee and dirt covered clothes. "Are you okay? You look kind of banged up."

The tears started to flow now, and Ariel couldn't stop. All her feelings of panic and pain flooded into her at once. "I hit a hole and broke my bike. I can't move my arm or stand up."

Kyle moved the flashlight, and she watched him as he looked at her twisted arm. "That looks broken. It kinda looks like my arm did when I broke it wrestling with my brother." He seemed to be thinking for a moment and looked over at the bike. "If you can sit on the bike, I could roll you back to your house."

Ariel shook her head. "The chain came off and the wheels are stuck."

Kyle tugged at his ear, looking as if he was trying to come up with a new idea. "Okay. Let me go get my mom's garden wagon. We live on the next street over, just outside the woods. It has big wheels, and we should be able to pull you out of here. It will be like your own personal princess carriage."

In between her sniffles and hiccupping sobs Ariel whispered, "I'm not a princess."

Kyle frowned. "Oh. How about just being my princess then?"

Ariel gazed into Kyle's sky-blue eyes. She was looking to see if he was making fun of her too, but she didn't see the mean intent that she saw with so many others. "Would that make you my prince?"

Kyle smiled and nodded. "Yup, and this would be our enchanted tree. This could be the place we could always come to find each other, no matter how lost we are. Does that sound good?"

Ariel nodded. "Yes."

"I'm going to leave you here to get the wagon, and I will be right back, okay?"

"Okay, but please hurry."

"I promise, my princess," he responded with a small bow.

Ariel watched him walk away and the beam of light grew dimmer with each step, putting distance between them. She tried to pass the time and keep herself from being afraid by singing songs and playing with the rips in her pants, fraying the fabric even more. It wasn't long before she heard footsteps and two figures with flashlights coming towards her down the hill. Finally, she was able to see Kyle's smiling face and another man standing behind him.

Ariel tried to scoot back, but Kyle crouched down next to her. "Hey, it's okay. That is just my dad. When I told him what I needed the wagon for, he said he wanted to come and help me. My mom is getting your parents to let them know we found you."

"They knew I was gone?"

"Yup. They were driving around town calling out your name trying to find you."

"Oh. I am going to be in so much trouble," Ariel said with tears starting again.

Kyle's dad came over and sat beside her. "No, sweetie. They were just worried about you. Your brother too. He was probably the most upset."

"Derek was upset?"

"Derek and I went out looking for you a couple minutes after you left. We thought you would just ride around the block and come right back. He said if I found you to let you know he was sorry, and he won't be mean to you again," Kyle said in a soft, soothing tone.

"Okay. Can we go home now?"

Kyle's dad carefully reached out to Ariel. "Hello, Ariel. I'm Mark Ashford. It is so nice to finally meet you."

Ariel nodded. "Thanks. Nice to meet you too."

"Well, pretty girl... we are getting drenched out here. Do you mind if I pick you up and put you in the wagon?"

"No, that's okay."

Mark easily scooped her up and put her in the wagon. Kyle took the handle of the wagon and began to pull her up the hill, while Mark picked up the broken bike and they began the trek back out of the woods. Once they reached the edge, Kyle reached in the wagon and pulled out an umbrella. He handed it over to Ariel, and she took it with her good arm. Kyle gave a wink and whispered, "A princess should never have to suffer in the rain."

THE NEXT MORNING, WHEN Ariel was trying to get dressed with her large pink cast on her arm, Derek knocked on her door. Her brother had already apologized several times for how he'd acted the day before and seemed to feel worse that she got hurt and was lost for so long. She had repeatedly told him that it was okay, but he kept trying to help her all night and was driving her crazy.

KNOCK. KNOCK. KNOCK. She knew that knock was his again.

"Go away, Derek. I can get dressed on my own."

There was a slight pause before she heard his voice. "Gross, Ariel. I don't want to help you get dressed, but you have a visitor. Let us know when you are ready."

She had a visitor? Who would come visit her? Nobody from school would come. They all liked to make fun of her and weren't really her friends. Curious, she tried to wiggle into pants faster, but the side where her cast was, wouldn't cooperate. She was able to partially get them up, but only halfway because she couldn't bend her dumb arm. Then she tried to use her good arm and hop and wiggle her way in. HOP... HOP... THUD. Great, now she was on the floor, half dressed and probably going to get a fresh bruise on her butt.

The door burst open, and Derek came rushing in with... oh no... Kyle. Of course, Kyle would see her looking like an idiot. God, she hoped he couldn't see her cartoon panties. She wanted more grown-up underwear, but her mom had put her foot down and said she was too young for satin and lace and it would be over her dead body that her "baby girl" would be wearing that at her age. "Oh my god, Derek, get out!"

Derek looked confused. "But you need help. You fell."

Ariel growled in frustration. "Where's Mom and Dad?"

"Dad is at work and Mom is at the store getting stuff for dinner."

Ariel looked helplessly at her pants and then back to Kyle, who was looking at the ground with his hands in his pockets. She needed to get dressed, and as much as she hated to admit it, she was going to need her stupid brother's help. She thought for a minute she was going to cry again, but she sucked it up and took a deep breath. "Fine. I just need help pulling up this side of my pants."

She looked at Kyle and could feel her face growing red. He rocked back and forth on his heels for a few seconds and said, "I am just going to go downstairs until you're ready."

Ariel put on her best smile and told him a quick thank you.

After Kyle left, Derek helped her to stand up and turned his head while he pulled her pants up. Once he was done, he sat on the bed looking at her with his head slightly tilted.

"Why didn't you just wear one of your dresses? I thought that would be easier."

Ariel frowned. "Yeah, but my legs are ugly."

"What? They're not ugly."

"Yes, they are. They're all scraped up and I have bloody scabs. I am not pretty enough for my dresses now."

"Hey. You will always be pretty enough for dresses. You wear whatever you want to wear. That stuff on your legs just shows that you are strong. Think about all those superheroes like Wonder Woman. Do you think she isn't pretty because she might get banged up during a fight?"

"No. She is always pretty."

"Exactly. Now come on. You ready to see Kyle?"

"He came to visit you, not me."

Derek shook his head. "Nope. He came here to visit you. He even brought you a present."

Ariel practically bounced on her feet. "Okay. Let's go."

Derek laughed, followed her out the bedroom door and down the stairs into the living room. Ariel felt her face blushing when she saw Kyle quickly stand up and wave to her.

"Hey, Ariel. I thought I would, uh... check to see how you are doing. Oh, and I brought you something."

Beaming, Ariel went over to Kyle and sat on the couch next to where he was sitting just before. She politely waited as he still kept standing next to her. After an awkward few seconds, she said, "You got me a present?"

"Oh, right." Kyle sat down and picked up the bag that was on the coffee table. She could tell it was from Estelle's bakery from the pink letters and donut printed on the bag. "Here. Mom and I thought you would like this."

She opened the bag and found a butter cookie with icing that was made in the shape of a tiara. On each point of the tiara were those little silver ball candies and pink glitter had been added on the outline of the cookie. "Wow. When did Estelle start decorating these with sparkles and candies?"

"Um... She didn't. I added those on there so it wouldn't be like the others. I wanted it to be extra special since you had such a bad day."

Ariel wanted to squeal and stomp her feet in excitement. This was so awesome, and Kyle was the sweetest and cutest boy she had ever known. She told herself not to overdo it. That wouldn't be cool. Reminding herself to calm down, she smiled brightly and said, "This is the best cookie I have ever seen. Thank you so much. I love it."

Kyle let out a woosh of air. Did he really think she wouldn't like it? She loved this cookie. She wasn't even sure she would eat it. She wanted to keep it forever, but that probably wouldn't be a good idea. It might end up like that mystery sandwich they found under Derek's bed that one time when his room started to smell funny.

"Would you sign my cast?"

Kyle smiled. "Sure. Do you have a marker?"

Ariel looked at Derek, who nodded and left the room to get one. It only took a few seconds before he was back and handed it over to Kyle. Kyle studied the cast, which was mostly blank except for three signatures that belonged to her parents and brother. Kyle gently held her hand while he continued his inspection. Finally satisfied, he took off the lid and rested her arm on his leg.

"Do you mind if I make a drawing too?"

"No, I would love that."

"Okay." Kyle bent his head and started the drawing with two long lines. "Um... could you look away until I'm done? I want it to be a surprise."

She was not good with surprises. Oh, she loved them, but if she knew about them, she was a nosy little thing. Her parents had to start hiding Christmas presents at their friend's houses. She already scoped out all the good spots in their house and their grandparent's house. She turned her head just enough so she could still peek around the corner of her eye.

Derek's voice startled her. "Cheater. Turn your head all the way."

Ariel stuck out her bottom lip. "You're mean, Derek McKenna. He wouldn't have noticed."

She felt Kyle give a soft chuckle. "I noticed."

"Hmph." Ariel turned her head completely to the side and tried to be patient. It was only a few minutes before she heard Kyle say that he was done. She turned and looked to see he drew a pine tree just like the tree he found her under. It was amazing for a three-minute drawing, and below the trunk he signed his name that was entwined with vine and leaves. She finally whispered, "Our enchanted tree."

Kyle quirked up the corner of his mouth. "Yup. I drew it so you could look at it anytime you want since you aren't supposed to go to the woods for now."

"And you're still my prince, right?"

Kyle looked embarrassed. Ariel watched him blush and look over at her brother, who was looking at his friend with his eyes drawn together in confusion. He finally fidgeted and answered. "Yeah, um... right."

Ariel could tell that he didn't want to talk about their conversation in the woods in front of her brother, so she let it go. "Well, thanks for finding me."

Kyle gave a big warm smile. "Anytime, Princess."

Chapter 1

Ariel stood in the middle of the dancefloor at Chase and Dixie's wedding alone... again. Why did she keep putting herself through this? She has been playing this push and pull game with the same man for nearly twenty-three years. They were having a good night. Kyle had her wrapped in his arms with her head resting on his chest. She could feel his heart beating fast even though they were both barely moving. She wasn't a complete idiot. She knew when a man was turned on, when they wanted more. But then, like a cold bucket of water had been tossed onto them, he stopped dancing with her and said he had to go.

It had been such an incredible day. The wedding was beautiful. Chase had used police cruisers to block off the whole street so they could use it for an open reception area. Ariel was the maid of honor, and Kyle was taking pictures since the town photographer, Dixie, was the bride. When couples started to dance, Kyle had approached her and asked her to dance. She wasn't the one who cornered him, at least not this time. He looked stunning in his button-down shirt, his wavy blond hair styled for once and his blue eyes shining with happiness. She was mesmerized. Kyle didn't often let happiness reach his eyes, at least not since he'd moved back from Philadelphia.

During the dance he held her close like he was afraid she would disappear if he let her go, but it had always been him letting go of her. He told her when she was a teenager that he couldn't be with her because she was too young. Then when she graduated, he told her that he couldn't be with her because she was his best friend's little sister, he was living far away for college, and she had a big life to live. And she did live a big life. She spent time in Europe and studied art with several different artists in her travels. When she came back home, she got her Associate Degree in business and opened her own card and gift shop. When Kyle finally moved back to Blossom Hills, he kept a distance from her romantically, but he was always there with their friendship. But it was a weird kind of friendship. It was like an emotional, romantic relationship—they had that deep connection but he never dared to touch her, and that was the most frustrating way to live.

Ariel's body was still vibrating from the swaying motions they shared when she heard Josie's voice beside her. "Prince Charming get spooked again?"

Ariel was still watching his retreating form walk past the cruiser and a man who had been watching the wedding from just past the barriers. "Yeah. I need to just accept that he doesn't want me."

Josie put her hand on Ariel's arm. "I don't think that's the problem. I think he has some messed up stuff he needs to deal with and doesn't know how to talk to you about it."

Ariel sighed. "And how long am I supposed to wait for him to figure it out and open up to me?"

"That is something only you can know. Is he worth waiting another twenty years for?"

"If you would have asked me that question ten years ago, I would have said that I would wait a lifetime for him."

"And now?"

"I'm not so sure anymore. I want a family. I want what Zoey and Dixie have. I want a man who puts me first and gives back the love and devotion that I give to him."

Ariel and Josie watched as Zoey and Tyler danced, wrapped up in each other. When you looked at the two of them, there was no denying the magic that glowed from them. Tyler had fallen in love with Zoey at first sight. He took the time to gain her trust and earn her love. She had moved to town after leaving a verbally abusive ex-boyfriend and had met Tyler on her first day in town. Even with her slightly skittish nature and self-doubts, Zoey fell hard for Kyle's brother. The two of them were already engaged and the whole town was excited about the town baker and computer geek's upcoming wedding.

Josie's voice once again broke through her thoughts. "Well, until we find our men like that, let's go drown our sorrows in more of Zoey's cake and wine."

Ariel smiled. "That sounds like the best idea you've ever had."

They made their way over to the cake table just as the bride and groom said their goodbyes and took off in one of the cruisers. After grabbing their slice, they joined Derek at an empty table.

Ariel watched in horror as Derek dragged his finger across the edge of Ariel's cake, scraped up some icing and sucked it clean off. "Hey! That was my cake, butthead."

Derek just shrugged. "I didn't want another whole piece. Just some icing." He tilted his head and batted his eyelashes. "Besides, I knew my darling little sister wouldn't deny me."

Ariel huffed. "Maybe not, but I at least would have used my fork to scrape some off for you instead of your nasty finger. Who knows where that thing has been today?"

Derek shook his head. "Don't worry. I have kept my hands to myself all day. You know I don't play with the locals."

"Ugh. You are such a Neanderthal." Ariel knew that her brother never dated anyone local. He would always just hook up with one of the tourists, have a quick affair while they were in town, and then kindly send them on their way. She hoped that someday soon he would meet a woman who would knock him on his ass.

Derek looked around the reception and asked, "Where's Kyle? I saw him dancing with you a few minutes ago."

Ariel shrugged. "Went home, I guess."

"I just don't understand his quick exits all the time."

Josie seemed to notice Ariel's discomfort and decided to steer the conversation elsewhere. "So, are we taking bets on who gets pregnant first, Dixie or Zoey?"

Derek's face turned down, and he looked over at his best friend, Zoey. "No bets for that one." Both Ariel and Josie looked at Derek with questions in their eyes. Derek looked down at the table. "I mean it. No pregnancy bets."

Ariel quickly picked up on the undertones in her brother's voice and looked at her friend who was smiling up at Tyler. "Oh. I didn't know."

Derek looked into her eyes with that determined look he always gave her when she knew he meant business. "And you still don't. Just don't bet on it or push her about it."

Josie's clear voice was the first one to respond. "We understand."

Ariel thought she heard Josie's voice crack at the end, but she wasn't sure if that was from sympathy for her friend or something a little more personal. Instead of pushing it with her in front of them, she decided to concentrate on finishing off her cake.

Soon after, the song ended, and Zoey and Tyler joined them at the table. Tyler looked around and asked, "Where's Kyle?"

"He made one of his discreet exits," Derek said with a shrug.

"We would have driven him home if he would have waited." Tyler turned to Josie. "You want a ride home?"

"Yup. Do you think Chase's dad will mind if I leave my car in the driveway? I've had a few too many glasses of wine."

"He'll be fine with it. You going to have a hangover tomorrow?"

"Maybe a small one, but it would help if you two love birds would take your noisy sex over to your apartment tonight. I don't think the headboard hitting our shared wall would help me any."

Ariel giggled. Zoey and Josie lived in the same apartment building, and their bedrooms shared a wall. Josie often would spill all their dirty little secrets to Ariel the next day during breakfast at the bakery. Turning to Derek she asked, "You ready to go, brother dear?"

"Yeah, just let me check with Tiny if he needs any help closing up." Tiny was Derek's head cook at the bar. His nickname was one of those ironic names. Tiny was actually Tim Cooper who was a giant at just over six foot five inches. He was an intimidating man with tattoos on his neck and arms, but once you got to know him, he was sweet and a bit overprotective of the women. It was his overprotective streak that got him thrown in prison when he had explained with his fists to a man that you don't hit women, especially his sister. Derek had given him a job once he got out of prison at the recommendation of the warden, and the large man was now very loyal to Derek and his family.

"Oh. Tell Tiny thanks for cooking tonight and that the food was amazing, like always," Ariel said.

Derek nodded and walked back to the table of food where Tiny was already packing up the leftovers. Ariel said her goodbyes to Josie, Tyler and Zoey. She sighed as she looked around at all the couples leaving the reception. She had some hard decisions to make. There was no denying that she wanted a future with someone who would love her completely. Kyle was supposed to be that someone, but if he wasn't, she needed to start making different choices.

Derek walked up beside her with a covered serving pan. "We get to take some leftovers home?" Ariel asked in a hopeful tone.

"Yup. It's Tiny's mac and cheese."

Ariel squealed in delight. "Oh yes, please!" Ariel looked around and finally found her mom, Amanda, talking to Tiny. "Are we taking Mom home?"

"No. She wanted to help with the clean-up and Tiny said he would take her home."

That was her mom. Always wanting to step in and help everyone. Amanda always tried to take over and make everyone else feel at home, no matter where they were. Ariel knew that her mom was an amazing and beautiful woman. She would never understand why their dad cheated on their mom, and she just hoped that her mom would find her own happiness someday.

"Okay brother dear, let's go."

KYLE WAS PISSED OFF. He had Ariel in his arms. She was fitted to him perfectly on the dancefloor, and for those few minutes gently swaying to the music, he allowed himself to believe this was how it would always be. Her cherry scented shampoo drifted up to his nose, intoxicating his mind. She looked stunning in her pale-blue dress and her hair partially swept up to show off the graceful line of her neck. When he looked up during a pause in the music, and saw his reminder that he couldn't have her, he did what he always did. He told her he was sorry and sprinted off the dancefloor to go home... alone... again. How long could he keep this up?

He walked past the man who had been watching the reception from across the street and didn't bother to address him. There was nothing left to say, but that sure didn't stop the man from following him. They had walked a full block before the short man spoke. "Hey, Mr. Olsen. Zeke would be interested to know if you have been tasting the little princess."

"Fuck off, Pablo." He hated the nickname Pablo and his other friends had given him. They all called him Jimmy or Mr. Olsen referencing the journalist from the Superman comics. It was dumb. They all knew his name, and they all loved making his life a living hell. After so many of Zeke's friends had paid him a visit and didn't give their names, he returned the favor and called all of them Pablo.

"You know the rules, Jimmy. You can look, but you can't have what you want. Ever."

Kyle turned with his fists clenched. "Do you really think I could ever forget that? You can tell Zeke he can stop with his little visits. Don't you guys have something better to do?"

Pablo stepped closer into Kyle's space. "Of course, we do, but it seems like we have to keep coming down here to remind you that you made a deal. Everybody lives, but you, you get to suffer every day. If you break that promise, that sweet little princess dies, and just for good measure maybe your brother and his little baker too. But that little princess... she shines bright like the sun, and you're the idiot who keeps standing close and getting burned."

"I was going to leave, but it was your boss's bright idea that I have to stay here." He had meant it too. At the time he was going to pack his things and move away to keep Ariel and his family safe, but Zeke put a stop to that, saying that he wouldn't suffer enough if he didn't see what he couldn't have every day.

"And you know why you can't leave. So just live your small little life and watch as that precious little thing grows to resent you and finds her comfort with someone else."

Kyle wanted to get sick. The bile was churning in his stomach. That would kill off the last piece of his soul. He knew that. He lost so much of himself in Philadelphia, and he had come back to Blossom Hills hoping to press the reset button and finally allow himself to have the one girl who had captured his heart. He wished he could go back in time. If he could change it, he would have come back home after he graduated and set things right with Ariel, but he got that amazing job offer in Philadelphia as an investigative reporter. It was his dream job. He figured he would take the chance, and if he hated it, he could always come back home. There were so many times he was tired of seeing the violence and death that he thought about leaving Philadelphia. At one point he had even tried to put in his notice, but his boss kept pulling him back in with a bigger story and even bigger empty promises. By the time he got a lead on the internal rumblings going on with the Sangres Nobles, a local and powerful street gang, he told his boss that this was his last story. He was moving back home and going to win over the woman he was supposed to be with for the rest of his life. There was no longer any interest in working for a large paper; he was going to take over the local paper and live a quiet good life.

"I'm going home, Pablo. Go back to Zeke and let him know that I am still playing by his rules. I'm here, but not with her."

"You need to remember this was all your fault. You could have had your girl. You could have had everything, but you took everything away from him, so he is taking only what you took from him."

"I am doing everything he has asked of me."

"Good to know. We hate making the little trips back here to remind you about your responsibilities. Now I would love to stay and chat, but we have other business to take care of back home. Remember, we see you... *we are the magnificent.*"

Chapter 2

Ariel started the next morning with a pounding headache. The light that was pouring in from her open curtains wasn't helping either. She was suddenly appreciating that she wasn't working in the shop today. It took everything she had to make it out of her dress last night when she came home. She was exhausted physically and mentally from Kyle's emotional whiplash again. Getting up, she considered going to Zoey's bakery for donuts and coffee, but her motivation to get a shower and to get dressed just wasn't there.

Once she managed to get the coffee brewing, she picked up her phone to send a text to her brother to let him know she would make breakfast with the coffee if he wanted to come upstairs. When she opened the messaging app, she saw that Kyle had texted in the middle of the night.

Kyle: Thanks for the dance. Hope you made it home okay. Sorry I left so quickly.

Really? How many times had she gotten a text like this from him? This was probably about the sixth or seventh time in just as many months. She didn't want to respond to his sorry excuse, but she was never mean or held grudges.

Ariel: It's okay.

She watched the cursor blink after her last word, just waiting for her to say something more, but if she typed out the words floating around in her head, it wouldn't end well. Sighing, she pressed send and then sent an invitation to her brother for breakfast.

It wasn't long after she started cooking the bacon that she heard her door open. Derek's gruff morning voice came from around the corner. "Is that bacon?"

"Yes, you big goof. Get in here and get the plates out."

Derek appeared, looking like he'd just rolled out of bed five minutes ago. His brown hair was curling up around the edges of his hat, he was shirtless and had on low hanging athletic shorts. Ariel rolled her eyes. "Ugh. Go put a shirt on. I don't need to see your man boobs while we eat breakfast."

Derek looked down at his bare chest. "These are not man boobs. They're pecs, and it isn't like you haven't seen it before."

"Yeah, but not at my dining table. Now go! I have one of your shirts on top of my dryer."

Derek tousled her hair as he walked by. "Thanks, sis. You're the best."

Ariel gave a slight groan as he walked down the hallway to the laundry room. "And you can stop trying to sneak in your clothes with mine to wash. If you try it one more time, I'm going to throw your clothes out the window, and you can pick up your underwear from the front lawn before one of your groupies scoops it up."

Derek walked back in and was pulling his University of Kentucky t-shirt over his head. "Don't be mean."

"Okay, then stop being lazy."

Derek stuck out his bottom lip. "But you are so good at it, and you love me."

"Fine, but I'm not paying for food anymore at the bar."

Derek brightened. "Deal."

They sat down and started eating. She watched as Derek inhaled his breakfast in nearly five bites. "You've been hanging out with Chase too much."

"What?" he asked mumbling through his food. "I was hungry."

"Uh-huh. So, are you going out to the trails with Kyle today?" Derek and Kyle often went hiking on his days off. Ariel was usually invited, but most of the time she passed letting the guys have their bonding time.

"Nah. I am hanging out with Zoey after the breakfast rush. Tyler has some client he is meeting with today in Raleigh, so he will be gone most of the day. Kyle texted last night and said he couldn't make it today, so it worked out well. What are you going to do?"

That was a good question. Chase and Dixie were going to be busy celebrating their newly wedded bliss, and she didn't want to bother them. Josie was busy entertaining one of Dixie's relatives who was staying with her until tomorrow. Dixie's relatives nearly took over the whole town. The B&B was booked and many of them stayed with Dixie and Chase's friends and family. Derek even let his vacant apartment above the bar get used for a couple of cousins. "I don't know. Maybe I will see if Dad wants to meet for lunch. I haven't seen him in a while."

"Dad doesn't deserve a minute of your attention. He couldn't keep his dick in his pants and broke Mom's heart."

Ariel sighed. "Derek." This was an age-old fight with them. She knew her dad wasn't perfect, and he made his mistakes, but he was still their dad. While she understood her mom not wanting to talk to him, he wasn't a bad father. Not really. After he moved out, he had some trouble learning to adjust to not seeing his kids every day and how to keep a connection. Derek had so much anger towards him, and still only tolerated him.

"No. Ariel, you didn't see what it did to Mom. Mom told him to leave after she found out about his second affair. She cried every night for at least a month. She was always strong whenever we were near, but at night when she would close her door, I would hear her cry. Then that asshole decided to date every woman in town and didn't even hide how much he was enjoying his new single life without her, without us. I watched the love in Mom's eyes slowly die."

"Mom is okay. She is happy now. She has a job she loves, and she has us."

"Then you aren't looking close enough. Watch her eyes when no one is looking. Watch how they drift out to memories that tear at her heart. I can't forgive him. I won't."

Ariel knew this war was not going to be won today, so she let it go. They finished their breakfast and Derek took the dishes over to the sink.

"You going to the store today?"

Ariel thought about it for a minute. "I wasn't planning on it, but I can, why?"

"Figured if you bought steak, I would grill for us tonight."

Ariel brightened. "You got yourself a deal."

ARIEL SAT AT A SMALL booth by the window at Casperelli's waiting on her dad to show up. Normally, he was early waiting on her. This wasn't like him. She looked at her phone again. He was now ten minutes late and hadn't called or texted. The waiter came by her table again asking if she wanted to place an order while she waited, but she declined and looked out the window hoping to see him approach.

She heard high heels clicking on the floor before she heard the overly feminine voice. "Oh, hi Ariel. Dining alone again?"

Ariel looked up to see Amber Kiley. Amber was dressed in her usual low-cut tight blouse and too short skirt. Ariel had known her since high school and had tried to get along with her several times, but Amber only used Ariel to get to know her brother and his friends. Dixie had even gone to a dance with her ex-boyfriend, Mike, but Amber made him ditch her at the dance if he wanted to get back together with her. Ariel straightened and looked Amber directly in her fake contact-colored blue eyes and said, "No, I am waiting for someone. They are just a little late. It was a pleasure as always... Goodbye, Amber."

Amber narrowed her eyes. "Well, I just hope that you don't get stood up yet again. It's so sad to have that continually happening to you."

Ariel's hand itched to reach for the saltshaker and throw it at her. Why were some people perpetually stuck in high school? "I appreciate your concern, but it isn't needed."

Finally, a man joined Amber and whispered in her ear that caused her smile to widen and show her teeth. "As you can see my date is ready for us to leave. I *do* hope you enjoy your lunch."

Ariel drummed her fingers on the table as she watched Amber leave with her date. He must have been a tourist because she didn't recognize the attractive man. When you lived in a small town, you tended to know who all the attractive single men were. "*I do hope you enjoy your lunch,*" Ariel said in a frustrated mocking tone. "I would enjoy it better if I could slap you with a breadstick."

"Sweetheart, I know I'm a little late, but does it really deserve a breadstick slap?"

Ariel turned to see her dad standing beside her. "Oh, hey, Daddy. Sorry, I didn't see you come in." She stood up and gave him a big hug. They both sat back down, and she continued. "The breadstick wasn't about you. Amber Kiley was gracious enough to stop by my table to say hello."

Her dad smiled warmly at her. "Is she still giving you trouble? I thought she would grow out of her personality issues."

"Some people never grow up."

Jeremy laughed. "Well, I know that, but I kind of wished you would stay little forever. Plus, I know I wouldn't have minded if the gray would have stayed away a bit longer for me too."

"You still look good, Dad." And she meant that too. He was still physically active, and while his muscles were no longer as defined as they used to be, he was still an attractive, fit man. His brown hair had flecks of gray throughout with a bigger cluster around his temples and his golden skin only showed lines around his eyes from when he smiled.

"Thank you, honey. How was Dixie's wedding?"

Ariel's eyes grew soft, and her lips turned up at the corners. "It was amazing. She wore Chase's mom's wedding dress, and Chase blocked off the entire street with the cruisers so she could use it for the walk between the two houses as an aisle. I've never seen her so happy. You should have come."

"Nah. Your mother was there, and I didn't want to spoil the day. She deserved to have a good time with you girls. Dixie is like another daughter to her. I don't know Dixie as well as she does. We had already... well you know by the time you were good friends with her... your mom and I..."

Ariel put her hand on her dad's arm. "It's okay, Dad. I know."

The waiter approached, clearing the awkward moment, and took their order. Once he left, Jeremy cleared his throat. "So, what about you? Any closer to getting married and giving me a grandchild? Has that boy woken up and realized you are the perfect woman?"

Ariel giggled. "Geez, dad. That is a bit over the top."

"What? You are perfect. Everyone needs to know that. I will stand up right now and tell everyone what a perfect daughter I have." He started to rise, but she grabbed him by the arm.

"Sit down." She shook her head. "You are impossible."

"Yes, I know. So, tell me what's going on."

"Much of the same. We get close, but then it is like those magnets I used to play with—if we get too close it is like some powerful force quickly shoves him in the other direction. It is always an instant mood shift. I wish I knew what the trigger was. Maybe we could work it out together, but anytime I bring it up he closes down even more and then disappears for days."

"I hate to say it, but maybe it is time to let the boy go. He obviously isn't going to do the right thing by either moving forward or letting go completely, so this might be something you have to do for the both of you."

The waiter returned with the bread and trio of dipping sauces and placed it in between them. Ariel just looked at the breadsticks and got lost in her own thoughts.

"Uh oh. If you are not devouring the breadsticks, I know it is bad."

Ariel did a mental shake off and smiled at her dad. "I am never too upset for breadsticks, and keep your grubby hands off my Alfredo sauce."

Laughing he replied, "That's my girl."

The remainder of lunch was filled with ordinary updates about their jobs and town gossip. Ariel told her dad how well the gift shop was doing, and that the influx of tourists this summer had been a huge boost to her sales. Her dad was a local insurance agent, and he always seemed busy. He had two partners join him within the past five years claiming that he wanted to slow down and learn to enjoy life more. Most of the town was insured through his agency for everything from home, auto and businesses. After the truth came out about his affairs, he started to see a drop in business, but Amanda had urged her friends to not drop him as an agent. While he was cheating on her, he was still a good, fair and caring professional. He had even developed a program with the fire department to help families with clothes and toys for children after devastating fires. Ariel was proud of the man he was, she just wished that he could have remained faithful to her mom.

As their meal ended Jeremy began shifting around in his seat uncomfortably. Ariel started to get worried. He never seemed so jumpy before. "Daddy, are you okay?"

"Yes, sweetheart. I... just have something to tell you." He looked really uncomfortable now. He began playing with the watch on his wrist, seemingly not able to sit still.

"Daddy, are you sick?"

His eyes jumped immediately to hers. He put his hand into her small one, and gave a gentle smile. "Oh God, no. Sorry, it isn't anything like that."

"Then what is it like?"

He took a deep exhale. "Well, I've met someone. Someone who means a lot to me."

That certainly wasn't what she was expecting to hear today. She blinked a couple of times and could feel her mouth fall open. Thinking she should probably close it, or at least say something, she struggled to hold on to a solid thought. Nope, she couldn't—there just were no words.

Jeremy must have realized she wasn't going to speak or react, so he continued. "Her name is Miranda. She is a retired social worker and moved in with her mom, to help with her Alzheimer's. She is really nice, and I think you will like her."

She was still just staring at him. She was listening to his words, but her body wouldn't react. That little girl inside of her always thought that her parents would find their way back to each other. They both still had respect for each other and were civil even when they first separated. She knew her dad was no saint, and he had his share of women through the past years after the divorce, but never before did he mention someone specifically. This was a big deal. Now he came and said that he found a woman who used to be a social worker and is helping her sick mother. She couldn't hate the woman for winning her dad's heart. That would make her a horrible person.

"Ariel?"

Right, she should say something. "I'm happy for you." She plastered on her best "this is not a fake smile" smile. "What is her last name?"

"Starr."

Ariel racked her brain. She couldn't remember anyone from a family with that last name. Usually in small towns you knew just about all the families. "I don't know that family."

"I wouldn't expect you to. She didn't have any children of her own. She can't. She's never been married before and her mom stayed home most of the time, with an at home daycare."

"Oh. How did you guys meet?"

"She came into my office with Power of Attorney paperwork for her mom and said she wanted to go over the policies for possible changes. We ended up talking in my office for a few hours, and it was time to close so I asked her to dinner. And I have been asking her to dinner a lot for the past couple of months now. She is amazing and has a genuine love for people."

"Yeah, well Mom has a genuine love for people too, but that didn't help her."

The corners of Jeremy's face fell into a frown. Ariel winced. She didn't really mean to say that out loud, but what would make this woman so special that he could be better to her than to her mom?

"I messed up with your mom. That was my fault. I had my own issues to work out, and I failed multiple times. She deserves to be happy with someone who hasn't broken her heart."

Ariel thought back to what Derek had told her about how she cried every night after their separation and tried to suppress her annoyance. "What makes this woman different? Why will you be able to be with her and not break her heart?"

"It isn't the woman who is different, it's me. I haven't told anyone this, but I am trusting you as my little girl to understand."

She couldn't respond, but instead just gave a small nod of acknowledgment.

"After your mom and I divorced, I went to a counselor for a few years. I know where my mistakes were, how and why they happened. I had to learn to change the person I was, and how to be good enough to be your dad. You have the biggest heart and allowed me to stay in your life. Your brother's heart is big too, but it's like mine and doesn't heal or trust like yours does. I want to be a man that you can be proud of."

Releasing a breath Ariel replied, "Of course I am proud of you, Dad. Yes, I hate what happened with you and Mom, but you have always been kind and generous to everyone.... Maybe a little too generous with other women."

"Ariel!"

Ariel bit her lip. "Sorry. That was the last one. I promise."

"I have one other request."

"Okay."

"Can you tell your brother about Miranda? I don't want him to find out about it at the bar or around town."

"Hmmm... I don't know. That is a big ask. See... this is where buying me that pony when I was twelve would have come in handy."

Jeremy chuckled. "Are you ever going to let that go?"

"No. I would have been a good pony mom. I would have spoiled him with the best hay, apples and carrots. Plus, it would have made the dog happy. I would have stopped trying to ride him around the house."

"Andre didn't mind, he was about the size of a miniature horse anyway." Jeremy paused. "So, are you going to help me with Derek?"

Ariel put her small hand into her dad's and nodded. "Of course, Daddy, but you need to buy me a tiramisu to go."

With a twinkle in his eye he said, "I can do that."

AFTER A TERRIBLE NIGHT'S sleep Kyle found himself at his second least favorite place, the grocery store. Blossom Hills didn't have a large franchise grocery store, so everyone shopped at the same place, Johnson's Market. It was started by the current Mr. Johnson's great-grandfather and each son took over as the elder retired. It had grown considerably over the years, and at least the latest Mr. Johnson had decided to carry a bigger selection of food. His father refused to order certain food in stock simply because he didn't like it, and he always told everyone that if he didn't like it, they didn't need to eat it either.

Kyle stood by the produce section waiting for an old woman to select her cantaloupe so he could have his turn. He learned the hard way that people here were not like they were in Philadelphia. You couldn't crowd them while they selected their fruit and veggies. Once he got whacked in the shin with a cane by Mr. Mellott when he tried to slide in beside him for a quick random grab.

Kyle saw more produce being brought out by the youngest Johnson, Bryce, as the boy smiled and nodded. "Hey, Mr. Ashford."

Being called Mr. Ashford freaked him out. That is what people called his dad, but whenever he tried to correct the boy, he just smiled and said, "Okay, Mr. Ashford."

"Hey. Have you talked to you dad about offering online shopping and pick up yet? I am sure Tyler would be happy to help get him set up with a website." Kyle's brother, Tyler, was a computer programmer and software developer, whose business concentrated mostly on larger companies, but he often would help local merchants set up an online presence.

"Yeah, I mentioned it." Bryce answered, "But he didn't like it very much. He said that people spend more money when they walk in the store, and he would have to hire extra people to make the orders. I think it is a great idea and we need to grow, but he said I am just a kid and don't understand business yet."

"I think you know more than either of you think, but he is the boss."

Bryce nodded. "Yeah... for now."

Kyle couldn't miss the smile widening on Bryce's face. He could tell he had big plans for the store when it would come time for him to run it.

Then like a switch, Bryce's eyes glazed over, and he stared over Kyle's shoulder. Bryce's cheeks flooded with a reddish pink shade and he said with a squeak, "Hi, Miss McKenna."

Ariel. Of course. Lots of men lost their functionality for speech when they would see her. Kyle turned around to see her approaching in a white skater dress with cherries printed throughout. She had on matching red heels and a red ribbon headband pulling back her blonde curls. She looked like a fifties' pin up. Just lean her against any classic car and she could be posing for a calendar. Well, this image of her would haunt him later tonight. He heard her soft melodic voice greet Bryce before Kyle could decide to speak. Finally, he shook his head clear and smiled. "Hey, Ariel. You look nice today."

She bit her lip and looked down for a minute before offering a quiet one word of thanks.

Uh-oh. He knew he was in trouble. Normally, she was a happy chatterbox. He might have some damage control to do after the wedding. "You having a good day?"

Ariel gave him a fake smile. "Yes. I am having a great day. I got to have lunch with Dad and Derek is making steaks for dinner."

Kyle waited for a few seconds. Usually, this is where she would invite him to join them for dinner, especially if Derek was cooking, but not this time. No invitation. Nothing, except an uncomfortable silence.

Forgetting that Bryce was standing there, Kyle startled a bit when he finally said, "Dad was just slicing up some fresh ribeyes. Do you want me to grab you some from the back?"

Ariel beamed. "That would be great. Thanks, Bryce."

Brushing a hand through his hair the teen smiled. "Anything for you, Miss McKenna, just follow me."

Before Kyle could say anything else, Ariel followed behind Bryce to the back of the store. Great. He looked like a jackass now, not knowing how to talk to one of his oldest friends, and the girl he had loved for most of his life.

Kyle walked the produce section like a man on a mission. He was throwing random items in his basket not even caring for how fresh it was, or even if it was something he liked. After a couple minutes of angry shopping, he made his way to the back of the store and stopped cold by the seafood counter. Just about twenty feet in front on him was Ariel talking to Austin Sutton, the fireman. He stared motionless as she laughed at something Austin had said and she put her hand on his arm. Kyle wanted to tackle the guy and punch his face in for flirting with her. He wouldn't feel the least bit sorry for it either. Sure, Austin was a nice guy, and he knew the women all thought he was attractive, but everyone in town knew that Ariel belonged with him. While he was staring daggers into Austin's back, he felt a hand on his shoulder.

Bryce was beside him again, this time shaking his head. "You really messed up big time, huh?"

Kyle gripped his hand into a fist and made a low growling noise. "Oh, yeah? And what do you know about it?"

With a slight chuckle he said, "I know that I have a date tonight, you don't, and Miss McKenna might have one coming up soon."

"Don't you have produce to stack?"

"Yup." Bryce gave one more slight clap on Kyle's back and disappeared down the aisle.

Kyle watched Ariel and Austin talk animatedly. What on earth could they be talking about for so long? All that man did all day is eat, sleep and put out fires. It wasn't that great. Well... okay it was great, but she didn't need the overly beefy hero type; she needed him. Only she couldn't have him, because he was a greedy, overly ambitious jackass who messed up everything. He was losing his appetite. He didn't want to shop for groceries anymore. Looking in his basket, it seemed like it was going to be salad for dinner... no juicy grilled steaks. Awesome.

ARIEL WAS READING HER latest steamy romance book. Just as she was getting to the part where her latest book boyfriend was going to try and win his woman back after screwing everything up, her heart gave a little pang of longing. She always loved seeing how the heroes would figure out how to win back their loves. It gave her hope that maybe someday Kyle would wake up and they could start their happily ever after.

The more she thought about it though, the more she thought that it may be time to find someone who could love her the way she needed. Maybe she romanticized their relationship too much. She thought they were the forever love.

She wasn't naïve though. There had been other boyfriends, especially while Kyle lived in Philadelphia, but she always compared them to Kyle, and they just didn't stack up.

Her mind drifted back to her weird encounter with Kyle earlier that day. She had been annoyed with him before, but never to the point where she didn't know what to say anymore. Was there anything left to be said? Drifting her gaze down to her charm bracelet with the lone pine tree she rubbed it, hoping it would provide some kind of direction. Kyle had given her that charm bracelet for her graduation present. He had left her a note on her dresser on graduation day asking her to meet him at the enchanted tree at midnight. When she arrived, he was still wearing his button-down shirt and tie, sitting on the ground with a lantern flickering a warm glow around him.

Kyle had smiled widely and quickly stood up to greet her. She had given him a big hug and reveled in how her body fit to his. He had wrapped his arms around her and held for a couple of minutes. Once they separated, he handed her the long rectangular box wrapped in red and white paper and bows. She had eagerly opened it to see the silver reflecting from the lantern's light that Kyle was now holding. "It's our enchanted tree, mobile edition."

Ariel laughed; she couldn't help it. "Mobile edition?"

Kyle shrugged. "Yeah. I might not always be able to meet you at the tree when you are lost since I will be in Philadelphia for at least a couple more years. I wanted to leave you something that would remind you that I am always here with you. And if you feel even a little lost, just rub the tree and know if you need me, I will find you."

The sound of her door opening broke her from the memories of that night. She turned in her seat to see Derek walking in with a dessert box from Zoey's bakery. Ariel threw her book on the coffee table and ran to tear the box away from Derek.

"Geez. Watch the claws. You nearly ripped flesh from my hands trying to get the box."

"Quit being such a baby. What did she give us?"

"Strawberry cheesecake."

Ariel set the box on the counter and lifted the lid. Almost immediately it was slammed back down with Derek's hand. "Hey! Watch it. You almost smooshed the goodies."

"Dinner first. Then dessert."

Ariel crossed her arms and stuck out her lower lip. "Okay, *Dad.*"

"Hey... don't call me dad. I am better than that asshole."

Ariel looked down and regretted bringing him up.

Derek sighed. "Sorry. I didn't think... How was your lunch with him anyway?"

Oh, goodie, she gets to ruin his appetite before dinner. "He is good. The agency is doing well, and he just talked to the knitting club about donating some blankets for the emergency kits."

Derek was mixing spices and butter in a bowl while it seemed like he was half listening. "Uh-huh. At least he does some things right."

While washing the lettuce, she watched as he set the bowl down and went for the mallet to tenderize the steaks. Well, he could at least take out his aggression on the food so she might as well spill it now. "And he has a pretty serious new girlfriend."

He stopped his rhythmic banging only to follow up with one loud hard bang. "Please tell me that you are kidding. He has some slut he is showing off around town?"

Ariel lost her temper. Between Kyle and her brother acting like idiots, she needed to release some negative energy. She grabbed the sink sprayer, aimed it at his head, and let it fly. Water spewed out hitting him on the temple and ran down his shirt.

"What the hell, Ariel? Have you lost your mind?"

She frowned and sprayed him again. He ran from the water like a little girl and gaped at her from the other side of the kitchen.

"I have not lost my mind. I am sick and tired of this crap you pull about Dad. Kyle is being an idiot. My best friend just got married to a man we all thought would never settle down. I still haven't dated anyone who wants me for more than my body, and I have had it! You are going to have dinner with me and Dad, and we are going to meet his new girlfriend who sounds like a perfectly lovely woman. *And* if you screw this up in any way, I will make you regret it. Do you understand me?"

He didn't answer. Mostly he just stood there staring at her like he didn't comprehend any of her ranting meltdown... so, she sprayed him again.

"Okay... Okay. I will meet her and be nice." He walked over to the drawer and pulled out a fork and handed it to her. "Here, have a bite of cheesecake before you kill me."

Swiping the fork out of his hand she glared at him. "I wouldn't kill you. I love your dumb butt too much for that."

Derek looked from her to the sprayer and back to her. "Clearly."

Once dinner was over, they both stood by the sink washing the dishes. "I talked to Austin Sutton today," Ariel finally said.

"Yeah? How's he doing?"

"Pretty good. He is hoping to get promoted to lieutenant when the chief retires. He thinks everyone is going to move up a step, and he is a good candidate for lieutenant."

"That's awesome. Austin is a great guy—has shit for luck sometimes, but still a good man."

Ariel giggled. "I remember when he hit on Zoey when she first moved here. I thought Tyler was going to rip his head off."

"Really? I missed that day."

"Josie told Tyler to calm down and wait. Then he got to see Zoey turn him down."

"Josie was the voice of reason? Now there's a scary thought."

"I think we have mellowed her a bit."

"Still, I wouldn't piss her off."

"Nope. Did you know her last name is Stabenow?"

Derek winced. "No. Kind of surprised she hasn't gone around stabbing people."

Ariel jumped up and slapped her hand on the counter. "See! That is funny. I made a joke to her about feeling a little stabby at Dixie's wedding and she nearly killed me."

"I can't believe you were dumb enough to say it directly to her."

"Yeah... not my brightest move. It kind of came out like word vomit. There was no stopping it."

"You need to work on that. Your filter is getting worse the older you get."

"It's from all the lack of orgasms," Ariel said with a shrug.

Derek dropped the dish towel and covered his ears. "Filter! Jesus."

Ariel pulled down his arms to uncover his ears and looked her brother in the eyes with her eyes narrowed. "If you want your sister to have a better filter, return the favor and put a gag on your conquests when you bring them home. I have heard better acting from thefourth graders at the spring play."

Derek's mouth turned into a sly smile. "That's no acting. They leave with a smile and pep in their step every time."

"Move in the apartment upstairs, he said. It will be fun, he said. I'm your brother... what could go wrong," Ariel said in a soft, sarcastic tone as Derek laughed and whipped her with the towel.

Chapter 3

It had been three days since Kyle had seen Ariel at the store. He was avoiding her. He knew it. His stomach had growled in objection that he wasn't eating breakfast. Going to the bakery held a high risk of running into Ariel, who often met up with Josie and Dixie there in the morning. When the bell clanging broke through the silence, he nearly jumped out of his skin. Tyler walked in wearing another new t-shirt, this time with Baby Yoda holding a coffee mug saying No Coffee No Workee. Kyle was so busy reading the shirt he nearly missed the bakery box.

Shaking his head Kyle said, "Thank god, you brought food." He snatched the box from Tyler and nodded. "Nice shirt."

Beaming Tyler replied, "You like it? Zoey got it for me."

"Where does she find these shirts?"

"Dunno. Somewhere off the internet. She won't tell me. She said she wants to be able to surprise me every now and then, and if she told me where to find it, I would read all the shirts they have, and it wouldn't be the same. She likes seeing my reaction."

Kyle walked to the back corner where he had a small fridge and pulled out a bottle of orange juice. He showed it to Tyler with an eyebrow raised and Tyler just nodded. He brought the two bottles over and leaned against the desk as they ate. Tyler began talking about his business and how it was really starting to pick up and he may have to consider hiring someone within about a year to help him out.

"You mean like a secretary?"

Tyler shook his head. "Nah. I can handle all the admin stuff. I am thinking a second coder and developer. I have heard rumblings about one of the larger contractor companies possibly dissolving in the next six months. They have several large clients here in North Carolina and I think I could really take advantage and expand my business."

"Is that what you really want though? I thought you came back here to reconnect to small town life?"

"I still do. I wouldn't relocate, but maybe hire a few people and make enough to support Zoey and build a family."

"I think you both make enough to support a family and it doesn't cost much to create a baby. Just go buy some candles and flowers and go seduce your fiancé."

Tyler's face fell, and he swirled the leftover juice in the bottom of the bottle in a circle. "Actually, it will cost a bit more... like ten thousand dollars more."

Kyle nearly choked on his donut. "Ten thousand?! For what?"

"Zoey has had some medical issues with her ovaries and uterus. For her to get pregnant, we would need to use in vitro fertilization, and that costs about ten grand per try."

"Per try?"

"Yeah, and there is no guarantee that it would work the first time. We read about couples who tried up to ten times and still didn't have any children."

Kyle blew out a long breath. He couldn't imagine paying a hundred thousand dollars just to have a child. The donut was now threatening to revolt. "When did she tell you about all this?"

Tyler looked down at the ground, suddenly finding the tiled floor interesting. "She told me when we first started dating. Do you remember when I went out of town while her ex was still stalking around?"

Kyle nodded. Everyone had been so concerned about Zoey's safety, and for good reason. That crazy asshole came back, beat her and shot her when she jumped in front of the gun when it was pointed at Tyler.

Tyler's voice broke into his memories. "Well, we talked as much as we could at night. She told me one night when we started talking about kids. She wanted me to know right away so I wouldn't be taken by surprise later. She was very candid about her history and the chances of us having a child naturally. I'm okay with it. The most important thing is being with her. However, we want to try at least a couple of times. If it doesn't work, then we will look at adoption."

Kyle looked at his brother who was trying hard not to show that this was affecting him, but he knew better. "I'm sorry. Just know that if you need help with money, I have quite a bit stashed. If it helps me be an uncle, I would spend that money happily."

"Thanks, I appreciate that, but I think we got this. At least most of it anyway."

It broke Kyle's heart to see his brother worry about being able to create his own family. When it came to family, Kyle knew he had basically won the lottery. His parents were kind and loving people, and they were still happily married. Mark and Hannah were that couple who raised the standards for a good marriage. They rarely fought and when they did, it was usually because his dad did it on purpose to watch his mom get flustered and a get a bit pushy. He always told her that he loved her "bluster" as he called it.

Tyler was just as good as his parents. Growing up, Tyler was always kind and patient to Kyle even when he didn't deserve it. Tyler was a bit of a nerd, while Kyle had been popular and athletic in school, but it was always Tyler helping Kyle keep up the grades to stay in sports, and he didn't make a big deal of it when Kyle ignored him at school. There was only two years separating them, and Kyle didn't really appreciate their relationship until it was almost time for Tyler to go to college. Kyle missed him so much, he ended up choosing his college to be in the same city as his brother. Now, Tyler was getting married, which he still couldn't believe. If he were honest, he thought that he would be the first to get married, to Ariel, but he fucked that all up.

Tyler threw away their remnants from breakfast and started to leave. As he grabbed for the door he quickly turned around and said, "Oh, Mom said to remind you that she is working with Amanda on the annual Senior Center Charity Bachelor Auction that is next weekend. Now that I am off limits, she needs you more than ever."

Kyle couldn't believe that was coming up already. Every year their mom worked with Amanda, Ariel's mom, on the bachelor auction. Even when he lived in Philadelphia, she made both boys come home to visit and participate in the event. It was always a bright spot in the year. Ariel always outbid the competition, and wouldn't allow him to spend time with anyone else. Would she bid on him again? Of course, she would. He had a great date planned for this year. Sure, it would be torture to be close to her and not really having her, but he sure didn't want some other schmuck taking her out. "Tell Mom I am still good to go, and I will run the article promoting the event Sunday."

"Don't forget to give out the flyers she dropped off for all the businesses."

"And why can't you walk your lazy ass around town to hand them out?"

Puffing up his chest he smiled and said, "Because I still help Dad with chores around the house... and I am her favorite."

Kyle reached over behind him and pulled out the Nerf gun and shot at Tyler's forehead. "Get out, asshole."

IT WAS NEARLY MIDNIGHT by the time Kyle got home that night. He had worked late trying to get his mind off Ariel. He even skipped meeting everyone at the bar that night claiming that work was busy. Right. He ran a small-town newspaper, and nothing was going on. Busy. Most of the time he enjoyed the quiet, but there were times the quiet brought back the images of violence and chaos from the city when he reported for the major paper. It was the last dead girl that broke him.

Kyle walked over to his desk and pulled out a manilla folder with his hurried handwriting on the tab reading "Sangres Nobles." On top was an article with a photograph taken in Northeast Philly by a local restaurant. The headline read, *Local Woman's Life Taken by Gang Violence*. The picture was taken by a staff photographer and captured an image of Kyle talking to the police officer while standing next to the body draped in a white sheet. Kyle remembered seeing her brazenly laid across the corner sidewalk. They weren't even trying to hide what they did. No, it was out on grand display for the world to see. It had only been fifteen minutes before that he received a text from her asking for him to meet her there. When he found the body, he knew that text wasn't from her, but it was definitely a message to him. The poor girl, Gianna, had been helping him with information to bring down the Sangres Nobles, a Latino gang who ruled that area of Philly.

Under the article was another picture of Gianna. She was beautiful with dark flowing hair and golden skin. Her large brown eyes seemed intelligent beyond her young age. She worked at the restaurant just a few feet from where she was found that awful night. Everyone seemed to love her and all she wanted in the world was to see the people she loved safe, her little brother and her fiancé. Seeing her smiling image brought back a flood of memories from when they'd first met, after he received an anonymous email promising the information he needed to complete his series of articles about the local gang activity.

"PEOPLE HAVE TOLD ME that you can be trusted, but what I have to tell you could get me and the people I love into a lot of trouble if it isn't handled in just the right way. What can you tell me that is going to make me feel like I am doing the right thing?"

Kyle studied the young girl as she sat on the bench next to him at the park just a few blocks from his office. She was nervous. Her fidgeting fingers gave that away. "I will answer any questions you have. I have nothing to hide, and remember you contacted me." He was trying to portray confidence in his tone, but he was scared he was going to lose this contact. Nearly all of the community was tight lipped and wouldn't talk to him. And really, he didn't blame them. He stuck out like a sore thumb. Being a middle-class, attractive, white male walking around in a nearly exclusively Latino community did not get much in conversation from others.

Gianna slowly exhaled. "Even personal questions? Just to get to know you better?"

Kyle gave a small laugh. "Sure. I don't have anything to hide."

"Have you always lived out here?"

"No."

"Yeah. Figured. You have an accent."

Kyle quirked a brow. "I have an accent?"

She imitated his brow quirk. "Yeah. You don't sound like you're from Philly, and you talk slower."

"I didn't know I was talking slow."

She shrugged. "More like you aren't in a hurry like the rest of us."

"Huh." Kyle never really noticed that before, but the more he thought about it he could see what she was saying.

"So, where ya from?"

"Blossom Hills, North Carolina."

"Seriously? That sounds like a made-up Hallmark Channel town. You got a wife?"

Kyle thought about Ariel. He was almost done. This was going to be his last investigative series and then he was quitting and moving back home. He was going to get his princess, as long as she didn't let some other guy swoop in and take his place. He sighed. "No. I don't have a wife."

Gianna smiled. "Oh, but there is someone. I see that spark that my Zeke gets when he sees me for the first time each day. What's her name? Does she live here?"

Kyle could feel his eyes crinkle from his big smile. "Her name is Ariel, and she doesn't live here."

"Like that mermaid? Man, she had cruel parents."

Laughing, Kyle said, "No, actually they are incredible people. They're amazing parents and good to just about everyone they know."

Gianna's eyes dropped slightly. "Must be nice. All I have is my mom, my brother and Zeke. Dad left us when I was a baby. Zeke takes good care of me, and my mom. He gives her extra money, so we don't have to worry about keeping the electric on."

"I'm sorry."

"Don't feel sorry for me. There are plenty others around here who are worse off than us. So, when did you know you loved this girl?"

Kyle shrugged. "When we were kids. She's my best friend's little sister. One time, she got lost in the woods and broke her arm. I was the one who found her. She was a mess, but when I found her, she looked at me as if I could make her whole world better. And while I didn't completely understand it at the time, I wanted to always make her look at me that way. When we are having a hard time, we always go back to that tree. I can't tell you how many times she has found me there, or I have found her. We call it our enchanted tree."

"Wow, now that is some real fairy tale shit right there."

Kyle laughed. "Well, to get my happily ever after I need to finish this last story I promised my editor, and then I am moving back home to get my girl."

Gianna grew quiet and didn't answer Kyle. A tear fell down her cheek, and she began to fidget again.

"Gianna, tell me, what do you need to get you your happily ever after? You called me for a reason, and I am thinking that I am supposed to help you with that somehow."

"Zeke was getting ready to leave Sangres Nobles. He was all set to make our escape, but then my little brother joined, and he stayed to keep an eye out for him. I want them both out. The only way to make that happen is to help bring them down. We could all leave, and no one would try to find us. I made a connection in Ohio, where I can get a good job for both me and Zeke. Mom said she would come too and bring my brother, so we could live a normal life."

"Okay, so tell me what I can do to help make that happen."

"I heard information about a specific shipment that is coming up. Everyone will be there except Zeke, my brother and two others. I also have videos that are proof of a couple of murders for several members. I give you this, and you give it to a cop that you trust and won't screw us over. I know a lot of cops are dirty, and I don't want to mess up in which one to trust."

"Okay, but you will need to time this just right when you leave."

Gianna nodded. "I already have it all planned out. I shipped some of our important things to my friend in Ohio and we will leave that night with just some duffel bags. The crappy furniture can stay with whoever takes over the apartment."

She handed over an envelope that Kyle figured out had a key inside.

Gianna pointed to his hand that held the envelope. "Take care of that. Our lives are literally in your hands. I need this to work."

"I promise I will take care of this."

"Follow the instructions exactly and we all should get our happy endings."

KYLE HAD FOLLOWED THE instructions exactly and Gianna didn't get her happily ever after. Instead, she was murdered, Zeke and her brother were now deeper in the life of violence and her mother was still living in that crappy apartment. And Kyle? He was living a half-life of work and daily torture of what he couldn't have. He remembered how he went to the train station and retrieved the memory card full of videos, pictures and detailed shipment information of drugs and guns for the next two months. It was an investigative jackpot. He could have been back home in a month at the most. What happened instead was burned into his mind. Gianna was dead, the files went missing, his story was squashed by his editor and Sangres Nobles didn't diminish in presence but instead grew only stronger and more violent.

Kyle carefully put all the documents back into the folder and dropped it into his desk drawer, where the other folder held all the evidence of threats to Ariel and his family. He picked up the glass blown Cinderella slipper that was left with the last picture of Ariel from the wedding with a red "X" drawn across her face. It was the latest glass trinket and picture that had been left as a warning. Quickly, all the frustration, rage and feeling of helplessness washed over him and he picked up the figurine and threw it across the room hitting the wall and smashing into a million shards of glass on the floor.

Chapter 4

It was Sunday morning and Ariel was already having a bad day. The latest shipment of glass blown figurines was late, Myrna called in sick and she had four guys giggling in the corner over the risqué cards with scantily clad men and women on the covers. Yeah, she knew they were vulgar and honestly some were quite funny, but really couldn't people be adults about it? At one point she thought about discontinuing them in her store, but then she ran the reports and found out how much money she was making off of them. The profit margin on cards was ridiculous, and she was living quite comfortably in part because of them.

After hearing hushed tones and whispers for the millionth time, she rolled her eyes and sent a text requesting some nourishment.

Ariel: Myrna called in and it is just me. Please rescue me with some doughnuts.

Zoey: That bad?

Ariel: Yes. I have a bunch of morons laughing over the sexy cards. You would think they never saw a woman in a bikini before.

Zoey: Teenagers?

Ariel: No. A bunch of dumb men in their late twenties who will probably be bald and fat by thirty-five.

Zoey: Locals?

Ariel: Don't think so. They look like stragglers from last night's wedding at the gazebo.

Zoey: Ugh. Ok. Sending Phil with goodies.

Ariel: You are the best.

It was only about five minutes before she heard the bell chime on the front door as Phil walked in with a small white box.

"Here you go, Miss McKenna."

"Oh. Thank you so much Phil, and please just call me Ariel."

"No, sorry, ma'am. My momma would kick my ass if I didn't show you the proper respect. I can call you Miss Ariel if that helps."

Opening the box, she shook her head. "Not really, but if you stop calling me ma'am, I will take Miss Ariel."

Grinning, he replied, "Yes ma'am."

Ariel gave him a glaring look. "Phillip!"

Phil wisely backed up a few steps and laughed. "Sorry, Miss Ariel. I have to get back to the bakery now." He looked back at the men in the far corner and studied them for a minute. "Do you need me to help you with anything before I go?"

Ariel gave a quick glance at the men and watched as one started swaying back and forth. "No. I've got this, but thanks, Phil."

The teenager gave a quick nod of his head and left out the front door. Ariel sighed and sat on her stool to finish her breakfast with the water she had stored under the counter. The men were still in the corner, but they didn't seem to be reading the cards anymore. She hated to be one of those clerks that hovered over their customers, but seriously, they had been looking around over there for well over twenty minutes now.

Finally, after finishing her second donut she walked over to the men who seemed to be hiding something. She was only a few feet away when she caught that unmistakable rancid smell. She reached the first man and tapped him on his shoulder. "Excuse me, but—"

The man stepped aside and there was no mistaking the vomit that was now covering her cards and floor. It was obvious to see who the culprit was. The shortest man with thinning dark hair was now shirtless and using the pole for support. The tallest of the men finally cleared his throat and was the first to speak. "Our friend got sick. I think he had too much to drink last night."

Ariel glared up at the man who was almost a foot taller than her. "I figured that out, thank you."

"We're really sorry."

"Yeah, well did you see that sign up front that said you break it you buy it?"

Another man who was also covered partially in vomit holding up his friend asked, "Yeah?"

"Well, I also have a 'you puke you pay' policy."

The men all looked at the cards that had been sprayed in vomit and shook their heads. The tall man who appeared to be the most sober looked to be doing math in his head. "That could be almost five hundred dollars."

"Bummer. You better dig deep boys." Ariel stood glaring at the men with her arms crossed.

A bell rang at the front of the store indicating a new customer was walking in. Ariel momentarily tried to look behind her to see who walked in, and that is when the tallest man decided to bolt. He quickly pushed Ariel to the side causing her to fall into the display of cards. She gave a gasp that was more from shock, than it was from getting hurt.

As she was pulling herself off the cards, she heard a couple of male voices arguing. She heard the man complaining about wanting to be let go, and then Kyle's angry voice echoing through the store. "You never put your hands on a woman." Suddenly, there was a solid thud of what sounded like a body slamming into a surface. Then Kyle's deep growling voice rose through the air again, "Especially, this woman."

Ariel started to panic. Kyle was going to end up doing something stupid if she didn't get up there. She turned to the other two men and pointed her finger. "Stay!"

The man who got sick was still leaning on his friend and the pole, and just shrugged. "Couldn't, even if I wanted to."

By the time she got back to the front, she saw Kyle pressing the man's chest into the counter. "Kyle, let him go. He won't go anywhere, *and* he is sorry." She bent over to tilt her head in the same direction his was being held to meet his eyes. With a smile she asked, "Right?"

The man gave a slight nod of his head.

Ariel rolled her eyes. "Use grown up words, please."

Kyle seemed to be loosening his grip on the man. He cleared his throat. "I'm sorry, and I'm not going anywhere. I promise."

Kyle's face suddenly seemed to refocus, and he looked around seemingly searching for something. "God, what is that smell?"

Ariel sighed. "Oh, that would be me, those two idiots back there and probably several hundred dollars' worth of greeting cards are covered in vomit."

Kyle's grip tightened on the man's neck. "You vomited on her?"

Gasping for breath he replied, "Not me."

A small male voice could be heard from the back. "That would be me."

Ariel tilted her head back down again to look at the man under Kyle's grip. "Are you going to stay put if I run next door for a couple of minutes?"

Kyle looked confused. "Are you going to get a snack to eat while covered in puke?"

Ariel stood up and glared. "No, dummy. I am going to get a pair of latex gloves I know Zoey keeps on hand. I need to handle all the cards to figure out how much these guys owe me."

Kyle nodded and then nudged the man still pinned to the counter. "And they will happily pay an extra hundred-dollar inconvenience fee, and a little extra to clean her dress. Right?"

Cleaning fee? She was throwing this dress away. Gross. The man in the back holding his friend up finally said, "We will pay whatever. Just let him up, and can we get a chair for him?" He was now nodding at his friend who was looking greener than ever.

Kyle finally let go of the man and they walked back to where the other men were still standing by the display.

Ariel said to Kyle, "Can you put the closed sign on the door and lock it? Also get him that plastic chair from the stock room while I go out the back door to the bakery. I don't want anyone to see me like this."

Kyle nodded his agreement, and Ariel exited out the back door. She took a minute to collect herself before walking the few steps to the bakery's back door. The smell on her dress was getting to her. As she approached, she saw the bakery's door was open with Zoey mixing what looked like icing. Josie was leaning on the prep counter eating a bear claw, looking as perfect as ever in her button-down ivory blouse and navy pencil skirt.

Josie immediately stopped eating and put down the pastry. "What's wrong? What happened?

Ariel's stress levels just flared up all at once and her hormones decided now was a good time for a breakdown. Her lip quivered as she looked up and said, "I am having such a bad day." Her breath shuddered as she turned to Zoey. "Can I have a few pairs of gloves, please?"

Zoey nodded quickly. "Of course, hon." She grabbed a few from the box on the shelf and started to walk over, but abruptly stopped. "Oh God, what is that smell?"

Ariel hung her head down. "That would be me. I got shoved into a pile of puke." She slowly turned around and the two women gasped as they saw the remnants of the offending odor. After a few quiet moments Josie broke the silence.

"Wait, some asshole shoved you into puke?"

"Yup. His buddy puked all over the cards and then in his attempt to escape he shoved me aside and I landed all in it."

Josie started to walk towards the door. "I am going to slice his dick with paper cuts using those damned nasty cards."

While that sounded like a fun idea Ariel knew she had to stop Josie from doing something to get her arrested. "No, Josie. Kyle is over there keeping an eye on them. He already shoved the guy's face into the counter. I don't need you *helping* him."

Josie took a deep breath. "Fine, but you really do take all the fun out of my day."

Ariel tilted her head to the side and studied her friend. "You really do scare me sometimes you know that?"

Josie shrugged. "Aren't you glad I love you? Just imagine if I didn't like you."

Then a male voice came from the corner. "I have seen what she does to people she doesn't like. It isn't pretty." Ariel turned to see Phil holding a couple empty trays, obviously overhearing the girls' conversation. "Miss Ariel, I have that garden hose and sprayer out back I use to clean up the alley. Do you want me to spray you off before you go back?"

Ariel looked down at her dress and took an inhale of breath to check how bad the odor was. Resigned she finally said, "Yeah, that is probably a good idea."

Josie stepped in between Phil and Ariel. "Oooo... let me do it."

Ariel, Zoey and Phil all provided a firm immediate answer of, "NO!"

Josie crossed her arms and narrowed her eyes at the three of them. "Fun killers."

KYLE HAD BEEN WAITING now for what seemed like ten minutes. How long does it take to get some gloves? The other men were still there, breaking the silence every now and then with a cough or awkward clearing of their throats. The smell was also starting to get a bit stronger. Thankfully, the years in college helped to build a strong tolerance to rancid smells. His roommates had their fair share of bad hangovers and they didn't always make it to the bathroom, not to mention they were not the cleanest of men. One of his roommates had left out an open milk carton, and for some inexplicable reason he put it behind the couch. It took hours for them to find out where that smell was coming from.

Finally, the back door opened, and Ariel walked in with her clothes all wet and her body glistening from water droplets. She pointed to the two men who had the puke still on their clothes and said, "You two, go out the back and get sprayed off. Phil and Josie are out there waiting on you. Then come back in here."

Kyle snorted. He could just imagine Josie's evil streak spraying them on full blast. After the two men left Kyle looked over at Ariel and asked incredulously, "You let Josie spray you off?"

Ariel scrunched up her face. "Do I look crazy? No. Phil did it, but I promised her she could torture the men." She handed over a pair of gloves to Kyle and retrieved a large garbage bag from the counter. "Do you want to play with the scanner?"

Grinning, Kyle reached over and grabbed the scanning gun. He looked down expecting to see a cord attached to the gun and smiled. "You upgraded."

"Yes. Myrna kept knocking stuff over with the cord, so I upgraded to the wireless. Come on, the sooner we get the damaged stuff scanned, the sooner we can kick them all out."

Ariel carefully pulled out the cards as Kyle scanned each barcode. He couldn't believe how many cards got hit. The rack vertically held eight rows, and the damage was about seven rows across. At some point in between each chirp of the scanner the two men returned drenched from head to toe. Kyle smirked and continued to trigger each card that Ariel held up.

The man who caused this whole mess still didn't seem to be looking any better. He looked at his friend and groaned. "That bitch kept pelting me in the head with the sprayer."

Ariel casually continued to pull each card out and replied, "Maybe next time you will try better to make it to a toilet. Or here's a thought... don't drink so damn much."

Kyle winced. Ariel was not much for cussing, so if she actually used a swear word she was pissed and barely holding her temper back. It reminded him a lot of his mom. She was the most patient and kind person, but once she reached her breaking point everyone hid from her.

Finally, all the cards had been scanned, and they walked to the register to see the total. "Six hundred forty-two dollars and eighty-seven cents."

Kyle cleared his throat. "Don't forget the hundred-dollar inconvenience fee and a little extra for the dress."

The three men all pulled out their wallets and combined their cash for a total of eight hundred dollars. After grumbling their complaints, they finally left leaving Kyle alone with Ariel. She sighed and started walking to the stock room. Without turning her head, she said, "You can go home if you want. I can take care of the rest of this."

Kyle did a slight jog and caught up to her. "Nah. I can stay and help. Besides, there is no big news going on in town today. I would just be sitting up at home... alone... all by myself."

Ariel shook her head and her slightly damp hair stuck to her cheek. "That was pathetic."

Kyle shrugged. "That's what I was going for."

"Well, if you help me, I can at least get a shower sooner." She started filling a small bucket with hot water and what looked like a floor cleaner. She then grabbed a scrub brush from the shelf and pointed to the top and asked, "Can you reach that big roll of paper towels?"

Nodding, he pulled them down and waited for further instruction. Ariel didn't say a word. She simply took her bucket and brush and walked back out into the shop. Kyle followed like an obedient puppy.

Ariel put the bucket down and stood with her hands on her hips. "Do you think that The Monkey's Wrench still has that steam cleaner for rent?" The Monkey's Wrench was the local hardware shop that seemed to have just a bit of everything. Mr. Mandrill always had a good sense of humor, and when he decided to open the hardware store, he wanted to play off his name since his last name was a type of monkey. Also, when he traveled to Asia, he found that monkeys also liked to collect and sometimes steal shiny objects, so he made it a point to carry just about every gadget and gizmo known to man. His son, Rafe, who was named after Rafiki, the mandrill monkey from *The Lion King*, now mostly ran the store.

Kyle thought for a minute and said, "I can call Rafe and ask him if he has it today. If he does, I will go pick it up for you."

"Oh, yes please. That would be helpful."

"Even if he doesn't, I can borrow Mom's cleaner."

Ariel gave a sad nod. "I really wish I would have listened to Derek when he said to install tile instead of carpet."

"Yeah, but we can't take all of our older brothers' advice. Then they get big egos."

Ariel snort laughed. "Yes, they do."

Kyle held up his phone. "I am going to step outside and get some air and make that call."

Ariel laughed. "Wuss."

Kyle was already almost to the front door. "Yup, and not ashamed of it."

ARIEL WAS ON HER SECOND bucket of cleaning mix when Kyle walked back in wheeling the big red carpet cleaning machine. She blew out a relieved breath. "Thank god. Just leave it by the counter and I will use it when I get done here."

Kyle set a bag on the counter and pulled out the carpet cleaning solution and a tub of bleach wipes. "I got these for you too... just for good measure."

"That was good thinking. Thanks."

Kyle and Ariel worked to wipe down the rack with the bleach wipes, when Ariel suddenly started laughing.

Shaking his head Kyle asked, "What's so funny?"

"Oh, I was just thinking about that time you and Derek were puking your guts out after trying alcohol for the first time."

"Hey... it wasn't my first time."

"Your dad letting you sip his beer doesn't count. How much did you guys have to drink that night?"

Kyle paused seemingly trying to concentrate. "Well maybe about four beers, a few shots, and a few blue mixed drinks."

"No wonder you guys got sick. You can't mix all that stuff at once. Especially, if you haven't drank before."

"Yeah. We figured that out, but to be fair nobody told us that before we started. They just kept pouring, and we kept drinking."

"You're lucky that Mom was out of town. She would have killed you both."

Kyle gave a small huff of laughter. "Yup. Especially after Derek missed the toilet and threw up on the bathroom rug."

"Have you been sick again since?"

"Oh yeah. College was a blur of drinking with a bit of studying until junior year. I finally realized that I had to focus so I could work at a big paper."

Ariel thoughtfully wiped at the bottom ledge and looked down. "I didn't think you were coming back. I thought that you would stay there, become famous and forget about all of us." Her heart panged as she remembered how she felt abandoned the first couple years after he graduated. She thought he was going to forget all about her. The dreams she had of making a life with Kyle had faded to a blurry vision packed away in the small corners of her heart. Then, when he came home, he wasn't the same happy easygoing person he was before. She knew she had to give him time to find himself and hopefully find his way to her. After almost a year she started dating again, at first hoping it would pull him out of the fog he always seemed lost in. She thought maybe he would figure his issues out and claim her, but it never happened. Eventually, those hopes faded too, and she settled into a life where she was a part of his world but would always have to stand at the edge and watch.

Kyle crouched down to the bottom, took off one of his gloves, and turned her face to look at him. "First, I would never forget you. I never stopped wanting you... and the others here to be in my life. I had always planned on coming back home. I just felt that being a journalist at an important paper was something I had to do, but I also knew myself well enough that I wouldn't want it forever." He brought his hand to her cheek, where he stroked it gently with his thumb.

Ariel didn't want to break the moment. Feeling Kyle's light touch on her cheek was like a zap of electricity leading straight to her heart. She took a deep breath in and closed her eyes, but then she started to waver in her balance. Kyle immediately caught her before she fell onto the floor.

"Careful. Here stand up for a minute."

Kyle helped her stand up, and she lifted her head to look directly at him. His eyes were soft and seemed to be searching for something in her face. Finally, she remembered his last words and before she could think better of it asked, "What do you want forever?"

Kyle grazed his hand along her jawline and then sunk his fingers into her still damp hair. "I want all the beautiful things that I can't have."

Ariel's heart was racing. She was trying to interpret what he was saying against what his body and eyes were telling her. "You know with me; you could have everything."

She waited, holding her breath, waiting for him to do something. He needed to move in and accept her with her heart in her hands, open to what he would be willing to give. After watching him internally struggle for a moment, he finally took his hand off the back of her neck and was breathing as if he'd just ran a marathon. Just when she thought he would leave her again he gave a whispered curse and lifted her up and leaned her against the pole. His mouth was suddenly on hers, but this was no gentle kiss of soft love. No, this was a needy, desperate claiming of her body. He was pressed up fully against her to help support her weight and his hands dug into her ass as she wrapped her arms around his neck meeting his desperation with equal force.

Kyle's tongue grazed along hers as she finally groaned into his mouth. This seemed to spark energy into Kyle as he adjusted to free one hand from her ass and weaved it back into her hair and neck. Their bodies were pressed so hard together she barely knew where she began and he started. It felt as if her heart would burst from her chest as she tried to breathe in between the hard press of their lips and tongues.

It was only a minute or so before she started to slide down the pole. Kyle tried to follow her down with his lips never leaving hers. She started to form a smile and laugh when he finally released her lips. With pure happiness she looked into his eyes. "Maybe we should continue this in the back."

Kyle nodded looking back at the front window. "Yes. Privacy would be great."

He followed her to the stock room and came to a dead stop staring at the shelf with the incoming inventory. Ariel watched as his face grew pale. She looked at him and back to the shelf confused. "Kyle?"

Her voice seemed to break his thoughts, and he looked at her with what looked like fear in his eyes. He pointed to the collection of glass and crystal pumpkin carriages. "When did you start carrying these?"

Ariel looked at the shelf and tried to remember. "Just this year. I think it was about the time Zoey moved to town. I had a customer asking for trinkets that would be related to queens and princesses. I showed him this line of collectables and he loved it. I ordered extra thinking they would be great to release for Christmas. You like them?"

For a moment Kyle studied the shelf, and he spoke in nearly a whisper. "I can't do this."

"What?" Her question came out as a pained squeak. He couldn't be doing this. Not again. He pulled her in again and was going to leave her with a hole in her chest where her heart should be.

"I'm sorry, Ariel. We can't... I can't." He was finally looking into her eyes and he looked almost as pained as she felt.

He was doing it again. He was leaving, only this time he had finally crossed that line that seemed to always be carved into the earth between them. She couldn't breathe. She watched as Kyle took two steps backwards, away from her, leaving her cold and empty. With her body trembling, she watched him take a slow turn and walk towards the stock room door. Just as he reached the threshold, she said in a small but still not quite quivering voice, "Kyle."

He stopped with his hand on the doorknob.

"If you walk away again, you will break us. You will break me."

Kyle's head dropped in defeat, but he never turned around. "At least you will heal. If you love me, you will end up worse than broken. I... I am so sorry, Princess."

Ariel watched as he walked through the shop and out the front door. It was only when she had lost him from her sight, that she finally tried to take a deep breath only to stutter in several gulps of air as she slid down the wall to the ground, and finally allowed herself to let the tears pull out from her soul.

KYLE WALKED HOME WITH his soul shattered in pieces. He did the one thing he knew he couldn't. He was weak. He let his body have a taste of her. Even worse, he let her have hope that they could finally be what they were always meant to be... together. She told him that if he left, he would break them, but the whole problem was that he had been broken for years. His spirit broke when he was told he could never have her.

The short couple of blocks back to his office were filled with people smiling at him and wishing him well. He couldn't talk to anyone. He just gave a small smile and nod as he passed by, evading all small talk. Finally, he made it back to his office and grabbed the bottle of bourbon that was given to him as a present from the mayor, picked up his truck keys and quickly left to go home.

As he drove, his hands were itching to open the liquor bottle and begin the process of wiping all these feelings from his chest. He hadn't washed away pain with liquor in a long time, but he just wanted to stop the pain, even if it was just for one night. Once he crossed the threshold of his door, the bottle was immediately opened, and he gulped the drink as if it provided precious air to his lungs.

He dropped himself to his desk chair, opened the bottom drawer and pulled out a small glass and crystal tiara. It was similar to the carriages he saw on Ariel's stock room shelf. He immediately knew it was from the same line of products. That bastard had been in her shop. He'd talked to her and bought this to taunt Kyle.

Kyle remembered back to the day he found that tiara and a picture of Ariel with a giant red X across her face. The conversation between him and Zeke echoed in his head as if it were yesterday.

KYLE HAD WALKED IN the door still wearing his toga from McKenna's Ides of March party. He had been in a good mood until he found a small glass tiara on his front porch with a manilla envelope. With shaky hands he'd opened the contents to find a picture of Ariel laughing and walking with Zoey by the town gazebo. A bright red X was across her face and a yellow Post-it Note was attached reading, "The princess could still die."

Kyle gripped the picture hard with one hand and threw his fist into the door with his free hand. "Shit!" He drew his hand back and clenched it a few times checking for injuries. He thought he was being watched at the bar but was never able to find anyone so he had shaken it off. His mind was now flooded with regret for not trusting his gut.

He finally opened the door and walked in to find Zeke already comfortably sitting on his couch with an arm draped across the back.

With eyes narrowed he dropped the tiara and picture on the entry table, and said to his intruder, "Get the fuck out of my house."

Zeke smiled with a knowing glint of someone who had the upper hand. "Now is that any way to greet your guest?"

"You are no guest of mine. I have been playing by your rules, so get the fuck out of my house and out of my life."

Zeke raised up from the couch and started to close into Kyle's space. "See, now I have heard that you might need to have a reminder from me about our deal. It seems that you and your little princess have been getting a little too close these days."

Kyle's anger got the best of him and he attempted to lunge at Zeke, but he was no match for the street-smart fighter. Kyle ended up with his back up against the wall and

Zeke's arm across his neck. The man angrily pushed harder as he said, "You are alive only by my grace, and that my queen liked you, but she isn't here. I can't be with her, so you can't be with yours. If I have to kill her to make that happen so be it. We both failed my love. She is dead because of both of us. Neither of us gets our happily ever after." He finally loosened his grip and took a step back.

Both men startled as the police scanner went off and the dispatcher advised about the break in and vandalism at Sweet Dreams Bakery. They looked at each other after the call was completed. Kyle clenched his fists and accusingly looked at Zeke. "You fucking destroyed the bakery?"

Zeke scoffed. "No!"

"Yeah, right."

Zeke shook his head and pointed at the scanner. "This was not us. We have been looking forward to having more than one place to have breakfast in this damn little town too. We have no reason to mess with the pretty little baker."

"Stay away from Zoey."

"Again. I am tired of your greasy spoon diner. We have no plans to mess with the baker."

Strangely, Kyle believed him. While Zeke was a violent gang criminal, he had never lied to Kyle during all their interactions. His intentions and actions were always proudly displayed for him to see.

Zeke finally made a move to get his jacket off the couch. "Looks like there is a story out there. Go do your job that is so fucking important to you."

Kyle winced. He knew that Zeke felt that Gianna died because Kyle had to have his story. The guilt that he felt over her death weighed on his conscience just as he knew it weighed on Zeke's. Stopping at the door with his hand on the knob Zeke finally said, "It was her birthday today. I thought you should know, and someone should feel a bit of the pain that I do." With those final words Zeke pulled the door closed and quietly slipped out into the cold, black night.

Chapter 5

Ariel was never so thankful to see a Monday morning in her life. She didn't have to work today. Lana was going to open the store and Myrna was closing. Ariel's head was pounding out a loud and harsh rhythm from crying all night. Seeing Kyle walk out on her again, only this time after giving her a taste of what they could be, had her picking up pieces of her heart off the floor. Then to add insult to injury she still had to steam clean the carpet from the idiot's puke.

She entered The Monkey's Wrench to return the carpet cleaner only to find Rafe behind the counter looking at her with great concern. Rafe was an attractive man with dark brown hair and matching eyes. The tattoos on his arms added an edge to him, but his eyes were always kind. When he had asked her what was wrong, she gave him a weak smile and just said that she was tired after the horrible day she was having. She wasn't convincing. Not even a little bit, but at this point she didn't care. Her plan for the day was to go home and change into her flannel pajamas and fluffy slippers and eat junk food. And no yoga today either. Today was for wallowing. Screw men.

Rafe's gentle smile seemed to ease her a little. He never talked much, but when he did, you knew whatever he was going to say, it was important. "Whatever he did, I'm sure he's sorry, or at least it wasn't intended to harm you."

Ariel sucked in a breath. "I don't know what you are talking about."

Rafe raised his eyebrows. "Well, the way I see it is, Kyle rented the machine, and you are returning it, and now you have that heartbreaking look on your face. So, I assume he screwed up... again."

Ariel sighed in resignation. "Could you do me a favor and not mention this to anyone else? The last thing I need is everyone hovering over me. I just want to take a couple days of quiet time and maybe eat a couple of gallons of ice cream."

Rafe nodded. "Boom Chocolatta."

Ariel gave a small huff of a laugh. "What?"

"Boom Chocolatta. It's a Ben and Jerry's flavor. My cousin swears by it every time she breaks up with the dumb ass of the week."

Ariel's smile widened. "I will have to go pick some up then. Thanks, Rafe."

"Anytime. Now go sugar it up."

Ariel left the store and approached her car when she saw that her passenger side tire was completely flat. "Fantastic," she muttered to herself. At least she wasn't wearing a dress today so she wouldn't get scraped up changing the tire. She opened her trunk and flipped up the blanket to reach the tire and jack. As she was pulling out the tire, she heard a deep voice behind her.

"Need some help?

Ariel knew that voice. She dreamed of that voice every night. Sighing, she tightened her grip on the tire and replied. "Nope. I've got this."

"Come on, Ariel. Don't be stubborn. Let me help you."

"I think you helped me enough this week." The tire finally broke free and thudded down to the pavement.

Ariel saw a flash of hurt in Kyle's eyes, but she wasn't going to fall for it this time. He walked out. Not her. And she didn't need him to rescue her. She could change a tire. Her dad had his faults, but he'd taught her many things so she could be strong and independent, and changing a tire was one of them.

Kyle wasn't moving, and she walked around him when she figured out that he wasn't going to get out of her way. She leaned the tire against the car and went back for the jack.

"Ariel, listen about last night. I just wanted to say..."

Ariel pulled out the jack and slammed down the trunk... hard. "Say what? You're sorry? You just can't do this with me? You don't want me like that? Jesus, Kyle I get it. You want me to move on, so get out of my way and let me do it. Let me change this stupid tire and get on with my day. Then after that, I will figure out how to get on with my life without you in it, because this," she started pointing between the two of them, "isn't working anymore either."

Kyle bowed his head and stuffed his hands in his pockets. Ariel stood with the jack in her hands waiting for him to do or say something. After a few minutes she shook her head. "Just go. I've got this." She started to walk past him, and he wrapped his hand around her arm stopping her.

"Ariel. Believe me I wish I could."

She lifted her head and looked in his eyes. She could only use a small whisper. "Then please explain it to me, because this is tearing both of us apart."

Kyle's hand slid down her arm to where the pine tree charm bracelet rested and he fingered the charm. Ariel wished some of the magic from their tree could change what was happening now, but there was this sharp pain that was stabbing in her chest searing into a deep feeling of loss. "Last chance, Kyle. Tell me now so we can fix this, or let me go." Ariel looked into his eyes as he seemed to struggle with himself, but it only took a moment before the corners of his eyes dropped and she knew she had lost him again.

Kyle finally released his grip on her but didn't release their locked gazes. He took a step back and exhaled a big breath. "I'm going, but know this Princess, if things were different, I'd never let you go." After taking a few more steps away he turned and disappeared around the corner.

Ariel was determined to hold it together. She slammed the jack under the car and lifted it to remove the tire. It wasn't until she tried to loosen the first lug nut that she finally started to cry. The damned thing wasn't budging, and she started pounding her fists onto the cross wrench. "Stupid tire. Stupid lugnut. Stupid Kyle. Stupid. Stupid. Stupid." With each word she kept pounding her fist harder and the tears just kept falling. Suddenly she felt strong arms wrapped around her and large hands stroking her hair trying to calm her down.

Another man's voice she knew so well was whispering words in calm tones until she was able to take in a deep breath.

"Daddy?" Ariel leaned her full weight into her dad's body and let her tears flow silently.

"Come on, sweetheart. Let's go inside. Okay?"

Ariel nodded, but then turned to see her tire still waiting to be changed. "I need to change…"

"No, you don't. I will take care of that after I take care of you."

Feeling safe in her dad's arms she stood up and leaned into his side as they walked to his building. She kept her head down as they walked past his assistant into his office. Jeremy pulled a box of tissues from his filing cabinet and handed them over to Ariel as he sat on the couch next to her.

"You still keep a stash of tissues in the cabinets?"

Jeremy tilted his head and gave a small deprecating smile. "I run an insurance company, sweetheart. People come in my office after a loved one dies, or they lost their home to a fire. If I just let the tears fall all crazy like, we would drown in my office."

Ariel gave a small huff of laughter.

"Ah. Now, there is my sweet girl. You want to tell your old Dad what happened?"

Shaking her shoulders in a small shrug she finally said, "I was returning the steam cleaner to Rafe, and when I came back out, the tire was flat."

Jeremy arched his eyebrow. It was the same look he used when his kids did something wrong and was waiting for someone to confess. Ariel sank a little in her seat. "And I had a fight with Kyle."

"A new fight or the same old thing?"

"Can I just say it's the same thing and not give details?"

"Of course, you can. I know all too well how it works with you two. But I have to say this time it doesn't seem the same."

Ariel gave a small sniff. "It doesn't feel the same to me either. I think I need to keep some space between us for a little while. Maybe I will calm down."

Ariel let a few more tears fall as she leaned her head on her dad's chest and worked on steeling her resolve about the stubborn idiot who couldn't love her back. She felt her dad squeeze his arm around her shoulders and finally spoke. "How about you and Derek come over for that dinner we talked about with Miranda this weekend?"

Ariel thought about it for a few minutes. "How about in a couple weeks? We have a lot going on and I want to be in a better frame of mind when I meet Miranda."

"Alright, sweetheart. Pick the day and we will be ready."

"Okay. Let me talk to Derek. I am going to McKenna's with the girls tonight for dinner, and to torture him while he works."

"Is Kyle going to be there too?"

"No. It is supposed to be girls only. Tyler and Chase are working late tonight, so that freed up Zoey and Dixie. We are going to get all the juicy honeymoon details from Dixie."

"I didn't realize Dixie and Chase went anywhere."

"They didn't, really. Chase had to get back to work after the wedding since he missed so much time the week before at the beach and then with Dixie at the hospital. They both decided just to hide out for alone time at his house for a week when they weren't working." Dixie and Chase had been friends since they were children. They both had been in love with each other for many years, but with the events around his sister and mother's deaths, Chase's guilt prevented him from claiming Dixie as his. Finally, after breaking up with her last boyfriend he decided he was going to grab his forever with Dixie. Chase nearly lost Dixie to another car accident after their time at the beach. He proposed right away when she woke up, and they got married two days after she was released from the hospital.

"I am happy for Dixie. Send her my congratulations when you see her tonight. I know Chase will take good care of her."

A masculine throat clearing broke the silence. Jeremy's assistant, Doug was standing in the door. "I called Tank's garage and they are sending Jay over to change the tire."

Ariel shook her head. "Oh, you don't need to bother them. I can..."

Doug softly interrupted her. "It isn't a bother, Ariel. Your Dad pays for a roadside service on your car, so let him get some use of the money he spends on you."

"Okay. Thanks Doug."

Doug left, quietly shutting the door to give them some privacy.

Looking at her dad with narrowed eyes she said, "I can't believe you told him that you pay for my insurance."

Jeremy shrugged. "He does all the in-house accounts billing and payable, so of course he knows. I still pay for Derek and your mom's car insurance too."

"I thought Derek said he was paying you."

"Well, he thinks he is paying me. I put all his money into an account so I can give it to his kids one day. I screwed up things with your mom and the two of you. This is the least I can do."

"Do you think he will ever settle down?"

Jeremy rubbed the back of his head. "I do. He isn't like me. He has close relationships that he's very loyal to. I never had that with my friends. Sure, we would drink or hang out to watch games, but it isn't anything like the friends the two of you have. He is right at the heart of all of you. Zoey is here because of him. Kyle has been his friend since they were young. And look at the two of you. He wanted to protect you and stay close. He bought that two-family house so you wouldn't be alone. He is afraid of turning into me, but he has never been anything like me, which is a good thing."

It wasn't long before they heard the unmistakable sound of the tow truck pulling up on the curb behind Ariel's car. Ariel gave her dad a hug and went out to meet Jay. As she approached the truck, Jay gave a small smile.

"Hi, Ariel. Heard you got a little problem with your tire."

Ariel felt bad for Jay. He had broken up with Dixie only weeks ago and now Dixie was already married to Chase. The whole town had known how Jay was in love with Dixie, but she never fell in love with him. "Yeah. I am not sure how it happened, but I came out and it was just completely flat."

Jay shook his head. "Didn't we just put these tires on a couple of months ago?"

"Yes, and I really haven't driven much since then, mostly just around town."

"Well damage can happen at any time. Let me take a look at it and we can get you on your way." Jay crouched down and ran his hand over the side of the tire and dipped his head with a sigh. "Ariel, have you upset anyone lately?"

"No, why?"

"Take a look at this. Do you see this line in the sidewall of your tire?"

Ariel squatted down beside Jay and took a closer look. "Yeah. Is that where the damage happened?"

Jay nodded. "The problem with this is that is do you see how the line is fairly straight and clean through?"

"Yes."

"This is a sign of a knife cutting through the tire. If it was road damage, you would normally see a crooked line with fraying on the edges where the object cut the tire."

Ariel's eyes grew wide in concern. "Oh. But I am just a gift shop owner. I'm not even dating anyone for a person to throw a jealous tantrum over."

Jay stood up and put his hands in his pockets. "I could be wrong, but I think you should take pictures and send them to the sheriff's office. I will put your spare on and take the tire with me. You should still be covered by the warranty, so you won't have to pay anything."

Ariel nodded as she took some quick snapshots with her phone. "Thanks, Jay."

Jay efficiently changed her tire with the spare and loaded the damaged one into the tow truck. "Will you be following me straight over or will you come by later?"

Ariel looked at the time on her phone and sighed. "I guess I will go now."

"If you do a night drop another day either me or Tank can drop it off to you."

"That's sweet of you, but I can sit in your waiting room today while you guys fix it. I have a book to read, so I'll be fine."

Once Ariel got into the car her phone pinged with a text message from Austin. She had forgotten to call him today. The men at the fire station had posed for pictures for a greeting card that gave the profits to Firelight Foundation, a local youth center that helped children, focusing on foster care and low-income families. The cards were selling well, and Ariel thought it would be a good idea if the guys would autograph the cards so she could charge an additional fee for those to give the proceeds to Firelight. She talked to Austin about her idea, and he offered to talk to the men.

Austin: The guys said they are in. Just bring the cards over and we can get them all signed tonight.

Ariel: That is great! I am on my way to Tank's right now but will stop by after I am done.

Austin: What's wrong with your car?

Ariel hovered over the phone for a minute. She considered telling him about the intentional damage but decided against it.

Ariel: Just your normal flat tire. Getting a new one.

Austin: Want one of us to pick you up, so you don't have to wait there?

Ariel: No thanks, I am going to get some reading done. I will drive over after they are done with my car.

Austin: Ok. If you change your mind, let me know.

Ariel: I will, thanks.

When Ariel pulled up to Tank's garage a few minutes later she found Chase standing by his cruiser with his arms crossed and a scowl on his face. Great, Jay ratted her out. She was going to call him, but she at least wanted to take care of some other things first. Putting on a fake smile, she got out of the car to greet Chase.

"Hey. What's with that face? Is Dixie not satiating your appetite enough?"

Chase's face softened, and he smiled at the mention of his new wife. "Oh, she feeds all my appetites, but that isn't why I am here... waiting on you."

"I can't believe Jay called you."

Chase looked behind him at Jay who was pulling Ariel's tire out of the truck. "Well, he didn't call me specifically. He called the station and Oliver told me he got a call that involved you. I think I am the last person Jay wants to talk to right now."

Ariel knew that was probably true. Just as Ariel was going to say something Jay started to approach the two of them.

Looking at Ariel he asked, "Do you want to give me the keys to your car so I can get you fixed up?"

Ariel extended her hand with the keys. "Sure, here. Take care of my baby."

With a crooked smile he replied. "Of course. Just go inside and see Tank to sign the warranty papers for the new tire." Ariel nodded a reply, and he turned to look at Chase and his eyes drew down to the ground. "Chase."

"Jay. Good to see ya."

Jay flipped the keys around in his hand. "Yeah, well I... uh... need to go."

Ariel watched as Jay's shoulders slumped and he walked over to Ariel's driver side door to get in. After he parked the car in the garage Ariel finally turned back to Chase who was still looking at the garage bay. "Well, that wasn't too awkward," Ariel said in a sarcastic tone.

"That is the first time we have seen each other since he found out about me and Dixie. I think he tried everything he could to make it work with her. I feel like an ass around him. Dixie and I are so happy together, and I want to apologize to him, but how does that conversation even start?"

Ariel leaned on the cruiser and shook her head. "Maybe it doesn't. They didn't break up because of you, at least not directly. He just needs some time, and maybe some good nasty rebound sex."

Laughing Chase replied, "Jesus, you and Dixie need to ease off the porn books."

"Really? Because I heard that you really liked what she learned in our 'porn books.'"

"Is nothing sacred between you women?"

"Not really."

Chase shuddered and then turned back into his stiffer posture. "Okay, back to why I am here. Jay said someone stabbed your tire and that you have pictures for me."

Ariel nodded and handed over her phone after unlocking and bringing up the first picture. Chase zoomed in and frowned.

"Have you had any disagreements with anyone lately, or dates that might have gone wrong?"

"No. I haven't had a date in a while. I was supposed to have a date with this guy named Cord, but we both had to keep rescheduling, and right now I am just not in the mood. I had some guy puke in my store, and I made him and his buddies pay for all the damages and a surcharge for cleaning."

Chase cringed. "I heard about that. When did that happen?"

"Yesterday. The whole reason I was parked on the street was so I could return the steam cleaner to The Monkey's Wrench."

Chase held up the phone. "Do you mind if I text these to my phone?"

"No. Go ahead."

"Did you know the puker?"

Ariel gave a small huff of laughter. "No, but I think they were here for the wedding at the gazebo on Saturday. I think they were the groomsmen."

"It probably isn't them, but I will ask around, just to be sure. Let me know if you think of anything else."

"Okay. Give Dixie my best."

"No problem." Chase gave Ariel a hug as his radio went off about another call. "I've gotta go. Just be careful."

With a small worried look she replied, "You too."

With a cocky smile and an impish glint in his eyes, he got into the cruiser and said, "Always."

IT HAD NEARLY BEEN two hours since Kyle had seen Ariel and felt the stabbing pain in his heart when he left her on the sidewalk. And now, his head was pounding. The whole mess had him tangled up in knots. He had tried staying away from Ariel a long time ago, but that left him so empty and cold inside he had decided to be close as her friend was the only way to ease his soul. Now he'd crossed that line he knew was carved between their friendship and something more, and trying to cross back over it to the other side again may be the thing that permanently rips them apart.

Hitting the power button, he turned on his laptop ready to do some research. He constantly was trying to keep feelers out in Philadelphia to see if his circumstances could change. But with each search of local news sites, it was more of the same... random shootings, increase in gang violence and people just destroying each other.

Jarring him out of a trance-like state his phone pinged with a text message.

Derek: WTF man?

Kyle hovered over the keyboard not knowing what to say. Did Ariel say something to her brother? Was he going to lose his best friend too? Holding his breath, he finally typed a response that he hoped conveyed more confidence than he was feeling.

Kyle: You are going to need to be more specific.

Derek: Really?!?

Then a link followed that Kyle clicked on. It directed him to Penny Nolan's Facebook page. Penny was an elderly woman who loved town gossip and had learned all about social media at the senior center and had been terrorizing Blossom Hills residents for years now with her posts. Once the page loaded, he found pictures of him and Ariel talking to each other, then a final shot of Ariel standing alone on the sidewalk by her flat tire with tears falling down her face. Kyle scrolled back up to the top to read the post and felt worse with each word he read.

Will Kyle and Ariel truly not get their fairy tale ending? Blossom Hills has waited for that inevitable day when these two would finally find their way to each other, but it looks like it may never happen. An anonymous source reported seeing the pair arguing in front of The Monkey's Wrench this afternoon, and Kyle left a distraught Ariel in tears. These pictures definitely say a thousand words. Will this finally allow Ariel to move on and find love with someone else? Will Derek remain friends with a man who could hurt his little sister time and time again? Call me old-fashioned but I still hold out hope for these two.

Kyle: I will fix it.

Derek: You better fix it. I have sat by for years letting you guys work this out, but you are fucking it all up.

Shit. Derek sounded pissed. Not that he really blamed him. He always wanted to hurt anyone who made Ariel cry too. He needed to come up with a plan. How could he make it up to Ariel without making it look like a romantic gesture? His head was hurting, and he still had things to do for the paper. Maybe inspiration would come to him while writing. He hovered his finger over Ariel's contact information and finally decided to text her instead.

Kyle: I am so sorry about the past couple of days. I wish I could be everything you think I am.

He could see that she had instantly read his text message. He waited for a response and finally got it almost ten minutes later.

Ariel: I wish you could see how I normally see you too, but right now...

Then an image of a frog with a prince's crown appeared on his phone. He had to laugh. There might be some hope if she was teasing him and having a bit of humor with all of this. He just wondered if her humor would still be there once she read Penny's post.

IT WAS ONLY ABOUT AN hour after arriving at Tank's Garage that Ariel was pulling into the fire station's lot. She saw Austin's Jeep and parked beside it. She lifted the box holding the greeting cards that needed to be signed and carefully walked through the front garage doors.

The fire station was always clean and had what she called the man cave in the back. They had recently had their area remodeled after saving an important medical lab from being completely destroyed by a fire just outside of the main town. The company donated furnishings and upgraded their kitchen that rivaled any gourmet restaurant. The kitchen now had oversized stainless-steel appliances, new cabinets, and granite countertops. The living area had a new leather couch and recliners, a big screen television and even a new pool table.

Austin was behind the counter slicing peppers with a wide grin upon seeing Ariel. "Well, hi. I didn't think you would get here so soon." He really was quite charming. His smile was always genuine, and his slight southern drawl from his younger years in Texas wrapped around you like a warm hug.

Ariel placed the box on the counter and smiled when she caught the aroma of dinner. "Smells good. Is that fajitas?"

Austin nodded his head back towards the pan where steak and more peppers were frying. "Yup. It was my turn to cook, and this was our neighbor, Carlos' recipe. Tex-Mex at its best. You should stay for dinner. We have plenty."

Ariel looked around at the others who were engrossed in TV and playing pool. "Oh, I don't want to impose. And besides I didn't bring anything with me to add to the dinner."

"Are you kiddin'? Having you here would be a blessing. I am tired of eating with just these knuckleheads."

A gruff "I heard that," came from the couch and Ariel giggled.

"Well, how about I stay? But only if I can help you cook."

"You do drive a hard bargain, but deal."

Ariel really did have a good time helping Austin in the kitchen. She grated cheese and helped to plate the meals. The other men came in and helped bring everything to the table. Before she knew it, she was sitting between several men and really enjoying the banter they all had with one another. After they had all finished their meals, Chris finally asked her, "So I guess you won't be bidding on Kyle this weekend for the auction, huh?"

Ariel tilted her head. "What makes you say that?"

"Well, I just figured after reading Penny's post—" He was suddenly cut off after receiving an elbow to the ribs.

Ariel's eyes widened, and she felt a lump growing in her throat. "Penny posted something about me?" She started to grab her phone, but Austin gently put his hand around her arm to stop her.

"You don't need to read that garbage."

Ariel stiffened her spine and looked him directly in the eyes. "Yes, I really do. Please excuse me." She softly pushed the chair back as the table grew quiet and walked into the kitchen to open her phone and read the latest post from Penny. As she read each word, she could feel her cheeks heat in embarrassment and hurt. Briefly she wondered if Kyle had read the post already, or even her brother or friends. Sure, everyone knew how she felt about Kyle but now it was all out there for the whole town to see. And for them to see her rejection. She finally closed the screen and walked back to the table where she left the men.

"I want to thank you for your hospitality gentlemen, but if you will excuse me, I need to get home now. Austin, just drop off the signed cards to me later this week, okay?"

Austin stood and began walking to her. "Sure, I'll call you."

With great effort she gave a small smile and said good night as she made what she hoped looked like a dignified quick exit.

Chapter 6

Ariel pulled into her driveway and breathed a sigh of relief. This day just needed to be over. She still had another day off tomorrow and resolved to stay home in her pajamas and maybe bribe someone to deliver some groceries. That Boom Chocolatta ice cream sounded like the best idea ever now.

She turned her key, but paused as she heard the television on. She listened more closely. It was some kind of sports game. Figures. She steeled her resolve and walked into her place with a smile she completely was not feeling.

"Hello, brother dear. To what do I owe the pleasure of your company?"

Derek quickly grabbed the remote and pressed pause on the baseball game. "Hey, sis. I'm here because..." He seemed to be trying to decide what reason to give since she was pretending that her world wasn't falling apart. "Well, I saw Penny's post."

Ariel waived a dismissive hand as Derek walked around to the back of the couch. "Oh, that. It was misunderstood what happened. I'm fine. I just got upset about my tire being flat."

Derek leaned back crossing his arms and narrowing his brown eyes like he always did when he knew she was lying. "Bullshit."

Dropping her keys and purse with a thud, Ariel spun around. "Excuse me?"

"Bullshit. You think I don't know the messed up tangled emotions you have with Kyle? You guys don't fight, and those pictures show you in fight mode. What did he do? Do I need to kick his ass?"

Ariel's headache was coming back. "No, you big idiot. When and if anything is going on with me and Kyle, you will keep your nosy butt out of it, and I don't want to put a divide in between your friendship. We either go forward with clear hearts or we don't at all. None of this half in half out crap anymore."

"Good. And just so you know, Kyle put a divide between me and him many years ago. He changed in Philadelphia. Did I ever tell you about when he finally came to visit me in Lexington?"

Ariel shook her head and leaned on the couch beside him.

"It was just before Zoey's boyfriend died. I was close with my roommates and even closer with Zoey and Trevor. Kyle visited during a weekend holiday when we were all there celebrating with an almost non-stop two-night party. Kyle had told me about how he had won an internship with the major newspaper there and some of the horrible things he had seen while shadowing the lead investigative reporter. His first day he saw a dead body. He wasn't sleeping well and wanted to have some fun, but he was having a hard time fitting in with the guys and didn't know quite how to connect with Zoey. I think he felt like he had been replaced. He only came back one other time, but that was about a couple weeks after Trevor died. Zoey wasn't eating and was just losing herself in grief. Her roommates were horrible people and didn't care about her. When Kyle came, I was preoccupied trying to check in on Zoey all the time and I was dealing with my own grief over losing a friend."

Ariel looped her arm around Derek's and squeezed as she leaned her head against him. "I'm sorry. I didn't know it got that bad for you guys back then."

"I know. It wasn't something I really wanted to talk about, especially with my little sister. I was supposed to be the big, strong older brother. A lot of things happened the last half of college that just made things harder, and remember I had several friends to lean on. I know Kyle didn't make many friends out there. He concentrated so much on working at the paper and school he pretty much isolated himself. Tyler even lived out there with him and he said he would only see Kyle maybe once every couple of months the rest of their time out there."

"I never really thought about it, but being a reporter is probably pretty lonely. I mean you talk to people all day, but they are sources of stories and you can't talk to many people about who you talk to or what you are investigating."

"You and I both know it took a while for him to get back to even the guy we have today. We get these glimpses of the happy-go-lucky guy we knew in high school, but he still struggles."

Ariel closed her eyes and took a deep breath. "I know he does. He has talked to me about it a couple times. Before Josie, Tyler and Zoey moved here Kyle and I spent a lot of time alone at your bar."

"Yeah, I know."

"Anyway, for a time I felt like we were getting closer. I know he isn't the same man I fell in love with as a kid, but I still fell for who he is now too. I waited for a long time when he came back, but he gave me nothing, so I started dating again. Still nothing, and the other men were just horrible."

Derek looked uncomfortable for a minute and cleared his throat. "You didn't wait for... I mean you're not still a... uh..."

"Ugh. Stop. To answer your question, no I am not a virgin."

Making a small gagging noise Derek replied, "I think my dinner is coming back up."

"You asked, dumbass."

Derek paused before he continued. "I don't remember you having any big relationships."

Ariel rolled her eyes. "Just because I had sex with someone doesn't mean we had a relationship. It was college. He was cute, we went out a few times, and I decided I didn't want to wait forever so we did it. And there have been others since, but I have done much the same as you. Usually, a tourist that I found attractive, only I am much more discreet about it than you are."

"Christ Ariel, of all the things you could have learned from me that is what you picked up?"

"It's hard being the small-town princess. Everyone has certain expectations and won't touch me with a ten-foot pole either because of you or Kyle. Or there are the ones who will, but then they only want one thing from me."

A sudden knock came from Ariel's door and she was immediately grateful for the person stopping her from confessing more to her brother.

"Open up, Pip Squeak. We know you are home. That ridiculous car of yours is parked out front." Everyone always made fun of her car, but she loved her little Karmann Ghia.

Derek laughed. "You better open the door before Josie breaks it down."

Ariel barely had a crack open before Josie pushed her way in followed by Dixie and Zoey. The girls all walked in armed with grocery bags and made their way to the kitchen.

Derek jumped up and rubbed his hands together. "Ooo... goodies. What do you have for me?"

Zoey shook her head which caused more of her strawberry blonde curls to escape from her hair clip. She picked up a small round container and handed it over to Derek. "This is your 'go away' bribery of raspberry white chocolate cheesecake."

Derek quickly strode over to Zoey and kissed her on the cheek as he greedily took the cheesecake. "Bribery accepted. I'm outta here. Have fun girls."

After Derek left the girls, Zoey unpacked more containers and began to open them. "Okay, I have more cheesecake like that one, broken hearted brownies and Boston cream pie cupcakes."

Josie held up two wine bottles and smirked. "And I have the dessert wine."

Dixie snatched the bottle and looked at the label. "Josie, this is Chateau Mouton."

"Yes, Shortbread, I can read."

"No, I mean this is *Chateau Mouton*," she said the name like it was it was the latest hot movie star. "Depending on the year this can cost anywhere from a grand to thirty thousand dollars."

The room suddenly grew silent until Zoey could be heard making a choking sound. Everyone looked at her with concern. She started shaking her hand back and forth. "I'm... okay. Just need a minute."

Josie finally shrugged after the stares returned to her. "What? It's just money, and it was on sale."

With wide eyes Dixie whispered, "Just money. Really?"

Josie slowly took the bottle from Dixie. "Give it here, before you go into shock and drop the damned thing."

Zoey grabbed the bottle opener from Ariel's drawer and held her hand out. "Here, give it to me and I'll open it."

All three girls quickly said, "No!"

Zoey's bottom lip pouted out. "Why?"

Ariel smirked. "Sweetie, how many times did you drop something today?"

Zoey's eyes looked up as she seemed to pull the number from her memory. Sighing she said, "Only twice today."

Josie smirked. "And to think she plays with knives for a living." She held out her hand to Zoey for the bottle opener while Ariel got the wine glasses down.

It wasn't long before each woman had a glass of wine and dessert in front of them. Ariel knew she just had to start talking about everything with Kyle before they all pounced on her. "So, I guess you all saw Penny's post."

Zoey was the first to speak. "Yeah. I was with Derek and Tyler when we found out about it. Someone texted Derek and ask if he knew his sister was Penny's latest target. He was pretty pissed off."

Dixie reached over to comfort Ariel. "Chase found out from one of his deputies, then he told me and I was with Josie. So, we decided to grab Zoey and have a girl's night with you. Wine and sugar makes everything better."

"The last time I saw you, Kyle had been helping you with the puker," Josie said with a questioning look.

Ariel scrunched up her nose. Being reminded of that just made her shudder. It would be a long time before she could forget that smell. "Well, he did help me with that, but after everyone left, he kissed me. And we are not talking about the small inconsequential kisses he has given me before. Oh no, he finally kissed me with a possession and hunger that I could feel everywhere. It felt like all those moments of something greater to come was finally happening. But then he stopped cold. It was like someone threw a cold bucket of ice water on us and all the magic was gone. The spark in his eyes left and returned to that haunted, empty look that he has had since he moved back home."

"Okay. Since I haven't lived here all my life to see everything, I just have a couple questions to ask."

Ariel looked at Josie who seemed to have concern in her eyes. "Okay. What?"

"Has he ever given you a real kiss before?"

Ariel traced her finger around the rim of her wine glass and sighed. "Just once."

Dixie's head whipped to the side, and she nearly fell out of her chair. "What? When? And why didn't you tell me about it?"

Ariel shrugged. "You were still recovering from your accident with Chase's mom and sister, and you still had bad days. It was such a weird and special moment with Kyle I almost felt like if I told others about it, the dreamlike moment would go away forever."

Dixie's eyes grew sad, and she reached for her friend. "I would never want you to not tell me things. We're friends, and I want to celebrate your moments with you."

"I know that now, but back then we were all kind of a hot mess."

Josie snapped her fingers. "Enough of the sad memories. Let's hear about this weird special moment."

"It was the year after high school. Tyler and Kyle were going to school in Philadelphia, Derek was going to school in Lexington with Zoey, Dixie was still having a hard time with her hip and leg and Chase was spending a lot of time helping her. I was supposed to have dinner for my birthday with Mom and Dad. They were going through a patch where they were trying to be civil to each other after the divorce and still doing things with me as family, but it was always a disaster. This time Dad's ex-girlfriend made an appearance at Casperelli's. She made a big show about how she wanted him back and how he said he loved her. Mom got annoyed and said, 'He said he loved me too before. You'll get over it.' It was mortifying."

Dixie shook her head. "I remember hearing about that. Grams had her friend over just after that happened, and she was the biggest gossip."

"Yeah, well I could hear the whispers all through the restaurant and I just wanted to go home and hide. Once I got home, I called Kyle and left him a voicemail. Only it was one of those horrible blubbering messages where you could only make out every other word of what I was saying. He seemed to understand blubber alien speak because two days later I woke up to a room full of pink and gold balloons with ribbons and little silver stars tied to them. There must have been two hundred of them covering my ceiling almost two deep."

Zoey sighed. "Awe. That is so sweet."

"It was. My heart was melting as I looked around the room. When I finally looked to the side of my bed, there was Kyle holding a muffin with a lit candle. He held it out and told me to make a wish. He said that I deserved a better birthday than the one I had, and he was there to give me a do-over. We spent two hours in my room lying in bed and talking, all while wearing my ugly oversized pajamas and fluffy unicorn socks. He held my hand while we laughed and told stories about things that had been going on since he left. When he finally said he had to go so he could drive back to school, he asked what I wished for. I told him that if I told him my wish it wouldn't come true. He said that he would try to make all my wishes come true. I was embarrassed. I certainly wasn't going to tell him that I wished he would kiss me, but then he leaned in close and cupped his hands around my face and said I deserve a world of wishes. Before I knew what to think his lips were on mine. It was a sweet tender kiss, but also felt like love and as if my body was coming alive for the first time."

Ariel paused remembering the sweet moment and how happy she was. Dixie broke her thoughts. "And then what happened?"

"He didn't take it any further. He stroked my cheek with his thumb, put his forehead to mine, said he had to go, gave me another light kiss and then backed his way out of my room with this small, incredibly charming smile."

Josie was the first to speak. "Well, shit. I think I love the guy a little now. At least I don't want to punch him any-more."

"That's just it. I can't hate him just because he isn't giving our relationship a chance, but how much more can I take? I don't want to be forty years old and still have my life on hold. I want a family. I want to be loved by a man who loves me as much as I love him. I deserve that."

Zoey tilted her head. "Of course, you do honey. And I don't think this is a situation where he doesn't love you. I have been around him a lot because of Tyler. He may joke about his big game with women around the guys, but he doesn't go out. Ever."

Dixie grabbed a cupcake and asked, "I thought he went to Greko's bar like Chase used to."

Zoey shook her head. "Tyler said he hasn't been with anyone for at least a year that he knew of. He watches you when he thinks you aren't looking, but he forgets about the rest of us. We see him, and lately it has just gotten even sadder. We kind of hoped that he would wake up when Chase did and see that he was just wasting time."

Josie took a swirl of her wine glass and looked thoughtfully at Ariel. "How many times a day do you think a guy has to tickle his pickle if he hasn't had sex in a year?"

Dixie nearly choked on her cupcake. "Oh my god, Josie!"

"What? It isn't like we don't know that all men do it? Should I have said it another way? How about doing the knuckle shuffle?"

Ariel laughed. "Ew. That just made me think of the truffle shuffle. Can you image a combo of the truffle shuffle while doing the knuckle shuffle?"

Zoey smiled brightly. "He could call it doing the truffle shuffle with One-Eyed Willy."

While holding her ribs from laughing so hard Ariel asked, "Does anyone else want to watch *Goonies* now?"

All the others raised their wine glasses in agreement.

They all settled into the living room and pulled up *Goonies* on the television. It wasn't long before they were all well past a little tipsy. Josie pulled out the drinking game rules and assigned each of them a character to drink when they did something on the drinking list. Ariel was used to her brother knowing when to switch her to virgin drinks, so she found her tolerance to be significantly less than the others. By the end of the movie her head was on Dixie's lap and her legs were draped over Zoey's lap. She leaned over to the coffee table and grabbed the last cupcake. "I solemnly swear by this incredibly delicious cupcake that I am done chasing that man. No more. I am putting my happiness first, and if it isn't with him, I will find it with someone else!"

Josie raised her glass. "Amen, sister. Want to send a clear message to him?"

"Yes, I do." Ariel sat straight up, nearly falling off her couch. "How can we do that?"

"I think you need to make a clear statement at the auction this weekend, and I have the perfect way to do that. You game?"

Ariel straightened up her spine and tried to project a sober resolve. "Absolutely."

Chapter 7

The next day Ariel slept in until ten. She didn't quite remember everything from the night before. Wine. There was definitely wine. Oh, but what was the second liquor? Vodka? Tequila? No, not tequila, she would have definitely been vomiting by now if she drank that. She made her way into the kitchen rubbing the sleep out of her eyes. When she gazed into the living room, she saw Dixie only about halfway on the couch. Her head was nearing the edge with her feet and legs off the couch resting on the pillow on the floor. She remembered Tyler coming to get Zoey and Josie but didn't remember how Dixie ended up staying.

Ariel began making coffee and cringed when she looked at her selection for breakfast. Grease and eggs were not an option this morning. Maybe she would have some leftover cheesecake. Just as she plated a slice, a knock came from her door. Opening it she saw Chase standing in his full uniform with a big smile on his face.

"I am here for my wife."

Ariel's heart just went all soft. He looked so happy calling her his wife. They had only been married now for about a week and a half and their happiness just radiated off of them.

Ariel opened the door to allow him in when he suddenly made a near sprint to her kitchen.

Before she could object Chase had the cheesecake on a fork and he was getting ready to take his first bite. Ariel put her hands on her hips. "Hey, I was going to eat that."

"But I need food. I'm dying." He began to raise his fork again when she didn't object further, but then stopped. "Wait, Tyler didn't make this did he?"

"No. I'm not trying to poison you."

"Thank God." He finished the slice in just about four bites and then looked at Dixie now snoring on the couch.

"Sorry I couldn't get her last night. Everything was a mess, and I just wanted to get all the paperwork done before I came home since I have tomorrow off."

Ariel smiled warmly at her friend. "Don't worry about it. You know I love having Dixie here. Besides, how much time will I have with her now that she is a married woman?"

Chase frowned. "I would never come between your friendship. I know how important you both are to each other."

"Thanks, I appreciate that."

Suddenly they heard groaning coming from the couch. "Chase, is that you?"

Chase immediately went next to Dixie. "Yeah, babe. It's me. You ready to come home?"

"Mmm... Can't move. I'm dying."

Chuckling Chase scooped her up and stood cradling her in his arms. He kissed the top of her head. "Well, how about I take you home and we can die together in bed."

Dixie nuzzled into his chest. "Okay. That sounds good."

Ariel grabbed Dixie's purse and cell phone from the counter and nodded towards the door. "Go on. I'll follow you out with her stuff."

Chase nodded and said thanks as he made his way out the door.

As Ariel waved to Chase as he drove off with a sleeping Dixie, she heard her cell ringing in the house. "Shoot."

She scrambled up the walkway and back to her kitchen only to just miss the call. She saw that the missed call came from Austin. She wanted to fill him in on their little plan for this weekend, so she immediately called him back.

Austin picked up on the first ring and greeted her with his normal easy Texan soft drawl. "Hey there Ariel, I was just leaving you a voicemail."

"Ugh. Don't ever leave me voicemail. I never listen to it. Then I have that annoying little tape icon in the corner that just taunts me."

With a small laugh he replied, "You sound like the chief. He says to either text him if he doesn't answer or wait for him to call us back when he feels like it."

"I knew I liked that man."

"Well, that's good. He sure loves you. He doesn't let just anyone eat dinner with us at the station."

"Aw, well that's nice to hear."

"Yup. Anyway, I just wanted to let you know we got all the cards signed, and I thought I could drop them off to you. Are you working today?"

"No, but I will be at McKenna's later for lunch. You want to just drop them off there?"

"Sure. How about I see you there at 12:30?"

"Great. See you then."

KYLE WAS ATTEMPTING to stay busy. He was also trying to avoid his parents' phone calls after seeing Penny's posts. His dad was resorting to trying to send funny text messages. The latest had Kyle's face plastered on those old missing child pictures on a milk carton. As he was grabbing his camera to head out and take pictures for a story about crop circles that "mysteriously" appeared in Mr. Tepet's farm, his phone rang yet again. Seeing that it was Tyler again, he finally resigned to answering it.

"Hey, what's up?"

"Hello to you too, Butthead."

"I am getting ready to head out to Mr. Tepet's farm. Do you need something?"

"Actually, you need something, but the farm? Let me guess crop circles again?"

"Yup. Let's just hope he hid the evidence better this time."

"Why are you even bothering?"

Kyle shrugged but then realized that Tyler couldn't see him. "I am having a hard enough time scraping up stories. It is good enough, or at least it was this or feature Rose's creepy doll collection."

"Oh. Yeah. Crop circles definitely win over the creepy kill-you-at-night dolls. How did her husband die again?"

"Fell down the stairs, but my favorite part was when Chase showed up, she surrounded his body with the dolls who all had their heads turned towards the entry, so they were staring at him as he came in."

"And why did she do that?"

"She said that it would keep the soul collector from stealing her husband's soul until the pastor could bless his body."

"Do me a favor, if you ever go and do another story there, take backup."

Laughing Kyle said, "Didn't you know that you would be my wingman for that one?"

"Not funny."

"Okay, why did you call?"

"So... I went to pick up lunch for me and Zoey at McKenna's and I saw Ariel there."

"Ariel is always there."

"Yeah, but she looked like she was on a date."

Kyle stopped dead in his tracks. His feet felt like hundred-pound weights had just been dropped on them. "A date... with who?"

There was a big pause on the line before Tyler finally responded. "Austin Sutton."

There were no words. Shit. Was she really moving on to someone else finally? He knew that was for the best, but his heart felt as if it was free-falling into his gut. He dropped his hand to his side and then Tyler's voice echoed from below.

"Kyle? Hello? Did you hear me?"

Clinching his fist, he brought the phone back to his ear. "Thanks for letting me know. I've got to go."

"Kyle you have to get—"

Kyle hung up the phone before Tyler could finish the sentence. He knew what he needed to do, or at least what everyone thought he should do, and if it were up to him, he would have done it the minute he moved back home.

As he walked out of the office, he dared to take a look down the street where he could see McKenna's Pub. It was only a moment before he saw Ariel coming out of the front door followed by Austin who was carrying a large cardboard box. She looked amazing, and she had a big smile for Austin. A smile that reached far and wide, so much so that he could see it nearly a block away. When he finally looked away from her face, he saw the dress. Not just any dress, but the dress *he* bought her. His focus faded as he remembered when he bought that for her.

KYLE HADN'T MOVED BACK to Blossom Hills for long, but he was already feeling at ease with his small paper and reconnecting with old friends and family. Many people just stopped in to say hello and welcome back or wanted to give him story ideas. That was the funny thing about small towns. Everyone knew you and couldn't help but still think of you as the teenager who still needed help with everything. He didn't mind it though. With each person that came in it just reinforced to him that he had made the right decision.

It was raining again, and Kyle grabbed his hoodie getting ready to leave when his door burst open. Walking in with rain-soaked hair, a button-down white blouse, and faded denim capris was Ariel. Even in this state of disarray she was still the most beautiful woman he had ever seen. He quickly went to her and wrapped his hoodie around her. "Ariel, what's going on?"

She wiped away a lock of golden hair from her face and looked up at him. Sighing she said, "Can you take me home?"

Kyle was still looking at her up and down, wondering if he would see any injuries. She looked frazzled and upset. "Of course, but where is your car?"

"At home. I had Dixie drop me off at McKenna's and figured I would have Derek take me home after I had dinner and some drinks."

"Okay, so what happened?"

"He's a slut-puppy that's what happened."

Kyle bit his lips together trying not to laugh or smile. "So that's why he couldn't take you home?"

Ariel started using the hood of the jacket to dry off her hair. "Yes. He took some blonde bimbo up to the apartment to have his way with her, and then some creeps started hitting on me at the bar. I didn't feel like putting up with them and they weren't taking my not-so-subtle hints, so I left. I thought I would walk home, but then God thought it would be funny to dump an ocean's worth of water on me, so I came here. You were the closest person."

Grinning like an idiot, he was only more than happy to spend some time with her. He pulled his keys out of his pocket and nodded to the door. "Okay. Let's go then."

The ride over was pleasant. Ariel talked about some people they knew from high school and what they were doing now. Kyle talked about what it was like to work for a major paper and skipped over the not- so-pleasant parts.

Pulling into her driveway, she invited him in for a drink. He nodded and followed her in. She left him in the kitchen, saying that she was going to change into some dry clothes. After only being gone a few minutes, he heard her belting out an aggravated scream.

Kyle went running down the hallway with his heart sinking. Did she get hurt? Once he burst through the bedroom door, he saw Ariel having a standoff with a hissing black and gray cat standing on what looked like it used to be a dress.

Ariel began to pull the garment away from the cat and was now growling almost as much as the scary feline. "Give it up you evil ball of fur."

Kyle bent over to help release the cat from the dress. When he reached down to remove the claw from the dress, the cat took a swipe at his arm and drew a bit of blood.

Ariel threw down the dress in frustration and shoved what little was free towards the cat. "Fine keep it you little monster."

Kyle scratched the back of his head in confusion. "You got a cat?"

"No. This is my Dad's girlfriend's cat, Hecate."

Kyle looked at Hecate who was still guarding the dress and giving a low growl to the two of them. "Wasn't Hecate the Greek goddess of the underworld?"

Ariel pointed at Hecate, who now had settled onto the dress and was watching the two of them with narrowed eyes. "Yup. Who does that? Why give an animal or even a child a name that you know is just asking for trouble?"

"Yeah. Remember Damien?"

"Right? I mean, did his parents not watch *The Omen*? Or how do your friends and family not warn you about that?"

Ariel sat on the bed and gave an exasperated sigh. "I was supposed to wear that dress tomorrow for helping out at the senior center's prom revisited. I didn't have enough money to get a new dress because I just bought a bunch of new inventory for the store and money is tight. I added some lace and sequins to make the dress nicer, and now look at it."

Kyle looked back at the dress where Hecate had now taken to licking herself and not giving any mind to the humans. He just started laughing. He couldn't help it.

Ariel glared at him. "So glad to see that you are enjoying my misery."

"I'm sorry, but it just reminded me of Cinderella and how the step-sisters ripped up the nice dress that the animals helped her make."

Shaking her head, she looked back at the mangled material. "Yeah, well, do you know a fairy godmother who can fix this?" Just then Hecate stood, stretched and proceeded to pee on said dress and then strut out of the room.

Kyle gave out a little snort trying to hold in his laughter. "Well, maybe we should just ask for a new dress instead of fixing *that* one."

"Gee, ya think?"

Thankfully the rest of the evening went by uneventfully since Hecate seemed satisfied with her reign of destruction for the night. As Kyle left, he gave her a hug and told her everything would work out, and he would see her later.

It was early the next morning when Kyle found himself balancing a bakery box and a garment bag while knocking on

Ariel's door. When she finally answered, she was wearing pajamas and had her hair pulled back in a ponytail.

Kyle extended his hand with the bakery box. "I brought breakfast from Estelle's." Then extending his other arm with the garment bag he continued, "And a present."

Ariel excitedly took the items from Kyle and left the door open for him to follow her in. She placed the donuts on the hall table and hung the dress from the closet door. She quickly looked over at him while holding her fingers on the zipper. "May I?"

With a chuckle Kyle nodded. He watched as she quickly unzipped the bag to reveal the dress. It was a retro skater dress with a black plunging top that faded into a deep red starting at the waist and down the skirt. The skirt was also layered with a black lace overlay.

Ariel glided her hand down the dress and gasped. "Kyle, this is amazing. How did you get this dress? Everything was closed by the time we got home last night."

"I may have bribed the owner of A Stitch Above to open up for me in exchange for a feature in the paper."

Ariel quirked a brow. "I thought you were going to do a feature on the store anyway?"

"Oh, I was, but she didn't know that."

"How much do I owe you?"

"I don't want your money. I just want a small favor."

"What's that?"

"Let me take you to the dance and help out with the festivities."

Extending her hand, she beamed at him. "Deal."

KYLE'S MEMORY WAS INTERRUPTED by a gruff voice. "Snap out of it, kid."

Kyle stopped looking at Ariel and turned to see Mr. Glover, Tyler and Zoey's landlord standing beside him looking down the street with him. "Hey, Mr. Glover. Sorry I didn't see you there."

"Son, I don't think you saw anyone but her down there. Can I give you some advice?"

"If I said no, would it stop you?"

"Nope. Not really." Mr. Glover put his hand on Kyle's arm. "Women like her don't come around more than once in a lifetime. You look at her the way I look at my wife. It was always her for me, and if I am not mistaken, it has always been Ariel for you. Time is precious, don't waste it."

Kyle nodded. "But what if she is better off without me?"

Mr. Glover gazed over at Ariel who was now standing still looking at them with a sad look of longing on her face. "Does it look like she is better off without you?"

Kyle looked down the street again at Ariel who now had raised her hand up to her heart and was starting to clench her fist. The pain was radiating off her in waves. It mirrored his own. "I don't know if she is anymore or not."

"Well, when a woman looks at you with that much longing and hurt, I have to believe there is a way to figure out how to fix what is stopping the two of you from being where you belong."

Kyle watched as she walked to her car and ran his hands through his hair. "What makes you think that there is something to fix?"

"I've been around a long time, Kyle. It isn't your head or heart that is stopping you, it is something bigger. But know this, there is always a solution to outside problems. You just need to decide to take that first step to solve it."

"What if while I am trying to fix it, I make it worse?"

"There is always that risk. Did you know that I eloped with my wife when we were seventeen?"

"No."

Paul's smile crinkled his eyes as he seemed to remember how he married his wife. "Oh, she was a wild spitfire that came from a good family. They were high society types, and I was just a steelworker's son. My family adored her, but her family felt that I wasn't good enough. It was a strange twist of fate that one day I found a woman stranded on the side of the road who was giving birth. I was able to help her deliver her son and get her to the hospital. She was traveling back home to Raleigh after visiting her family. Her husband was so grateful that he wanted to give me anything I asked for. When I told him that he couldn't give me what I wanted, he challenged me and said that he knew he could help me achieve anything. I told him how I wanted to marry Edna and that I didn't have the means to support her. As it turns out he was a prominent attorney in Raleigh and told me to go get Edna and move to Raleigh where I could work as a law clerk in his office, and if I liked it, he would put me through school."

Kyle smiled at the old man. He never heard this story before, and if circumstances were different, he would be asking to do a complete interview for a feature article.

Paul cleared his throat and continued. "So, I had Edna meet me that night and we moved and got married in Raleigh. I ended up working at that firm for the rest of my professional career and opened the second office here. Mr. and Mrs. Harrison ended up being our family down here. Edna even worked as a nanny for Mrs. Harrison for many years. My point is... that fate has a way of helping to make things right, but you also need to take steps to help her out every now and then."

Kyle watched the taillights of Ariel's car drive off away from him. Almost in a whisper he said, "Help her out."

Mr. Glover clasped a hand on Kyle's shoulder and nodded. "Now you've got it."

As Kyle began to get lost in his thoughts, he heard the shuffling of Mr. Glover's feet walking back towards the town square. Kyle pulled out his cell phone and dialed a number he hadn't used since he moved back to Blossom Hills.

It rang only twice before a gruff voice answered. "This is Anders."

Kyle flinched and pulled the phone away from his face. Anders was the assistant editor and usually had an easy light tone when he was on the phone. "Anders? Hey, it's Kyle Ashford. I thought I called Alan's desk."

"Oh, hey Kyle. You did, but you didn't."

"What?"

"Alan quit. It's a shitshow up here. He quit a few of days ago just out of the blue. He said that he couldn't do this job anymore and just walked out with his laptop and some files. His wife is going crazy because he didn't go home. Rumors are flying everywhere."

"What kind of rumors?"

"Some people think he jumped off the Ben Franklin bridge, some are saying he ran off with some other woman, and there is even one floating around that he got mixed up with some gang and was forced out of town or killed."

"Shit. Have you tried his cell?"

"Do you really think none of us tried that? His wife even tried that lost my phone app, and it was left at some restaurant. His car is gone, and that old piece of crap doesn't have LoJack or anything like that. Now they have me as the editor when I was perfectly happy just being the assistant editor. I told them to find someone else. I liked my life and my free time. Don't suppose I could put your name in the ring?"

Kyle let an uncomfortable laugh escape. "God no. I like my life down here much better."

"Damn. It was worth a shot."

"Well thanks for the info. If you hear from him could you have him give me a call back?"

Anders let out a short laugh. "Yeah, you and nine hundred other people. Listen I would love to catch up, but I have three people standing outside my door who can't get dressed without instructions."

"Okay, well thanks. Talk to you later." Kyle had barely gotten his words out before Anders hung up.

Once Kyle got home, his reporter instincts were itching. Why had Alan disappeared? He was a reliable man. He went to work, stayed there too long and then went home to his wife. It was because of Alan's obvious love for his wife that Kyle found himself opening up to him one night about Ariel and all about their history. He grabbed a beer and opened his laptop.

Kyle started pouring over Alan's social media looking for something out of the ordinary, but there was nothing. The man didn't really post much. Just a few pictures here and there, or sometimes he would be tagged by someone else when he was out having dinner with others. His wife's social media didn't provide anything else either. It looked like they weren't going out as much over the past year. The group pictures started to trickle down to nearly nonexistent.

Kyle changed his searches to see if there were any updates about gang and gun violence. The most recent was an article about a four-year-old who was shot while riding with his uncle on a motorcycle. As he continued to read, it stated that it was a suspected drug deal that had gone wrong just as they drove by and got caught in the crosshairs. He knew this was Zeke's territory and wished he could have made a difference to this community. He started feeling that acid churning nausea in his stomach again and closed his laptop. This was why he'd moved back home. He no longer wanted to be around the senseless violence. He would much rather report on boring city council meetings or the quirks of the town's residents.

IT WAS ONLY A COUPLE days before the bachelor auction and Ariel was working in her shop unboxing some new inventory when Kyle's mom, Hannah, walked in with her mother, Amanda. The two looked beautiful. They both had been aging with a natural grace and her mom's blonde hair was just starting to show little peeks of gray that were in small areas that made it look more like highlights. They were giggling like schoolgirls as they approached Ariel.

Amanda leaned over to kiss Ariel on her cheek. "Hello, sweetheart. How is your day going?"

With a warmth in her chest, she smiled broadly. "Well apparently not as good as the day is going for the both of you."

Hannah's face blushed. "Oh, you know. Just a little girl talk."

Amanda laughed. "More like embarrassing sex talk."

Ariel felt her face flush. "Mom!"

"What? Did you think just because we're old we don't have sex anymore?" Hannah said as she tried to slow her laughter.

Amanda grimaced. "Well, some of us still have sex. Others of us have to talk about the sex we had eons ago."

Hannah placed her hand on Amanda's arm. "That is by your choice. I have seen men still salivate with one look at you."

Ariel put her hand up. "Could we stop the sex and mom talk? I prefer to think of both of you as non-sexual people."

Hannah smirked. "Well... we could focus on our children's sex lives. Would that be better?"

Ariel fidgeted behind the counter. "As long as it is anyone's but mine."

"You take all the fun out."

Ariel was still thinking about a better topic when a balding man in his late fifties walked in. He looked tired and as if he'd slept in his clothes for days. Seeing that helping this man had to be better than listening to her mom and Kyle's mom talk about sex, she rushed over to the man with an overly excited smile.

"Hello. How can I help you today?"

The man looked around at the store and then at the other women at the counter and cleared his throat with apprehension. Ariel looked at where she'd left her mom and Hannah and noticed that Hannah had her head tilted and was looking at the man thoughtfully. When Ariel brought her attention back to her customer, he was rubbing his hand on his pants leg as if he were wiping sweat off his palms. "Uh, yeah. I kind of upset my wife and need to give her a card. Maybe she will listen to me better in writing."

"Of course. Did you need an apology card, or just a card that reminds her that you love her?"

"Just the second one I think."

Ariel gave a warm smile hoping it would calm the man a bit and led him to the back of the store where he could find the appropriate card. "If you think you need a small gift too, just let me know. I am sure between the two of us we could find something special."

The man just nodded and appeared to randomly grab the first card to read. Ariel walked back up front to give the man some privacy while he shopped for his card.

When she got back to the counter, Hannah was still looking thoughtfully at the man, while Amanda was unpacking the inventory.

"Mom, you don't have to help. I can do that on my own."

"I know dear, but I love when you get new stock in. It's like Christmas, opening a present and not knowing what is inside."

Ariel felt the corners of her mouth lift. "Well, I ordered it so there's no surprise, and the joy of opening inventory has lost its luster. Seems more like work now."

"You working alone all day today?"

"Yes. I just had a couple days off and it is usually slow today. Plus, Myrna and Lana will be closing for me on Saturday so I can go to the auction."

"Bidding on Kyle again this year?"

With a devilish smile Ariel replied, "Only time will tell."

Hannah finally turned around after staring at Ariel's customer and started to help unpack the new inventory. "Ariel, do you know that man?"

Ariel looked again at the man who was reading yet another card and glancing at the back door to her stock room. "No. I've never seen him before."

Hannah put down the ceramic figurine and looked over to Amanda. "How about you?"

Amanda took a closer look. "No. Sorry. He is probably in town for one of the weddings."

Hannah started tapping her finger on the counter and paused. "Maybe. I suppose you're right."

After a few minutes the man came to the counter with his card. Ariel rang him up and asked the one question that would clear up if he was from town or close by. "Would you like to buy a stamp for the card?"

Startled the man looked Ariel in the eyes but recovered quickly. "You sell them here?"

"Of course. I am a card shop. Many people send cards through the mail and I like to save them the trip to the post office."

"Oh, yes please."

Hannah finally moved behind the counter with Ariel and put on a smile that Ariel knew was fake. "I am sorry sir, but you look so familiar. Have we met before?"

The man's hands were shaking as he pulled out his wallet. "No, I don't believe so." Then with what seemed like forced charm he smiled and gave a wink. "All of us bald men look the same."

The three women watched the man leave and stared at the door after he left. Amanda was the first to speak. "He was lying to us, wasn't he?"

Nodding Hannah said, "Oh yeah, and it concerns me as to why he needed to."

Chapter 8

Kyle was taking one last glance in the mirror before looking out at the crowd for the bachelor auction. His week had been busy between his regular duties for the paper and doing some internet research about his missing friend. He had talked to Alan's wife briefly and was surprised to find out about how his old boss's life had been going just before he left and since. She explained to him how she had been diagnosed with cancer a few months before Kyle had moved. They were near declaring bankruptcy when her husband finally was able to figure something out with the creditors and hospitals, but he had to work even longer hours and was always stressed out when coming home at night. Kyle's additional searches didn't provide any new leads, and he was beginning to believe the others that maybe he did take his life into his own hands.

Trying to clear his thoughts he felt a clap on his back. He turned to see his dad, Mark, smiling at him. "You going to earn your mom a ton of money again?"

"I'll do my best, Dad. I mean, who doesn't want all this?" Kyle gave a small flourish with his hands up and down his body as if to prove his point.

"Well, I guess I taught you how to be confident well enough."

"I think it helped that I am so damned handsome."

Mark rolled his eyes. "There is confidence, and then there is arrogance. Keep your arrogance in check, Kyle."

With a crooked grin Kyle put his hands in his pockets and tried to look out the open door to the crowd. "Is Ariel out there?"

"Yes. She's helping her mom and Zoey at the dessert and drink stand."

"How does she look?"

"Do you mean does she look heartbroken still?"

Kyle winced. "You saw Penny's post?"

"Everybody saw the post. She has more people following her page than we have residents."

"When did that happen?"

"Oh, shortly after Zoey nearly got killed by her ex-boyfriend. Everyone loves a good story with a happy ending. I can't believe you didn't know that."

Kyle shrugged. "The feed pops up on my timeline, but I never check on her stats. As much as I hate to say it, I get some good story leads from her."

"Being outdone by an old lady. Your skills are slipping."

"I think she has spies everywhere that send her pictures and stories. I haven't actually seen her out and about in at least a month.

The lights then started to dim, and a spotlight was turned on at the podium. Amanda walked up onto the stage and commanded everyone's attention. "Hello, and welcome to our annual Bachelor Auction benefiting the senior center.

This year we have fifteen men up for your bidding pleasure. Ladies, let's give the men a warm welcome to the stage."

Kyle looked at his ribbon and saw the number thirteen. Great, that didn't seem like a good number.

A loud bang echoed through the room, and Derek came sprinting in looking all flushed. "I'm here. You can rest easy, the big money maker is here to shake it."

Kyle leaned over and whispered to Derek. "Careful, or you will get a lecture from Dad about arrogance."

"I'm not arrogant. I'm charming."

"Geez. No wonder they put you last."

"Eh. Actually, I told Mom I might be late because I had an appointment with a new brewery opening up just outside of town."

"Really?"

"Yeah. It seems like it will be great. They are brewing on site and opening a restaurant that will feature their craft ales and local wines. It will have a great modern industrial vibe to it. They wanted to reach out to only a select few local pubs to carry their product to start out with. They are being very discriminatory about who they are choosing, but felt that our town with the built-in tourism and my pub were a perfect fit."

"Congrats. That's great."

They started walking up to the stage when Austin squeezed in between them. "Hey guys. Looks like I am back here with you."

Derek smiled at Austin. "Hi, Austin. How have you been? I heard I missed you at McKenna's the other day."

"Yeah. I met Ariel there for lunch. I had to drop off those cards that the guys at the station all autographed for her shop."

Kyle felt an ease of tension in his chest. It wasn't a date. It was business. Thank god. At least he didn't want to rip the guy's head off now. Their conversation stopped as they finally made it up on the stage. The audience of women roared in approval as they all presented themselves.

Amanda's voice again filled the room. "Okay, ladies. Take a good look and figure out your best strategy. Are you going to run up others' bids so you can get your man? Will you try the sneak attack strategy or just lay it all out there? Let's raise some money for a good cause!"

The event was going well. Kyle was actually having fun watching the women bid on all the men. At one point he saw Chase and Dixie in the corner with his arms wrapped protectively around her holding a ripped-up bidding sign. Tyler was sitting in a chair with Zoey on his lap behind the dessert table. He tried not to look at Ariel too much, but his eyes kept drifting back to her. At one point, she smiled and whispered something in Josie's ear.

It was during the bidding of Finn Kavanagh, the newest addition to the orchards, when he saw a couple enter the building. At first the lights prevented him from getting a clear picture of who was there, and then his heart sank. It was one of Zeke's men, but this time he looked different. He looked unsure and was holding the hand of a petite brunette with pale skin and blue eyes. He seemed to be looking to her for guidance and she simply pulled him forward into the crowd.

Before Kyle could jump off the stage to ask him what he was doing there, he heard Amanda's voice announce his name. "Ladies, here we have number thirteen, Kyle Ashford. You all know him as our local reporter, editor, and publisher, but he is so much more. He is charming, a hiker, skilled with hands for home renovations and is terrible at cards. So, challenge him to a game, ladies, and you will be sure to win."

Kyle shot a glance at Derek who was trying to cover his laugh with a cough. Asshole. He would get him back for that one.

"Let's start the bidding at one hundred dollars."

Several paddles quickly raised into the air, but not the most important one. Ariel's paddle stayed firmly in her lap. The bidding quickly rose to six hundred dollars and only a couple were still in the running. Greta, who was a nice woman that they all went to school with, but she was always a bit over eager and obvious with her crush for him and... he saw the next bidder go up and it was Josie's paddle. What was she doing bidding on him? Ariel was sitting next to her looking at her nails, trying to seem disinterested. She would certainly hop in at the last minute and outbid them.

Greta looked crestfallen. To win she would need to bid seven hundred dollars. The room grew quiet as Ariel walked over to Greta and handed her one of those bank cash envelopes, whispered into Greta's ear and then stood behind her with a triumphant smirk. Greta shot her paddle up in the air and shouted, "One thousand dollars."

Amanda repeated the bid to the room and began the final closure. Josie didn't bid again. She simply sat in her chair with her arms crossed grinning like the evil supervillain who just won a battle. He stood frozen in his spot. Ariel didn't want him. How could that be? She always bid on him. Had he finally pushed her too far?

"Kyle. Get back in line dear."

Kyle shook his head after hearing Amanda's direction and stood next to Finn who leaned over and whispered with his Irish accent, "Fair play, mate."

"Yeah thanks."

He listened as Amanda gave the description for Austin and the bidding started. Austin's bids started much the same as Kyle's had with several paddles starting and then dwindling as the bids grew higher. While Kyle had shifted his gaze to Zeke's man and his girlfriend, Josie's voice boomed over the crowd. "Two thousand dollars."

The room immediately grew still. Amanda didn't skip a beat though. "Okay. Two thousand dollars. Going once. Going twice... sold to Josie."

Josie stood and crossed her arms. "I want to donate my winning prize to Ariel McKenna."

Everyone's head whipped back to see Ariel who was still standing beside Greta. Ariel's face flushed, but she didn't look surprised at all.

"Okay, Ariel, Austin will be your date for the evening."

Kyle was itching to get off the stage. Not only did Ariel not bid on him, but she was going to go out with Austin. He still had to wait for Derek to be auctioned off before he could find out why Zeke sent another guy to mess with him now. Plus, he had to deal with his crazy jealousy ripping at his soul that Ariel was going on a date with Austin.

He caught Ariel looking at him several times in between Derek's antics on stage. Just before it was time to leave the stage their eyes locked, and he watched as she brought her hand down to rub the tree on her charm bracelet. There was still hope. She was still thinking about him.

As he was walking down the steps of the stage, he found Zeke's man waiting for him at the bottom, and Greta.

Kyle eased into that façade of charm he was just getting tired of. "Greta, do you mind if I have a couple minutes with my friend here? I haven't seen him in a long time and we just need a couple of minutes."

With a smile that almost seemed like it would split her open, she replied yes and went over to grab a drink from Zoey's station.

He turned to the man and tamped down his anger. "Okay. What are you doing here?"

"Let's go over there for some privacy," the man replied nodding to the corner.

They walked quietly over to the corner where several extra chairs and tables were stacked. Kyle was clenching his fists trying to hold in his frustration. "You guys have got to stop showing up all the damn time. I am just about done with all of this."

The man who stood much shorter than Kyle but still had an impressive muscular physique stood straighter and looked at the woman beside him with clear affection in his eyes. "You are done with all of this. You're free."

Kyle was ready to argue with him more but stopped. "Wait. What? Who are you?"

"I'm Pablo."

Kyle drew up a skeptical eyebrow. He called all of Zeke's men Pablo just to piss them off. "Pablo?"

The man gave a small huff of laughter. "Yeah. I know you called us all that, but I was the only one who actually had that name."

Well, that was funny. He felt a smile tug at his lips but quickly pulled it back. "Okay, Pablo. You said it is over. Why did Zeke change his mind?"

Pablo looked at the ground. "He didn't. He's dead."

Kyle's eyes widened. "He's dead? How did that happen?"

Pablo reached back out for his girlfriend's hand, who immediately took it in a show of support. "All of this is off the record. I am only here because of her," he said nodding to the woman beside him.

"Okay. Off the record. Tell me what happened."

"They're all dead. Every last one of us, except me."

Kyle fought with his conscience. While a large part of him wanted to rejoice about his newfound freedom, it was still senseless loss of life. "Why? How did that happen?"

"You really haven't been keeping up with things back home?"

"I have been a little preoccupied."

"Well, earlier this week there was a drug deal we had that went all kinds of sideways. One of our men accidentally shot and killed this kid who was riding on his uncle's motorcycle for his birthday."

"I did read about that. That was you?"

Pablo vehemently shook his head. "No. I was actually on my way down here doing a run. Then we found out that the kid was the grandson of the Prez for Reaper's Revenge."

"The MC?"

"Yeah. Anyway, the guy I was riding down here with drove back and left me to finish the run by myself. It wasn't uncommon for us to do solo runs. That is how I met Sarah. Anyway, Zeke tried to reach out to the Prez to try and make amends, but it ended up being a trap. They ambushed them. The guys were all at the house when it blew. They made it look like a meth lab accident. Zeke was out meeting the Prez, and he never came back. It was only dumb luck that I wasn't there."

Kyle was trying to process that mound of information that was handed over to him. He looked again to the woman at Pablo's side. "What does she have to do with this?"

Pablo looked to his side where she put a comforting touch on him. "Zeke kept on sending me down here to do runs with other suppliers. It was just your bad luck that it was so close otherwise he wouldn't have bothered with you as much as he did."

"Lucky me."

"Anyway, I met Sarah one night after I got into some trouble with some guys who thought they would make a little extra side profit. I was injured pretty bad, and she found me dumped at the side of the road driving home one night. I refused to go to the hospital, but she patched me up. I kept coming back to her when I would make runs and we fell in love. I was looking for a way out before all this happened."

Finally, Sarah spoke. "I followed him here one night. I thought he was cheating on me. I found him spying on your girl and we got into a fight about it. He finally confessed to me what he was doing down here. I told him we needed to help you, but then all this happened. I made him promise to come here and talk to you in person so you would know he was telling the truth."

Pablo put a stray hair behind her ear and then looked back at Kyle. "So, you're free to get your girl and live your life in peace. I just ask one favor."

Kyle crossed his arms. He didn't want to give this guy any favors. He was still bitter about all the time he had lost with Ariel. "What's that?"

"Don't tell anyone I am still alive. I have a new identity I can use. It was one of the true lives IDs we saved for emergencies."

"Is that one of those that is cultivated in real time from birth?"

"Yeah. I think Zeke was going to use it before Gianna got killed."

These IDs went for an insane amount of money. Kyle had seen a report on these during his college years. Fake births were given real birth certificates, and they were treated like real people. Taxes were filed with that child as a dependent for years. Social security cards were given but the person never existed and then they sold that identity with complete histories, education, credit histories, identification... everything a person needed to disappear.

Sarah's gentle voice broke through Kyle's thoughts. "Please, Mr. Ashford. Pablo has made mistakes but where he came from, he didn't have much of a choice. He has a chance to change everything and start a life with me. I don't have any family left and he is my everything."

Kyle looked between the two of them and nodded. "You won't be living here will you?"

Pablo shook his head. "No. We will be living in Willow Springs. We have no need to come back here again. I don't want to remind you of the past, just as I don't want you to remind me of mine."

Before Kyle could think any more about it, he extended his hand to Pablo. "Thank you. I wish you both the best."

Taking his hand firmly, Pablo shook it and said his good-bye.

Zeke was gone. Everyone who wanted to keep him and Ariel apart were gone. Ariel. Oh god. She was going out with Austin. He started to frantically look around the room when Greta popped into his line of vision.

"Looking for me?"

"Oh, uh Greta. I..."

"It says here we are going to Casperelli's for dinner. Are you ready?"

He looked around the room and found his mom standing just a few feet away. "Of course, he is. Your dinner reservation is all set, and the limo is waiting outside."

Kyle looked confused. "Limo?"

"Yes, dear. The two top bids got a limo ride. So, you and Austin get to take your dates in style."

Fantastic. "Mom, can I talk to you for a minute?"

With the brightest smile that he knew was trouble she said, "Sure, honey. After your date." She patted his cheek a little too harshly, so that he understood she meant business.

"Right." Gritting his teeth, he turned to Greta and asked, "Are you ready?"

She excitedly looped her arm around his and they walked out to the limo to go on their date.

ARIEL SAT ON THE LUXURIOUS soft seat in the limo and couldn't help but to be awed by the whole experience. The lights under the seats changed color and there was champagne waiting for them to enjoy. She ran her hand down the seat and breathed in the rich smell of new car and leather. "I've never been in a limo before."

Austin jerked his head back a little. "Really? I would have thought that you took at least one for a high school dance."

"Nope. I'm a simple girl, really. I am happy if a man would pick me up in a working CLEAN car, and if he would respect me."

"Well, shoot. If that is all it would have taken there would have been men lined up around the block for you."

Ariel looked out the window and bit her lower lip. "Well, there wasn't."

"That's because your heart was somewhere else, and everyone knew it."

"Hmm. Maybe your right."

The limo pulled off the main road and into the orchard. Ariel looked back at Austin in surprise. "Where are we going?"

"Let me have some surprises."

Ariel pouted her lower lip and looked up through her lashes doing her best to get her way.

"Good lord, woman. Put those eyes away. It won't work."

It wasn't long until they pulled up to a gazebo by the lake that was lit with white twinkle lights. A table and chairs were placed in the center and two covered dishes were waiting for them.

Laughing Ariel started walking to the romantic dinner setting and shook her head. "You thought you were going to get lucky with someone tonight."

"Well, I am not going to lie, it would have been nice, but to be honest I thought Ruby was going to be my highest bidder."

Ariel turned and tilted her head. "That sweet lady who just had her ninetiethbirthday?"

Austin rubbed the back of his neck. "Yeah. I helped her on an emergency call not so long ago and she said I reminded her of her late husband. She talked about how she missed him taking her to the lake and have a dinner there all prepared so they could enjoy the night stars. I saw a picture of him. He does look a lot like me. Anyway, when she heard that I was up for auction she said she was going to bid on me."

"What happened? I am sure she could have outbid Josie. I heard she has a ton of money."

"Oh, she does. Her granddaughter came in for an unexpected visit and so she texted me to say she wasn't coming."

Austin pulled out her chair and then took his seat. Once he opened the lids, there was a petite sirloin waiting with steamed asparagus and red potatoes. Ariel leaned over and took a deep inhale. "This smells amazing."

"Yes, it does. The catering chef for the Orchards Event Center prepared this for me."

"We should dig in before it gets cold," Ariel said while picking up her fork and stabbing into the asparagus.

Ariel felt at ease with Austin. Their conversation flowed naturally. Austin talked about some of the antics at the fire station and some of the crazy situations they got calls for. Ariel talked about growing up with Derek and some of the issues with her Dad and Mom's divorce. Finally, she asked the one question most women in town had about Austin. "How come you're still single? I mean, I can't remember you dating anyone in high school, and I know that you haven't had many women around since then either."

Austin leaned in closer and rested his palms on the table. "High school was kind of complicated. I was kind of in love with one girl, and she kept me at a distance, but I always had hope that we would work it out."

Nodding her head, Ariel whispered, "Summer." Summer was Chase's sister who died in a car accident with her mom and Dixie. Dixie was the only survivor of the accident and it left her with an injury to her hip and leg that gave her problems even now.

Austin popped his head up quickly. "You knew about Summer?"

"Sweetie, the whole school knew how you felt about her. Your face didn't really keep any secrets. Dixie and I have talked about it a few times."

"Did you know that originally I was supposed to hang out with her that day?"

With a slight gasp Ariel replied, "No. Does Dixie know?"

Austin shook his head. "I don't think so. I had talked her into having lunch with me that day, just the two of us, but I got really sick and had to cancel. I felt horrible and like I was throwing away my chance with her, but my mom had put her foot down since my fever was nearly a hundred and two. Anyway, she sent me over some soup from Daisy's diner and said that next time we would enjoy it together. So, instead of being with me she went with Dixie to the fields, and... you know the rest. You don't know how many times I said that if I wouldn't have cancelled on her, she would still be alive."

"Oh, you can't carry around that kind of guilt. It was not your fault. It wasn't Dixie's fault, or Chase's or his mom's. The man who hit them was responsible for their deaths."

Shrugging, Austin said, "Of course I know that, but telling that to my teenage brain and believing it took a while. I didn't want to date anyone for a long time."

"Have you had any serious girlfriends?"

"No. Not really. I'm pretty picky. I want an attractive woman, but I also want her to have a brain and a kind heart. But keep in mind, I'm no saint. I've had my fun too. The fire department helped me get this body, and I have used it a time or two to get my way."

"Oh, that is just awful."

"I'm a guy. I'm supposed to be awful."

Once they got back in the limousine to go home, she leaned against him feeling a bit sleepy. She looked up into his eyes and said, "I had a good time. I needed this; thank you so much."

"Of course. Can I try something?"

"Sure." Before she could interpret what his meaning was, his lips were on hers and her head tilted back. It was a lovely kiss. It had all the right mechanics. Soft giving lips with slight caresses on her cheek, but there was something missing. She grew a bit frustrated and tried to pull at his shirt to move him in even closer and deepen the kiss. He responded without question, but there still wasn't that deep pull at her heart wanting more. Wanting all of him. She let go of his shirt and looked at him with apologetic eyes. "I'm so sorry, Austin."

He put his fingers to her lips and shook his head. "Don't apologize. I really knew it wouldn't work ahead of time, but I hoped that maybe I could be wrong."

Ariel's eyes filled with tears. "I really wish I could give you my heart. It would be so much easier."

"Shhh. It's okay. I think the greatest love stories are not the easy ones, because once you overcome the things that prevent the happy ending, it is all the stronger for it."

"Ugh, can we just fast forward to the happy ending already?" Frustrated, Ariel sighed and leaned back into the crook of his arm, staring out the window as they passed by the houses.

It was only a couple minutes later when they pulled up to Ariel's house. Her car was already in the driveway and Kyle was sitting on her stairs. Austin leaned over her to see out the window at the anxious waiting form of Kyle staring at the limousine.

"Looks like someone pressed the fast-forward button."

"Oh, he is in for a rude awakening if he thinks all he has to do is show up on a doorstep this time."

Looking amused, Austin got out of the car and rounded to her door waving off the driver. Ariel took her hand in his as he helped her out of the car. Kyle immediately stood up waiting for her approach. Austin chuckled. "This ought to be fun."

"Hush," Ariel whisper-yelled at him.

She only took a few steps before Kyle rushed over to her, whispered her name like a prayer, picked her up off the ground and crashed his lips to hers. She was still mad, but this kiss—it was a kiss of possession and promise. His arms wrapped possessively around her and squeezed as she felt as if she would drown in her emotions. He slowly lowered her to the ground but didn't leave his lips from hers. He moved his now free hands to her cheeks and thrust his hands into her hair. Ariel's heart felt as if it would explode from inside her chest. Finally. Finally, he was showing her what they both knew in their souls—that they belonged together.

It took a moment, but her brain was slamming on the brakes and said that he needed to do this right. Do not give in easily, or he will just walk away again. Then the anger started to return. He left her crying at the door of her shop, and again at the sidewalk beside her broken car. She placed her hands on his chest and pushed. "No! You don't get to do this. You big jerk!" She slammed her hands against his chest and pushed him aside as she walked through her front door and slammed it shut.

KYLE STOOD THERE WITH a shocked expression. Did she really just tell him no? This is what they had waited for.

They could be together now. She should be happy. What just happened? It may have been only a minute or so since Ariel slammed the door on him when he heard Austin clear his throat.

"Didn't go as you planned, huh?"

Kyle rubbed the back of his head. "No, it didn't. I don't understand it."

Both men were now staring at the closed door. "Let me see if I can put this in words you can understand. You have been telling that poor girl no for years now. She's had to adjust to your rules of the relationship, bending to your moods. Now, you suddenly changed your mind, and you expect her to just fall in line. Basically, she jumped into a pool expecting it to be nice, cool water but got burned. Of course, she jumped out and sought refuge. Just because you flipped a switch on your emotions, you can't expect her to do the same thing. Ease her into it. Believe me, she still just wants you."

Without taking his eyes off the door Kyle asked, "Do I want to know how you know that?"

"Probably not. Good luck, man. Believe it or not I am rooting for the both of you to work this out."

Kyle heard Austin's footsteps behind him and then the sound of the limousine pulling away.

He looked over at Derek's door and knew that he had to talk to his friend about how he could fix what he broke. Derek was annoyed with him, but he hoped that with his help he could make everything right. Making his decision, he knocked on Derek's door and didn't get an answer. He looked around and didn't see Derek's car parked anywhere. Kyle pulled out his cell to call his friend.

"Hey, where are you?"

"Still on my bachelor date. What's up?"

"I need to talk to you about something. Are you coming home soon, or will you be partaking of extracurriculars?"

"Did you see who won my bid?"

"No. Sorry, I wasn't paying attention."

"I am out with Agnes Thorpes."

"The granddaughter or grandmother?" The family had named the first grandchild after the elder Agnes and the poor girl hated her name.

"Grandmother. She already fell asleep during the appetizer. I was afraid she would fall asleep in her soup and drown. I can meet you when I drop her off."

"Actually, I am already at your place."

"Oh, well just use your spare key and I will be there soon."

"Thanks, see you then."

Kyle walked into Derek's house where it looked like the persistent bachelor's apartment. Black leather furniture accented with industrial steel and wood tables. Kyle turned on the TV and plopped on the couch to get comfortable. He tried to keep his eyes open, but soon he found himself drifting off into a comfortable sleep.

He was dreaming about Ariel in his arms when it was quickly lost as he felt a short thump to his head. He jolted upright and then felt another pelt to the head and liquid running down his face. He wiped away at the side of his cheek and then turned to see Derek sitting on the coffee table with a Super Soaker. "What the...?"

Derek squirted him again only this time it zig-zagged across his face. "You're an asshole."

"Hey, come on, man. Knock it off."

"Knock it off? You made my sister cry. I wanted to break your nose; you should be grateful for this."

Kyle held out his hand trying to stop the impending additional douse of water, but failed miserably. "Okay, I'm sorry and I want to fix it. That's why I am here."

Derek put the gun down and placed his elbows on his knees. "What do you mean by fix it?"

"I mean, I'm all in. No more distance. No more push and pull. I'm here and I won't go anywhere."

Derek hung his head with an exasperated sigh. "And she is just supposed to roll over now and accept that?"

"Well, no."

"Good, I'm glad you're using your brain."

Kyle looked down ashamed to look his friend in the eye.

"Aw, shit. You already tried, and it didn't work, right?"

"Yeah. That pretty much covers it."

"Did she slap you?"

Kyle felt his lip turn up on one side. "I think she wanted to, but she just gave me a big shove instead."

"Good for her. Look, I'm going to be honest with you. I told her to move on from you a long time ago. I didn't want her wasting her time waiting for something that wasn't going to happen."

Kyle felt a stab in his heart. His best friend told her to move on. This, of course, was his own fault. He had been pushing her away for years without an explanation to anyone. Kyle started to get up off the couch. "Of course. I'm sorry, I shouldn't have asked—"

Before he could fully stand Derek was pushing him back on the couch. "Sit your ass back down. I'm not done." Derek was now pacing back and forth and running his hands through his hair. "First, you're a great friend, but you have been leading my sister on since we were kids." Kyle started to open his mouth to speak but Derek pointed at him and continued. "You don't deserve her, but for some stupid reason she still loves you. If you screw this up again, I will beat the ever-loving shit out of you. Got it?"

Kyle started to reply but looked at Derek. "Okay, you can speak now."

Kyle let out a long exhale. "I had something that kept me from making things right with her, but I'm all straight now. I want her to know that she will never see me walking away from her again. I can get her to forgive me, but I just need some help with getting an open door... so to speak."

"She slammed the door on your face, huh?"

"Yup. I thought it would break the glass."

"That's her classic super-pissed-off move. Remember in high school when I had that big goose egg on my forehead?"

"Yeah, you said it was from football."

"Nope. She slammed the door on me. I didn't want her to get in trouble with Mom and Dad so I said it was from football. Anyway, I have an idea for you two to spend some time together, but you are going to have to grovel, and use your best charms to get forgiveness."

"I can grovel, and I'm always charming," Kyle said with his head tilted and megawatt smile.

Derek crossed his arms and gave Kyle a blank stare.

"Sorry. That was autopilot. I won't do that again."

Shaking his head Derek reached for the Super Soaker again. "You got that right."

Chapter 9

Ariel awoke the next morning to the incredible aroma of bacon. There really wasn't a better smell in the morning. Some people love coffee, but to her, that just reminded her of the fact that she was getting ready to start her day to work. But, bacon... when it was cooked just right, when it was crispy and the fat just melted in your mouth, that was the perfect way to start your day. Derek must want something if he was cooking bacon, or he messed something up and needed to ask for forgiveness.

When she walked down the hallway, she heard the refrigerator door open and saw not just bacon, but home fries, eggs, and pancakes. She turned to the kitchen with narrowed eyes. "What did you do this time?"

The door shut, only to see Kyle standing with a milk jug and butter in his hands. "Good morning, Princess. Did you sleep well?"

Ariel couldn't move. She just stood there with her mouth opening and closing like a guppy. Words. Words would be good right about now. She should say something, but the man just kept setting the table like he belonged there, like she didn't just slam the door on him last night. Turning to follow him as he walked by, she finally said, "What do you think you are doing?"

Kyle gave a small lift to the left corner of his mouth and gave a gentle shake of his head. "Can't you tell? I am cooking breakfast for the both of us."

"Yeah, I got that, but WHAT are you doing here?"

He set down the milk and butter and brought his hand to her face where he stroked her cheek with his thumb responding with a smooth, low tone. "Trying to make my girl happy and feed her."

"But..."

Kyle ignored her baffled look and pulled out the dining chair. "Come on have a seat."

Not knowing what else to do, she sat down in the chair and stared at him in astonishment. She watched as he poured a glass of milk and started plating her servings. Finally, she asked a question, even though it wasn't the big question she wanted to ask. "How did you get into my apartment? You don't have a key."

Kyle tilted his head and gave her a look that said are you kidding?

"Right. My idiot brother."

"He's not an idiot. He got tested for that in school."

Ariel picked up her fork still trying to decide if she wanted to kick the man out or let him stay for breakfast. Well, he did take the time to make all her favorites and she would waste food if he didn't stay and eat too. She readjusted herself in her chair to look more confident and pointed her fork at him. "This amazing breakfast does not mean I forgive you."

"Of course, not." Kyle leaned in close and continued in nearly a whisper, "But you will forgive me, and then things are going to change, and I promise no more tears over us."

She was tired, and she didn't really want to talk to the big lug, but it would be rude to ignore him completely. "How was your date with Greta?" She gave a little smirk as satisfaction rolled over her for her part in his date.

"Greta is very nice. We went to Casperelli's, and she talked about her job as an assistant and her family."

"And things didn't get romantic." She looked at him and gave a smirk. "Or a little handsy?"

Kyle put down his fork and leaned forward. "She tried, but I told her all about this special girl in my life and how I had royally fucked things up with her. She understood and even gave me some pointers."

Ariel frowned. "She has been trying to outbid me for years for a date with you and she just fizzled out? Well, that's a disappointment."

Kyle leaned his head to the left and questioned, "You wanted me to be with someone else?"

Ariel looked down at her plate. "Can we talk about something else?"

Kyle scooted his chair closer and brought his hand to her chin to tilt her up. "No. Do you not want me anymore?"

Ariel closed her eyes. She couldn't look directly at him. That would be her downfall. He leaned over to whisper in her ear, "Maybe you didn't hear my question. Do you still want me?"

After she let out a shaky breath she replied, "Yes, but I don't trust you."

Kyle leaned back and held her gaze. "Okay. As long as you still want me, I can fix the rest."

Picking her fork back up she found her resolve again. She was going to make him work for this. She had been chasing him for years and if he was going to move them forward, she was going to make sure it was permanent this time. She shrugged up one shoulder. "We'll see."

With a look of victory Kyle leaned back in his chair and confidently said, "Yes, we will."

IT HAD BEEN THREE DAYS since the breakfast, and Kyle had been doing little things for Ariel to win her over. When she came home that night, she found the shelves up in her guest room that she had been intending to hang for nearly two months. On the top shelf was a classic bowler purse with the traditional heart tattoo art on the front. She had seen it at A Stitch Above, but it was nearly eighty dollars and she couldn't justify spending that kind of money on one purse. She nearly caved in after seeing it, but remembering how broken she felt watching him walk away, she kept herself busy to keep from calling him.

The other things Kyle kept doing after that were small things, like sending Phil over with a cupcake and latte, dropping off potted flowers for her front porch and even washing her car outside her house, shirtless, while she watched him from the window. The damn man and his tight abs.

Now, she was working with Lana on a reset to allow for a new merchandise line of gifts. The girls were dusting the shelves and placing them to the side so they could move the holders around to accommodate the new line of products.

Lana pushed back a loose strand of her auburn hair and reached the top holder for Ariel since she was easily able to reach at her 5'8" height. "So has Kyle left you any more surprises today?"

Ariel slotted the first holder in place and shook her head. "Nope, not yet. I assume he is working. He can't ignore the paper all the time to try and win me over."

"Are you going to put the poor guy out of his misery yet? He looks like a lost puppy dog. It really is kind of pathetic."

Ariel placed the last bracket in place and flattened the bottom of her skirt. "You know, every time I want to give in, I get freaked out. I mean he has never gone this far and said that he wants me so clearly, but why now? What changed?"

Lana set the first shelf on the bracket and bit her lip. "Do you really want to know that answer?"

"That answer terrifies me."

They both heard the door open and turned to see the man who had come into the store when her mom and Hannah where there last week. Ariel wiped her hands on her dress as she approached the man. "Hello, again. Do you still need to buy a gift for your wife?"

The man looked at her with bloodshot eyes and seemed as if he wasn't blinking. His wide-eyed expression made Ariel nervous. "Sir? Is there something we can help you find?"

He darted his eyes from her to Lana and looked around the store. "Uh, yeah. Do you have any keys?"

Drawing her eyebrows together Ariel was starting to feel uncomfortable. "Keys?"

The man's eyes dropped to her cleavage. "Yeah, like antique keys or fancy ones you wear around your neck?"

Ariel sighed in relief. Okay, so maybe he isn't crazy. "I'm so sorry. No keys. It's a cute idea though. Maybe with engraving or notes attached." Her mind was wandering already to new ideas for Valentine's Day or anniversary presents.

"Well, what about a charm like on your bracelet?" He started to reach out, but she pulled her hand back and held it close to her chest. "No, sorry. We don't carry these. This was given to me as a gift." She stopped herself from saying more because she was becoming uncomfortable. There was an eagerness to the man's face that was raising the bumps on the back of her neck in warning. "Tell you what... we are going to find something that is still fabulous for your wife." She motioned for Lana to come forward and approach. "Lana will help you find just what you need. I have to take care of something, and I will be back shortly."

Ariel quickly passed the pair, grabbed her cell phone from the area where they had been setting up the new product and walked into the back of the store. Once she knew she was clear, she quickly called Derek.

"Hey, what's up?"

"Hi. Are you still upstairs with Zoey?"

"Yeah. We just finished our early dinner before I go to the pub. Why?"

"I am at the shop and this man is giving me weird vibes, and I just think someone should be here with us." She immediately heard movement coming from Derek's line.

"I'm on my way. Meet me at your back door and don't hang up."

Rolling her eyes, she walked to the back door. "Wasn't planning on it."

As she opened the door, she heard a solid thud echoing off the walls of the back alley and then feet pounding in a quick pace. She took a deep breath as Derek came into view and hung up the phone. "Did you fall? I heard a big thud."

"I practically jumped down the fire escape to get to you."

"Okay. I want to have you take a look at this guy, so I am going back up front first then you discreetly follow me out."

Derek was already shaking his head and walking past her. "Like hell you're going first."

With a quick exhale Ariel muttered. "Brothers."

Derek walked through the door to the store front like he owned the place. So much for discretion. He walked up to Lana with all his charm and swagger and put his arms around her waist. "Hey there, hot stuff. How's work going today?"

Lana stiffened. Ariel couldn't believe he was using *this* plan. This was a dumb plan. Lana looked at Derek as if he lost his mind. Then, like watching a train wreck he leaned over and kissed her on the cheek. Ariel held her hand to prevent hiding her eyes in horror. Next time she was going to call Tyler, or even Tiny, Derek's ex-con cook. Either of them would have been more discreet.

Ariel's customer now was watching the scene in obvious befuddlement. Then he jumped back as Derek extended his hand in greeting. "Sorry. I'm Derek. Excuse the PDA, but I just can't keep my hands off this woman."

Lana must have got something in her throat because she started to cough. Derek rubbed her back in concern and cooed, "You okay, baby? Maybe you should go in back and get some water."

Ariel watched Lana look back at Derek and then to the customer and seemed to understand what was going on. "Yeah. Thanks... babe. I'll be right back."

Derek again extended his hand out to the man who finally took it. "Sorry about that. Like I said I'm Derek, and you are?"

Looking up the man finally answered, "Max. I was just trying to find something for my wife."

Derek smoothly went into an easy conversation mode that must come from his skills as a bartender. "Well, that is nice of you. What's her name?"

"What?"

"Name. What's your wife's name?"

"Oh... Erma."

Derek leaned back in that triumphant pose he always used when he was winning at a game and crossed his arms. It was usually annoying, but right now, Ariel loved it.

"Funny... like the restaurant."

Max's eyes widened. "What?"

"You know, that old restaurant, Max and Erma's?"

The man slowly shook his head. "Nope. Sorry."

"Huh. Oh, well. I'm just going to bug my sister over here at the counter for minute while you look around."

Derek gently pushed Ariel in her back to steer her towards the counter away from the man who was now watching them intently. Derek grabbed a box from the inventory that had not yet opened and began to open the new figurine.

Following his lead, Ariel grabbed for another box and did the same.

Nodding to the man at the back Derek growled in a low tone. "He's lying."

Ariel equally kept her voice in a low whisper. "Yeah, I got that but why? I mean why would he care about what I think, or why it matters to me who he is?"

"I don't know, but we can pull the security footage and show it to Chase and see if he knows anything."

Ariel winced. "Uh, yeah, about that."

Derek leaned back on the counter and crossed his arms. "Please tell me that you bought and had the system installed like I told you to."

"I got sidetracked and just didn't get around to it."

"Are you kidding me? After everything that happened with Zoey you still put it off?"

"Well, it isn't like I have some psycho ex who would come after me, and I don't sell anything that people would generally break into a store after hours for."

Derek reached around beside her to a shelf that held a porcelain figurine, read the bottom and pulled out his phone to pull up a third-party seller's app. Ariel watched in confusion as he pulled up what she was selling for forty dollars and gasped when she saw it was selling for eighty online.

Snatching the phone from Derek's hand her mouth gaped. "Oh my god. I didn't realize that this one was in such high demand."

Derek took his phone back and shook his head. "A lot of stuff you sell here usually sells out in the major cities and people sell them for a higher profit. Someone could steal this whole section of collectables and make a lot of money. Don't underestimate the value of your product. The right person would know what to do with it."

Ariel felt like a child being lectured by her parent. She hated it when he was right. Before she could respond to his thoughts, she heard Lana's voice piercing the quiet.

"Get out! You can't be back here. Get out!"

Ariel and Derek turned to see Max backing out of the stock room door with his palms up. "Sorry. I thought that the restroom was back here."

Lana was walking out right behind him. "We don't have restrooms for the public here."

The man was quickly walking towards the front door. He muttered an apology as he made his hasty exit out to the street.

Lana came up to the front and stood next to Derek placing her unsteady hands on the counter. She looked at Ariel obviously shaken up. "I thought I would take the trash out while I was back there, when I came back, he was looking around the stock room on the shelf above the computer. There is no way he was back there looking for the bathroom."

Derek looked over at his sister and ground his teeth. "Your security system is getting installed tomorrow."

Resigned Ariel took a deep breath. "Yeah, okay."

KYLE WAS CARRYING A box of the latest printed papers up front when he saw Derek walk in. Derek had stopped in his tracks with a bit of confusion on his face when he saw the teenaged boy with his head down into Kyle's laptop. Kyle was enjoying the moment. He hadn't had any help in the office since he took over the paper, but was happy to have his new assistant who approached him earlier that afternoon.

Derek finally turned his head and nodded at Kyle. "Thought maybe you found the fountain of youth for a minute. He kind of looks like a younger version of you."

Kyle shrugged. "Kind of weird isn't it?"

"Need help with the boxes?"

"Sure. I have three more in the back that Frank will be picking up for delivery."

The two men worked quietly bringing the stock up front and Kyle laughed as the teenager seemed to ignore them both and just furiously kept typing away. After the last box was up front, he walked over to the teenager. "Derek, this is Dimitri. He is the editor at the school paper and wanted to work for me to get additional experience before going to college."

Derek shook hands with the young man who looked to be in good shape under the obvious hand-me- down shirt and tie. The boy brightly smiled and extended his hand. "Hello, Mr. McKenna. Nice to meet you."

Kyle beamed. He really liked this kid, and now that his trouble with the gang was over, he felt comfortable allowing someone else to work with him.

Derek released the boy's hand and gave a wide smile. "Dimitri. That is unusual. Is your family from Russia?"

The kid rolled his eyes like he has had to explain this a million times. "No. My mom and grandmother used to watch some soap opera together and one of the main guy's name on the show was Dimitri. She says they used to make up fantasies about him, and when I was born grandma said I would be a heartbreaker, so they wanted to give me a name to match."

Laughing Derek asked, "Did your dad get jealous?"

"Don't know. He didn't stick around long enough to find out."

Derek frowned. "I'm sorry."

"Don't be. I like my life. My mom and grandma love me and now I have a nice stepdad too."

Kyle put his hand on Dimitri's shoulder. "Dimitri here is the high school editor and wants to attend Duke next year in their journalism program."

Derek leaned back on the wall and gave a welcoming smile. "Wow, that's great. Maybe now this knucklehead can take a day off or two every now and then."

Kyle nodded. "That's the plan. He's going out today to do an interview."

Dimitri stood up and grabbed his backpack and notepad off the table. "Yeah, I should probably head out now. I will send you my copy later tonight."

"Okay. Go ahead and have fun."

After Dimitri left Derek plopped down into a chair on the far side of the desk and Kyle sat in his chair. Kyle could see that Derek had something on his mind. "To what do I owe the pleasure of your visit today?"

"I was wondering if you would help Tiny install a security system in Ariel's shop tomorrow?"

Kyle leaned closer in his chair. "Of course. Did something happen?"

"Not really but there is a customer that has come in a couple of times and he just gives off weird vibes. Plus, I told her to do this a long time ago anyway."

"Let me guess. It went in one ear and out the other."

"Yup. I don't know why she just doesn't listen to me. I tell her logical things, or things to help her succeed and stay safe, and she just ignores me."

"You have to understand she wants to show her independence. She doesn't want to look like her success wasn't hers and that she needed your help. It killed her to get that small loan from you in the beginning."

Derek rolled his eyes. "It was so stupidly small. Just three thousand. She had all the rest for all her inventory, the first five months of operating expenses and a marketing budget."

"I remember you telling me about it. And didn't she pay you back within like three months?"

"Yeah. I told her to keep it and not worry about it, but that just pissed her off even more. She also yelled at me when I suggested that she live with me rent free."

Laughing Kyle remembered his mom telling him about that. "Yeah, Mom said you finally agreed to let her pay but only like four hundred a month."

"Actually, it's only three hundred a month, and I have been putting the money away for a college fund for her future kids. She can yell at me for that later."

"I know the pub is successful, but you should invest some for yourself. If you don't settle down and have a family, you will have to hire someone to take care of your old pathetic ass."

"Gee, thanks."

"Just saying."

Derek leaned forward and started bouncing his fist on Kyle's stapler, obviously wanting to change the subject of his personal life. "Anyway, I am getting ready to go to work and Tiny is going to drive and pick out the best system over at that security place that just opened up by Greko's."

"Does he know which one to get?"

Smirking Derek said, "His friend owns the place. You know, the one who got busted for breaking into high security corporate buildings."

"Oh, I remember him telling me about that guy. Didn't he do it just for the thrills? I remember him saying he never stole a single thing, and that he was just bored."

"Yup. That's the guy. Did you know that now big companies are paying him to actually break in and find the weaknesses of their security system?"

"Well, they always say find a job that you love. At least he will stop going to jail for it."

"Think there is a job out there for annoying your little sister?"

"Don't even try it. She will kill you if you make her your main focus."

Derek shrugged. "It amuses me. Okay, so can you meet Tiny at Ariel's shop around eight am?"

"Yeah. No problem."

Just as Derek stood to leave both men's phones pinged with a text message.

Zoey: Emergency wedding meeting. Everyone free tonight?

Josie: Darn. Now I have to release the guy from my new handcuffs to make it.

Derek and Kyle just looked at each other. Kyle was the first to dare to speak. "Do you think she is serious?"

"You dumb enough to go to her apartment to find out, or even just ask?"

"Nope."

Kyle: I am free.

Ariel: Yes

Dixie: Chase and I are good with that.

Derek: I have to work. Can we have the meeting at McKenna's?

The next round of messages came in with confirmations and agreements to meet at 7:30.

Derek started to walk out the door and then turned to ask, "Oh, I almost forgot, how is project Happily Ever After going?"

Kyle put his hands in his pockets and leaned back. "I think we are making progress. Just a little more of alone time and I should be able to win her over."

"Great. Just promise to spare me the details after you win her over. It might make me want to punch you."

Grinning like a loon, Kyle nodded. "I promise."

ARIEL WAS SITTING AT the table with Josie, Dixie and Chase while waiting for the others for Zoey's emergency meeting. "Do any of you know why we are here?"

Chase reached over and grabbed a wing and tore off a piece before he responded. "Nope, Tyler wouldn't give up the goods either. He said they would explain when they got here."

Kyle slid into the booth next to Ariel and nodded at everyone while he grabbed a wing. Josie handed over one of the ranch cups over to Kyle and said, "Maybe Zoey got knocked up and we are going to have a shotgun wedding."

Laughing Chase said, "I've got the shotgun if we need it."

Ariel watched Kyle frown and then put his head down. She could tell he knew something but wouldn't press it now.

It was only a few minutes later when Zoey and Tyler walked in and joined everyone. Derek's new waitress took their orders and said she would get him from the back.

Derek walked over with potato skins, mozzarella sticks, more wings and set most of it in front of Chase before sitting down.

Chase rubbed his hands together and looked over at Derek while batting his eyelashes. "I knew you were my favorite."

"Yeah, I am just protecting my friends. A hungry armed sheriff isn't good for any of us."

Putting a whole potato skin in his mouth, he just shrugged. "Whatever gets me more food."

Everyone was now looking expectantly at Zoey. She finally cleared her throat and began. "I know that we were going to wait and plan the wedding slowly and enjoy it all, but now we are moving up the date."

Pounding the table with her fist Josie exclaimed, "Ha! I knew it! Nerd boy knocked you up."

Zoey's face fell. "No. It's not that."

Josie immediate reached for Zoey's hand. "Shit. Are you okay? You're not dying on us, are you?"

Zoey jerked her head up quickly. "What? No. This is coming from the Queen on high command."

Everyone looked at Ariel in confusion. She looked at them all incredulously. "Not me. I'm Princess... not the Queen."

Their heads turned back to Zoey waiting for more. "My mom and dad are going to take a trip around the world for a month, and it's going to interfere with the time we had planned already for the wedding. She refuses to reschedule and said the time we chose for the wedding is just not convenient for her, and I just need to pick another date. When I tried to coordinate our schedules with the event center at the Orchards, it was a mess. I am not waiting another year and a half to get married." Now she was holding hands with Tyler who looked frustrated at the whole thing.

Derek was tapping the table with his fist. "Your mom drives me crazy."

Tyler shook his head. "Be grateful, I am marrying into this."

Zoey shot him a death glare.

"But I am marrying this woman who makes me the happiest man on earth." He then leaned over and kissed her temple.

Chase chuckled. "Oh man, you are going to pay for that one later."

"Thanks, asshole."

Zoey shook her head. "Anyway, there is an opening at the Orchards in three weeks. I wanted to check with all of you if we can move up the wedding and if you all will be able to accommodate the change."

They each looked around and gave yeses and nods. Ariel watched as Zoey relaxed back into Tyler's arms and continued, "We also have a change in the bridal party to make. Derek are you still ordained to perform weddings?"

"Yeah. I will double check to make sure, but I think so." Derek had performed a wedding for one of his friends from college a couple years ago and loved calling himself preacher when he gave lectures to others.

Zoey let out a sigh and looked over at Ariel. "The person we were going to use for the wedding isn't available for this new date, and if we use Derek as the officiant, he can't be my Man of Honor. Would you be my maid of honor?"

Ariel started bouncing in her seat with excitement. "I would love too, and I can help with whatever you need."

Looking more at ease Zoey said, "Good. I think we will need Kyle and you to help more than we originally intended before."

Ariel looked at her friend and felt true happiness that Zoey found someone so perfect for her. She peered over at Kyle who was now looking at her with a special twinkle in his eye. Then she dropped her eyes as she felt his hand slip into hers and he said, "We would be happy to help. In fact, give us anything. We are here for whatever you need."

Ariel was coming to a quick realization. She was doomed. She wasn't going to be able to hold out much longer. He was going to pull out the stops and helping to plan a romantic wedding together... yeah... she was doomed.

KYLE COULDN'T BELIEVE his luck. He was going to send a big thank you bouquet to Zoey's mom for making this perfect collision of events. Okay, maybe he wouldn't send her flowers. She always seemed to put Zoey on edge, but still, he couldn't have planned this better.

"I am taking most of the day off tomorrow. What can I do?" he asked Zoey as he started rubbing his thumb across Ariel's hand.

"Well, the first thing I think we need to do is maybe talk to the florist? I want to make sure she can work with the new date. Can you and Ariel talk to her? I'm not really all that into flowers. Ariel can pick the designs." She turned to Ariel. "Just pick what you think will be best. I have complete faith in you about this."

Ariel was almost bouncing out of her seat again. "What's my budget?"

Zoey frowned. "I don't know." She looked over at Tyler for assistance.

"Like I know what flowers cost?"

Chase's voice carried across the table. "If you aren't having them do center pieces, about eight hundred to a thousand, but if they need to do the centerpieces then probably more like two thousand." The table grew silent, and they all stared at Chase. "What? I know stuff. Besides, I just paid for the flowers for our wedding."

Josie smiled. "And here I thought you weren't really listening to me when I told you all that stuff."

"When it comes with a high price tag, of course, I listen."

"Okay, make the budget around a thousand then. I am going to make the center pieces out of desserts and dessert stands, and Tyler came up with a good idea for party favors," Zoey said.

Tyler laughed. "See, I know stuff too."

The rest of the night went really well with trying to plan out some details and just generally enjoying dinner. Kyle was so grateful for his friends. He knew that not everyone had such a great support system.

Then there was Ariel. He had been trying to make small advances throughout the night. He even found himself pulling out the lame high school yawning stretch to put his arm around Ariel. He knew how pathetic it looked, but he also knew she wouldn't make a scene in front of everyone to get him to stop. Was it his best idea? No, not really, but if he could get her to subconsciously put her defenses down, he would do whatever it took.

By the end of the night, he saw Ariel's face flush from the wine and that ever-present smile she had when she was on just the right side of tipsy. Derek had cut her off already, and the only people left with them were Josie, and Derek, who was still working the bar.

Ariel placed her head on Kyle's shoulder and yawned. "Sleepy now."

Kyle looked over at Derek who was still busy and whispered. "Do you want me to take you home now?"

"Mm-hmm."

Josie leaned back and smirked. "Go. I will let Derek know you took her home."

"Thanks. Tell him I can help him get her car back home later if he wants."

"Yup. Off with you now. I have to see if I can go seduce a tourist before it gets too late."

"If I didn't know better, I would say you are perfect for Derek."

Josie looked over at Derek who was now flirting with a curvy brunette. "No thanks. I need someone who isn't so soft and mushy inside. He needs a girl who will show him soft, supportive love. That isn't me."

Laughing Kyle said, "No, but as much as you try to hide it you have soft spots."

Looking down at her plate her eyes grew dark. "It is those soft spots that destroy me too though."

Kyle nodded knowingly. He had completed a background search on Josie when she first started getting close with Ariel. She had a horrible past before she moved to Blossom Hills, but it was her story to tell and in her time. He knew that all too well about secrets and respected her privacy, even though he knew that if she ever shared her past, everyone would be supportive and understanding.

He was taken aback when a loud snore came from Ariel, who was now slack against his body and if he wasn't mistaken drooling on him a little. "Okay. We better go. See you later, Josie."

She nodded while she took another sip of her wine, giving him a shooing motion as he slid himself and Ariel out of the booth.

Chapter 10

Ariel arrived at her shop the next morning to find her door unlocked. Alarmed, she grabbed her recently purchased taser and slowly peeked her head inside. She heard what she thought was the sound of a drill and two men talking. It only took a moment to realize that one was Kyle. Feeling at ease, she walked in the door. She found Tiny standing on a ladder while Kyle was handing screws up to him.

"What do you guys think you are doing?"

Tiny was the first speak in his incredibly deep voice. "Doing what Bossman told me to do."

"Derek told you to install my security system?"

He still didn't turn away from his task. He just drilled with the next screw to secure the camera in place. Ariel turned to Kyle and asked, "And why are you here?"

With a lift of one shoulder he said, "Derek asked me to help."

"Right."

Ariel set her purse down with a solid thud on the counter and looked suspiciously at the box where other cameras were still encased in Styrofoam. "Hey, this isn't the one I picked out. This is way more expensive." She turned and pointed a finger at Tiny. "You need to take this back."

"No, can do. Bossman said to get this one."

"Yeah, but I don't have the money to pay for this one."

"Take a look at your bank account. I only charged your card what you told him your budget was."

Ariel crossed her arms. She knew that the store wouldn't have given her that much of a discount. "And who paid for the rest of it?" She glared at Kyle.

Kyle put his hands up in a surrendering motion as he backed away to let Tiny get down from the ladder. "Don't look at me. I didn't do it."

She narrowed her eyes as he walked closer. Kyle wrapped his arm around her waist and pulled her until she was flush against him and he leaned down to whisper in her ear, "But believe me, Princess, I would have paid for all of it to keep you safe."

Ariel felt tingles down her spine as he still held her close and started nuzzling her neck, but just as she was giving in, she heard Tiny's voice coming from behind Kyle.

"Hey, I am all for you two finally getting together, but I would prefer not to be a witness for it. She is like my little sister, and I just don't need that image in my head."

Ariel slipped from Kyle's grip and grabbed her phone off the counter. "I need to go call big brother and have a little chat. Please, excuse me."

About ten minutes later Ariel walked back to the front of the store where Kyle was packing up the box and holding the manual to the overpriced system. She also saw that Tiny was putting up the last camera by the front door.

"Did you talk to Derek?"

Ariel gave out a huff of annoyance. "Yes, I did. The stubborn little asshole."

Kyle walked over and leaned on the counter next to her and wrapped his arm around her waist. "Hey, he just wants the best for you, and so do I. He told me about the weird guy who was hanging around and how he even went into the back."

"Yeah. He is a bit odd. He doesn't seem dangerous, but a bit off. I can't quite read him."

"Here is the thing though, people who are just a bit off can become dangerous rather quickly if they get desperate."

"Fine. Are we still going to the flower shop today?"

"Yeah, I figured we could go at eleven and then maybe get some lunch?"

Ariel thought for a minute. "Well, it should be slow today. I can take a couple of hours; Lana will be here."

"Great. I will see you at eleven then."

Before she could respond he leaned over and gave her a kiss on the cheek. She stood dumbfounded while he had a stupid charming smile across his face. She tilted her head and watched as he walked out of the shop, whistling to himself.

ARIEL ENTERED BLOSSOM Hills Blooms excited to be able to select the flowers for Zoey's wedding. She immediately saw Poppy, the owner's granddaughter, already sitting with Kyle who was paging through the folder of standard choices for bouquets. He looked up as she started towards him with a coy smile that always woke up the butterflies in her stomach.

Poppy was the first one to greet Ariel as she began to sit on the couch next to Kyle. She always was ready with a quick smile and was thought to be a bit quirky by others. "Hello Ariel, it's good to see you again."

"Hi, Poppy, thanks for being able to squeeze us in so quickly."

Poppy gave a dismissive wave of her hand. "I was happy to help. We have worked with Zoey on several weddings for cakes that wanted real flowers, and she is just so awesome. I was showing Kyle some of the samples that I think Zoey would love."

Ariel looked down as Kyle flipped through to some of the pages he had marked with Post-it Notes. The first was a bouquet bursting with color and vibrancy adorned with mostly wildflowers. The next few were a bit more subdued and tightly wound. Ariel looked over at Kyle. "I think maybe a combination of these two, what do you think?"

Kyle studied the two different options and gave a nod. "I think the second one is too formal for them, but the first is a bit too wild."

Ariel nodded. "Can you do a combination of the two? Maybe loosen up the formal bouquet to allow a little move-ment and add some color from the wildflowers?"

Poppy took a piece of paper and began sketching out a design. It was remarkable how quickly she was able to draw the flowers and give personality to the arrangement. Once completed, she handed the design to them and waited expec-tantly.

Ariel looked over at Kyle who was studying the drawing. He was the first to speak. "Can you make just smaller versions of this for the bridesmaids?"

Poppy sat back, obviously pleased that they liked her design. "Of course. Now, how about the men?"

Ariel looked at the folder thoughtfully. "I think just one simple white flower, but not a rose. It needs to be a little different."

"How about a stephanotis boutonniere?"

Both Ariel and Kyle looked at Poppy with blank expressions.

Looking a bit embarrassed, Poppy explained. "Right. Flower words, not normal human words. Sorry. It's a small five-pointed flower. We would usually wrap three together with some greens." She pulled out her phone and made quick movements with her fingers until she found what she was looking for and handed it over to Kyle.

"That looks great. If I brought over some charms can you add them to the front?"

Ariel looked at Kyle with her eyes crinkled in confusion.

"I bought these charms off the internet as a surprise for Tyler for all the men. They are different ships from Star Wars, like the Millennium Falcon, an X-Wing fighter and TIE fighter."

"Oh my god, Zoey's mom is going to hate that."

With a devilish grin Kyle replied, "Yup."

"How big are they?"

"Not very big. Less than a quarter of an inch or so."

"Think we could get them bigger? I want to make sure her mom can see them clearly from the front row."

Kyle leaned over and wrapped his arm around her waist and whispered, "I love your evil side. It's so damn sexy."

Ariel closed her eyes and let out a deep breath. She needed to get herself together, or she was going to straddle his lap and give Poppy a show she would never forget about. It was eventually Poppy's voice that pulled her out of the lust fog when she asked, "Are we ready to move on to the other arrangements?"

Clearing her throat Ariel replied, "Yes, please."

IT WAS ONLY ANOTHER twenty minutes when Kyle and Ariel finalized the flowers for the wedding, and they started walking towards town square. He was grateful Ariel didn't fight him when he reached for her hand when once they got to the sidewalk. It felt so right entwining their fingers together and walking side by side.

Ariel's soft voice finally broke the silence after a block. "So, where are we going for lunch? McKenna's or Daisy's?"

"Neither."

Ariel stopped in her tracks and pointed at her shoes. "I am not in the best footwear to walk to Casperelli's."

Kyle lightly tugged on her hand and laughed. "We're not going to Casperelli's. Now come on."

"Okay, so where are we going?"

"Would you just trust me and walk with me?"

Ariel stopped and crossed her arms. "But I want to know now."

Kyle stopped too and shook his head. "No. You have always loved surprises, so you can wait a couple more minutes and come with me."

He could see her fighting with herself not to give into him. He almost had her exactly where he wanted her. She started biting her lower lip while trying to pout at the same time. Kyle gave an exasperated huff and bent over and picked her up in a fireman's hold over his shoulder.

"Put me down you big idiot."

"Nope. You want to show off your cute stubborn streak, fine, but we are on a time crunch and need to get moving. Since you won't move, I will help you move."

"This is not helping; this is moving for me."

Kyle shrugged his free shoulder and just kept walking.

"My ass better not be showing to the whole town while you carry me like this."

"Maybe you should have thought about that before you insisted on stopping our walk. A few people might get a glimpse of your panties if we get a good gust of wind."

"Who said I was wearing panties?"

Kyle quickly placed her back down and tried to keep the dress from revealing her bottom half as she slid down. "Did you really just tell me that you are not wearing any panties?"

Ariel gave a sly smirk. "That isn't exactly what I said."

Kyle picked her up by placing his arms under her ass and leaned his forehead to hers. "So, are you, or aren't you wearing underwear?"

"If you are a good boy, maybe you can find out later. But you really need to feed me now."

Kyle quickly put her back down, put his hand back into hers and pulled her with him on the way to her surprise. He sure hoped Tyler had everything ready like he instructed, because he was about ready to lose his mind.

Once they rounded the other side of the gazebo, he saw it. He mentally sent a thank you to Tyler and heard a small gasp of delight coming from Ariel.

"We're having a picnic?"

"Yes, come on now before the food gets cold."

He helped Ariel down to the oversized blanket and opened the basket he'd bought earlier that morning. First, he pulled out two single serving bottles of champagne and glasses.

Ariel giggled looking at the bottles. "Look, they are small like me."

"The best things come in small packages." He continued to pull out food and then two plates. "Okay, we have lemon roasted chicken with red potatoes and carrots." He reached in and pulled out two more small boxes. "And for dessert we have mini-individual cherry pies."

"You cooked all this?"

"Most of it. I bought the mini pies from the bakery section at Johnson's."

"They are definitely cute."

"Thanks. I thought so too."

They began eating and enjoying the quiet comfort of just being with each other. This part was easy. It had always been easy. As their conversation flowed throughout the meal, he thought several times about telling her everything. How he had always had the intention of coming back home and to start a life with her, about how the life of reporting in a major city had slowly broken him in pieces, and how he was partially responsible for an innocent girl's life being taken away. But how could he confess all that now? Kyle was trying desperately to show Ariel he was the man she could count on, the man who would no longer walk away.

"Hey, where did you go?"

Kyle refocused his eyes on hers. "What?"

"We were talking and then you just kind of drifted away."

"Sorry. I just remembered something about work."

The light in Ariel's eyes dimmed a little. "Oh, you have to leave now?"

Kyle placed his fingers under her chin and lifted her to meet his gaze. "No. I am here with you. No more disappearing, or at least not before I can make sure that you know I would be coming back to you."

He watched as she studied his face, obviously looking for the truth of what he was saying. There was still sadness in her eyes. He hated it. He knew that the sadness was his fault through years of keeping her at a distance.

"I want to believe you, but how can you make me believe that you will come back again?"

Kyle slid his hand into her hair and gently grazed his thumb on her temple. "Because this will always be my promise to return to you."

He lowered his mouth to her trembling lips and tried to pour every ounce of assurance in his kiss. This kiss was his new unbreakable promise to her. Without losing contact with her lips, he pulled her into his lap and wound his other arm around her body. She melted at his touch. All the tension he felt from her before was gone. Now there was this woman with wanton desire. She was accepting his hunger, his need, and was healing his heart with every touch and caress of their tongues and lips. His arousal was now straining against his pants, and he had to slightly adjust Ariel to accommodate the new sensations.

She finally released her lips from his and gasped in a bit of air. She wrapped her arms around his neck and whispered, "I can feel your promise in other places now too."

Kyle gave a low groan. "That promise is going to have to wait. I think we have too much of an audience out here."

They both looked around and they indeed did have quite an audience. There were several town residents looking on with wide grins in the courtyard, and when Kyle looked over at the front of Zoey's bakery, he could see his brother, Zoey, Josie and several other patrons all stacked on top of each other looking out the front window.

Kyle nodded to the window. "Looks like half the gang already knows what happened."

Ariel looked over at the bakery and buried her head in his shoulder and she mumbled, "Look at Dixie's studio. Her and Chase are out front too."

Sure enough, when Kyle turned his head, he saw Chase in his uniform, standing with one arm around Dixie and his other eating an apple with a face of obvious amusement. "Don't they all have better things to do?"

Kyle felt Ariel's smile against his neck. "To be fair, we would have done the same to any of them if they did this so publicly."

Kyle sighed and squeezed her closer to him. "Okay, so how about we do this a little more privately tonight... dinner at my house?"

He felt Ariel playing with the small hairs on the back of his neck and giving a small nod of her head. "I would like that." She gave a small pause and then wiggled on his lap. "Should I bring anything?"

Kyle stroked her back and groaned. She was playing with him moving her petite little body in all the right places. "Just bring yourself." He leaned in closer and whispered in her ear, "Panties optional."

He felt her breath stutter and felt a small bit of victory. He still affected her, and soon she would understand just how much she affected him too.

Chapter 11

Ariel barely made it back into her shop before she heard Josie's voice booming from behind the counter. "Get your butt over here, Pip Squeak, and spill all the juicy details."

Ariel shook her head at her friend who was looking very comfortable behind the register with a helpless Lana standing off to the side. "Are you now working here too? I don't remember adding you to the payroll?"

"I knew you couldn't ignore me if I went behind the counter."

Ariel looked over at Lana who seemed to be at a loss of what to do with the intimidating woman. "Did she scare any customers away?"

"No, but one tried to hit on her."

Ariel looked over at Josie. "So, you have a date later tonight then?"

"Didn't you listen to her? He *tried* to hit on me. That man would snap like a twig if I played with him. I charmed him into buying some needless trinket and sent him on his merry little way."

A buzzing sound came from the counter and Josie picked up her phone to read the incoming text messages.

Ariel arched an eyebrow as several more messages came in. "I think you should respond to those."

"It's just Dixie."

"What does she want?"

"You'll see." Then as if they had planned this ahead of time, Dixie came bursting in the door with her face all flushed and out of breath.

"I'm here." She walked up to the now crowded counter and braced her hands on the edge as she gasped in a big breath. "Okay. You didn't let her start without me, did you?"

"No. But only because I didn't get a chance to get her started yet. God, Dix if you are that out of shape from running from the studio to here, we have bigger issues to talk about."

Dixie gave a self-satisfied smile. "Chase and I had a quick workout before I ran over here. He said that he was not 'going to be out romanced by the pretty boy.' Then I ran over here."

"Way to go Dix, and did he deliver?"

Dixie beamed as she nodded her head and lifted up two fingers. "He knows exactly where all the right buttons are."

A small throat clearing came from Lana. "I think I am going to... go clean something."

"Oh, Okay. Or you could take your lunch if you want. I can take care of things here for a while." Ariel felt bad for Lana. She knew that Lana wasn't comfortable with sex talk, and she had just recently found out that Lana was still a virgin. When she had asked about it, Lana had said it wasn't really by choice, but just that any time she got close things just kind of fell apart, and she didn't want to lose it to just any-one.

Once Lana was gone, Dixie started bouncing on her feet. "Okay. We want details."

"Really? I thought both of you got eyefuls earlier."

Josie rolled her eyes. "Of course, we watched. You didn't really think you could have a romantic picnic right in the middle of town square where most of us live or work, and we wouldn't watch the show, did you?"

"Well, I didn't get to pick where we had lunch."

"I know. I was having coffee with Tyler when Kyle showed up with the basket and gave instructions on setting it up so it would be ready when the two of you got done with the flowers."

Ariel looked over at Dixie who was smiling like an over excited teenager. "What? Josie texted me and told me about your lunch. As your best friend, it is my duty to spy on you to make sure the idiot didn't screw it up."

"And it didn't occur to either one of you to let us have a little bit of privacy?"

Josie snorted. "Privacy? Sweetie that kiss was live streamed on Penny's Facebook page."

"Live streamed? Oh my god. I hope my mom didn't see that."

Josie pulled out her phone and handed it to Ariel. "Not only did she see it, but she commented and applauded it."

Ariel scrolled through the comments and it seemed like half of the town put in their opinions. "God, that is mortify-ing."

Dixie reached for the phone and started reading the comments. "It is kind of romantic if you think about it. Kyle has been so private since he moved back to town. He pushed you away for so long now, but he is putting it out there for everyone to see. He wants everyone including you to know that he is choosing you."

"He definitely made an impression."

Smirking Josie asked, "Was that impression from a certain hard body part on your leg when you were on his lap?"

Ariel gasped half in laughter and half shock. "Josie!"

"What? Come on. Tell us. Is he deserving of his *cockiness*?"

Dixie was now laughing and nearly choking at the same time. "Oh, I am sure he has every reason to be proud as a *peacock*."

Ariel crossed her arms and glared at her friends. "I hate you both."

KYLE WAS PLATING DINNER when he heard a soft knock on his door. He quickly wiped his hands off on the towel and went to answer it. Once he opened it, he found Ariel standing looking like an incredible vision from his dreams, all grace and sunshine with a warm but nervous smile.

He was still standing in the doorway feeling a bit stunned. This was finally going to happen. No more obstacles, no more pushing her away. Tonight, he was going to claim her... mind, body and soul. He never wanted to see her greet him with a nervous smile again.

"Are you going to let me in?" She was fidgeting now, holding her bottle of wine like a lifeline.

"Oh, yes. Sorry come in."

She walked in the door into his entry way with a small tilt of her head, as if she was trying to figure out a puzzle. "I brought some wine."

Kyle gently took the bottle from her. "Perfect. This will go great with dinner."

Ariel took in a deep breath and closed her eyes. "It smells amazing. What are we having?"

"Beef bourguignons."

He watched as her eyes grew wide and lit with a spark. "Like that Julia Child recipe?"

"Not like her recipe. It is her recipe. I remember how much you wanted to try her recipes after watching that movie, so I thought tonight would be perfect."

Ariel walked into the dining room looking around at the dining table that was now completely set up with all of the food, lit candles and a small vase of flowers. Kyle quickly walked over to the table and extended out a chair for her to sit down. He worried if maybe all of this was a bit over the top, but he was just so happy that she was giving him a chance after he had screwed up so much with them the past couple of years.

As Kyle sliced some of the bread, he noticed how she was fidgeting with the bottom of her dress. She always did that when she was really nervous. She had once told him she had nightmares as a kid that she would be at some important function and her dress would just randomly fly up and em-barrass her in front of everyone. Now, she always played with the bottom when she would have problems calming down. He once suggested to her that maybe it would help if she wore pants instead. Not that he wanted her to, because he loved all her dresses, but she refused saying that she liked feeling feminine and pretty in her dresses.

Thinking that a glass of wine might help to calm her nerves he picked up the bottle and rose from the table. "I'll be right back. I am going to open the bottle of wine."

She nodded and folded her hands back into her lap. Kyle quickly prepared the glasses of wine and sat back down beside her. He took his hand and entwined their fingers together. "Are you okay?"

Her eyes slowly met his. "Yes. Everything looks amazing."

Kyle waited for her to continue, however she seemed to drift off inside of her own head as he looked at her. He didn't quite know what to say that would put her at ease. "Okay, well let's eat some of his *amazing* food." At least he hoped it was amazing. He got the recipe off the internet and watched a video while he prepared it, so he wouldn't mess it up.

He watched as she took her first bite and truly seemed to enjoy the dish. "This is really good. Was it hard to make?"

"No, surprisingly enough. I learned on the video that you have to have patience while cooking and not to rush things. That is how you burn the food, or overcook things. I found this amazing YouTube channel called Mindy's Meals. She recreates famous recipes and shows you how to make everything step by step. She also shows outtakes at the end, to show that even she sometimes messes up while cooking. She seems very relatable. I was thinking about asking her if she would like to be featured in our paper, so that others can see how great she is."

Soaking the juices with her bread she enthusiastically nodded. "You totally should. I think we are taught a few recipes by our parents that we can cook well, but when people try to branch out with online recipes and they fail it discourages them to try again. Having her mistakes at the end of the videos is a really good idea. Do you know how many times I have tried to make food or a craft from Pinterest and it turns into a total disaster? Even the neighbor's dog refused to eat the lime beef I made for the fajitas."

Kyle laughed. "That dog will eat anything. I am sure you are just exaggerating."

"No. I pulled the steak out of the oven and tried to slice it in thin strips, and I couldn't get it to cut. I got so frustrated I pulled out that crazy giant meat cleaver I never use and started hacking at it like I was chopping firewood. I could only get small cuts in when I finally gave up and opened the window and tossed it over the fence. I figured Rex is a big old mastiff with a good appetite and that he'd love it. And do you know what happened?"

Kyle was now biting desperately trying to not laugh too hard and shook his head.

"That poor dog took that big chunk of meat in his mouth and started chomping on it like this." Ariel made large up and down motions with her mouth while shaking her head. "This went on for almost five minutes before he flung that chunk of meat across at the fence where it fell to the ground. Then he took his paws and tried to cover it up with dirt. Then Derek had the nerve to walk in the door asking when I was serving him dinner."

"So, what did you have for dinner?"

Savoring a fork full of mashed potatoes, she gave a small shrug. "Cereal. I was in no mood to cook after that."

"Did Derek eat cereal too?"

"Yes, and he was a big giant baby about the whole thing too. I told him that if he wanted to cook, to go for it, but I was done for the day. Do you cook like this often?" she asked as she waved her fork around the table.

"No. I really don't see the point when it's just me. Usually, I will make a salad and throw some chicken on it or cook one of those ready meals that come frozen in a bag with meat, vegetables and pasta."

"Yup. I know those, I usually buy the cheesy chicken with broccoli."

"I have tried them all. They were great when I got in late back in Philly. Most of the time I wouldn't get home until after nine, and the thought of one more fast-food burger just turned my stomach."

"Did you eat a lot of cheesesteaks?"

"I did for a while. I went to get some with my old boss about a couple of times a month. There are a couple of places that are pretty famous right across the street from each other. It's a pretty big rivalry. Geno's is loud and commands your attention with a big sign and neon lights that would rival any place in Vegas. Pat's does have some neon and signage, but it is a much more subdued white building with picnic tables outside to eat on. Both places are great, and people usually pledge their devotion to one or the other, but I liked to rotate, and a lot of locals say it's for tourists."

"So, what makes a cheesesteak so much better there than what I can get from Daisy's?"

"No offense to Daisy's, but that is not a real cheesesteak. First, the cheese is all wrong."

"What's wrong with her cheese?"

"It's just slices of melted cheese. To be a true Philly cheesesteak you have to use Cheese Whiz."

Ariel stopped with her fork raised. "You mean that stuff that comes in a jar?"

"Yes. They drench the meat in the stuff so when you pick it up it's just oozing out the sides. You can get grilled onions or peppers on top too. And where the restaurants are is the weirdest little area. It's not the best neighborhood, but you will see ridiculously expensive cars pull up to get their sandwiches."

"Do the owners hate each other?"

"No. Actually, they are good friends. From what I remember they all grew up in the same area together and their wives are friends too. The media just hypes up the rivalry and they reap the benefits of that."

Kyle was really enjoying his night with Ariel. Her smile glowed with a natural radiance, and the longer they spent with each other, just being with each other, the more at ease she seemed. They were nearly done cleaning up from dinner when he heard a familiar song lift above the soft clink of dishes. Kyle put down the plate he was washing and stepped behind Ariel who was drying off a glass. He wrapped his arms around her waist and brought his lips to her ears as he started to sway them both back and forth to the music. "Do you remember this song?"

Ariel tilted her head just enough to allow him better access to nuzzle her neck. "Yes. This was the song we danced to in my parents' living room."

Kyle turned her in his arms and pulled her in close and found his body moving in a familiar rhythm. "Mmm hmmm. You were so nervous about going to your first dance."

Ariel rested her head on his chest as they slowly moved from side to side. "Derek was being a brat and wouldn't help me, but you promised to show me so I wouldn't look like stupid."

Kyle kissed her on the top of her head and smiled at the memory. "You want to know a secret?"

Ariel giggled against his chest. "Always."

"I didn't know how to dance either."

Ariel pulled away and looked up at Kyle with her eyes narrowed. "Liar. You floated around the floor like you had been doing it for years."

"If you remember, I didn't show you the same day. I made you wait a few days for your lessons."

Ariel crinkled her nose in confusion. "Yeah?"

"I didn't know how to dance that day, but I didn't want you to learn from some other guy, so I got a crash course from Mom and Dad. So, after a few days I came back and taught you." Before Ariel could respond he gave her a twirl and then a dip and brought his nose close to hers. "I wanted you to be mine, and the thought of someone else spending a couple hours holding you drove me crazy."

Ariel's eyes were dilating, and her breath was speeding up. "And now?"

Kyle pulled her up and put his hands on each side of her face so she could see his clear intentions. "Now, I need you. I want everything from you, your mind, body and soul. Because, Princess, you have owned every piece of me since the moment you gave me your first smile."

Ariel's eyes softened as he leaned in close and met his lips to hers. His hands gripped a little tighter as her mouth parted open and her body relaxed into his. He felt her arms go up his chest until they wrapped around his neck and she pulled him in closer. Kyle began to explore her mouth feeding the hunger that had been consuming his body for years. This was finally happening. He wanted to be closer to her body, to have nothing between the two of them. He walked her backwards as their mouths were still locked together, devouring every taste.

Kyle finally hit the wall with Ariel's back, and she wrapped her legs around his waist. He lifted her up just a bit to have her perfectly fit into his hold. Ariel's fingers were now running up his scalp as she finally grasped handfuls of hair and pulled. She was showing him just as much need as he felt; it was like an intoxicating drug. Kyle shifted slightly to brace her against the wall and freed one of his hands to glide it up her side and begin caressing his thumb over her breast. Ariel responded by thrusting out her chest trying to give him more.

Kyle's lips finally left hers as he trailed kisses down her neck and to her collarbone. He gently pulled down the strap of her dress and kissed her now bare shoulder. Ariel's legs began to loosen as she slid down to place her feet on the floor. Her lust-filled eyes met his, and she didn't look away as she grabbed the bottom of her dress and pulled it over her head. She was a beautiful vision as she stood before him in her matching blue and white lace bra and panties.

"You are trying to kill me," Kyle said as he traced his fingers along the lace edge of her bra.

Ariel began tugging at the bottom of Kyle's shirt as she shook her head. "No, actually I am trying to have sex with you."

With a quick tug Kyle took off his shirt and gave a possessive growl. "As you wish."

Ariel laughed at Kyle's *Princess Bride* reference and followed behind him as he held her hand and made their way to his bedroom. At first, they both stood by the bed hungrily gazing at each other's bodies. She was soft with amazing curves and abundant breasts that were spilling over the edge of her bra. Ariel began to gently graze her fingers up his chest feeling the ridges of muscles.

Kyle found that he was holding his breath. He was afraid that if he didn't, he would let his primal side take over and ravage her body too quickly. But this was their first time. He needed to take it slow and show her just how important she was to him. When she stopped at his nipple and began to trace it in slow sensual circles, he took her hand in his and gave a slow kiss to her palm.

She brought her other hand to his waistband and began to unbutton his jeans. "You have on too many clothes."

"Well, don't let me stop you from helping me," he responded as his hands found the hooks of her bra.

With almost exact timing her bra and his jeans hit the floor. With a devilish grin Kyle backed her up until she responded by crawling backwards up the bed. Kyle began moving up the bed but kissed his way up her legs and felt her begin to squirm the further up her body he went. He could tell she was seeking the friction of his touch with the small thrusts of her hips, but he had other things in mind first. He reached her core only to give a small warm breath and kiss to the top of her panties and continued his journey up her body tasting and licking her skin until he reached her breasts.

Her hands thrust back into his hair as his lips covered her nipple and began a slow rhythm of sucking and spiraling of his tongue. Her nipple hardened with the new sensations, and he felt her thrusting into his body wanting more. "You are a needy little princess. Should I grant your wish?"

"God yes."

Kyle turned to her other breast but now grazed his hand down to the edge of her panties. Ariel gave a slight moan as he teased her playing with the top edge, but not yet diving under the lacy fabric. Deciding to ease her need, he dove his finger under the lace and found her already wet and ready for him. He released her nipple only long enough to watch her as he took one finger and entered inside her warm channel. She sighed in what seemed like a relieved pleasure and began moving her body again as he moved his finger in and out.

Kyle returned his lips to her breast and joined a second finger with his first. Ariel gasped at the unexpected intrusion and gave a slight moan. He heard her whispered words of please and god increase as he quickened his pace. He could feel the beginnings of her orgasm but wanted to hold her off just a bit longer. He pulled out his fingers and readjusted as he heard her moan in protest.

"Not yet. I want to taste you as you come around my fingers."

Ariel seemed dazed, all she did was nod her head in response as he moved down her body and pulled her panties down and off her body. Ariel squirmed while waiting for him to fulfill his promise. He gazed up at her body and felt so much appreciation for this moment. Returning his attention to her core, he gently glided two fingers back in as he lightly brushed his tongue across her clit.

Ariel whimpered. "More."

"Believe me, you will have more until you beg me to stop." He gave another quick deep thrust with his fingers, latched onto her clit and began sucking and flicking it with his tongue. The walls around Kyle's finger began to pulse and squeeze. Her moans increased in volume and he reveled in the beginning of her first release as his fingers toyed with her g-spot. As she was climbing down from her orgasm, he replaced his fingers with his tongue where he stroked and savored in her juices. To his surprise she found a second orgasm and erratically thrusted her hips.

When her body finally slowed, he lifted his head and slowly moved back up to look her in the eyes. The hunger and need he saw in her eyes only made his desire to claim her intensify.

Ariel suddenly grabbed his hair and pulled him down to crash their lips together. She released one hand and trailed it down his chest only to place a firm grip on his erection. Kyle sucked in a breath as she scratched her nails over the cotton of his boxer briefs. The new stimulation nearly made this over too quickly. He felt her smile while she was kissing him and she said, "I really need you to take these off. I need you inside me, now." She wrapped her fingers around his cock and squeezed a lot harder.

"Jesus, woman."

Ariel had apparently run out of patience, because she was now tugging at the band and giving a frustrated growl. Kyle gave a small chuckle and helped her free himself from the offending clothing. Once he discarded them over the side of the bed his cock bounced, eager to find its home. He started to cover her body with his when he stopped and sighed. He looked over at his nightstand. "Hold on."

Ariel nodded in understanding and watched with rapt attention as he found the condom and rolled it down his length. He maneuvered back over the top of her and brushed a section of hair that was now partially covering her eye. She looked up and nodded her head, seeming to understand his unspoken question.

Kyle gave a small push into Ariel and felt the first breech of warmth and completeness. He pushed in slowly, inch by inch. Once he was fully seated inside of her, he took possession of her lips. Their tongues explored as he held still, wanting to feel this sense of belonging forever.

Ariel began moving her hips obviously needing more. Kyle kissed a path to her ear and whispered, "Ready?"

"I've been ready for this my whole life."

Kyle gave a slight nip on her ear lobe and laughed as he began moving in slow, steady thrusts. Ariel's hands began grasping at his back trying to find something to hold on to. She panted and said, "God you are so hard everywhere."

Kyle chuckled and gave a hard push. "It's all for you." Kyle picked up the pace and tilted her hips to give him a better angle and pumped back into her... hard. Ariel let out a surprised squeak of delight. He knew he hit that sensitive spot again. Her moans of pleasure only encouraged him to pump faster and harder.

It wasn't long before they were both sweaty and frantically grasping at each other as they approached their climax. Kyle felt his balls drawing up inside and he reached his hand down to circle her clit with his fingers. He was going to make sure they would reach their orgasms together. Ariel gave out a small cry and released his name to echo across the room. "Ky....le."

He was still inside her as he pulsed his release into the condom. They were going to have to have a discussion about protection, because he didn't want anything between them anymore. This was their forever, and he just needed to make sure she felt secure that he would always stay by her side from now on.

Kyle pulled out and kissed her on the cheek as he went to the bathroom to dispose of the condom. Once he returned, he found Ariel curled up on her side cuddled under his blanket. He lifted the cover and laid beside her wrapping his arm around her waist to pull her in close. "Stay with me."

He could hear the smile in her voice as she responded. "I don't think I could walk back to my car even if I wanted to."

Kyle gently glided his hand up her stomach to caress her breast and stroke his thumb over her nipple. "Does that mean you and your sexy body wouldn't be up for round two?"

Ariel responded by wiggling her ass into his crotch. "Oh, I think we could be convinced for a few more rounds."

Kyle kissed the side of her neck and whispered, "Thank God."

Chapter 12

"Ariel!" Dixie's voice rang out.

Ariel shook her head. She looked at Josie and Dixie who were staring her down with knowing smiles. They were all planning Zoey's bridal shower, but Ariel kept drifting off into memories from the night before. Kyle had been amazing and remembering his touch on her kept her mind wandering all morning. Not only had they had their first time together, but he also took her another time that night and again once they woke up. "What? I was listening."

Dixie giggled. "Really? Okay what did Josie just suggest we serve for dessert?"

Ariel searched her empty useless brain for the answer, but then got another image of Kyle leaning over her with his naked chest. Not helpful. She shook that thought and went with an obvious answer. "Cake."

"What kind of cake?"

"Um... chocolate."

Josie let out a snort. "Told you that Pip Squeak wasn't listening."

Ariel straightened. "I was listening."

"Honey, if you were listening you would have had an opinion about my choice of cake."

Ariel looked over at Dixie who was shaking her head making her brown curls dance back and forth. "She wants a penis cake."

Ariel's mouth dropped with a small gasp. "We can't have a penis cake."

Josie crossed her arms. "Why not? We are being forced to combine the shower with the bachelorette party, so why not?"

Dixie pointed between her and Ariel and rolled her eyes. "Because her mom and my grandmother are going to be there, and we don't need their weird sex talk."

"Oh, grow up, Dix. Old people have sex too, and Ariel's mom is young and gorgeous. She deserves a little fun."

Ariel grabbed a sip of her coffee. "Don't get me wrong, I want her to fall in love and have amazing sex, but I don't want to hear about it. Ever."

Josie shrugged. "My grams told me about her lovers when I was a kid. She even gave me pointers."

Dixie and Ariel both stopped eating and drinking and looked wide-eyed at Josie.

"What? Why are you guys looking at me like that?"

Dixie was the first to break the silence. "To be honest, I didn't think you had a past. I just assumed you were kind of dropped off at the border of town as a grownup. Like some weird miracle... or alien."

"Don't be ridiculous. Of course, I have a past, but it is just that, a past. I don't feel the need to prattle on about it."

After hearing the first nugget of information about Josie's history, Ariel latched on to it like a lifeline. "Do you ever visit your grandma?"

The corners of Josie's mouth dropped slightly, and she shook her head. "No. She died when I was eleven."

Ariel put a hand to her friend's arm. "Oh, I am so sorry."

Josie seemed to shake off a thought and reset her emotions. "It's okay. She loved her life. She was happy. She always said not to be sad, and that she would at least be reunited with Dad and Grandpa."

"Your Dad too?"

Josie took a deep sigh. "I am going to tell you only this one more thing, but then we go back to planning the shower."

There was no arguing with Josie's tone of voice. Ariel and Dixie nodded their agreement, both seeming to be grateful for even this small glimpse into their friend's life.

"I never got to meet my dad. He died before I was born. He was deployed to the Middle East and was killed by an IED. The day of his funeral was the day I was born. His name was Joe. I was named after him. Grams said that I was her son's gift to her, to have someone to love and care for."

Ariel sucked in her breath hoping that Josie would tell them more, but Josie simply picked up her coffee and asked, "So, tell me again why we can't have a penis cake?"

KYLE AND DEREK WERE driving in Kyle's truck to Raleigh. Ariel had called with a list of things that they wanted for the shower/bachelorette party and Kyle knew better than to refuse. He didn't want to make the long drive to the city alone, so he bribed Derek to come with him, plus it was his best friend who was getting married too.

"Explain to me why we can't get what we need in town? I don't get it. Buy a couple streamers, some balloons, maybe some confetti... and boom a decorated party."

Kyle shook his head. "Man, don't let your sister hear you say that. She is pulling out every Pinterest idea she ever had to make this perfect."

"And your dumbass volunteered to do the shopping?"

"She sounded a bit frantic and overwhelmed. She was working half a day alone today, and wouldn't get to the store before it closed, so I volunteered."

"She has your ass whipped already."

"I would do anything to make sure she knew I am not going to let her down again."

Derek didn't respond. Kyle let the quiet linger in the air for a moment before he decided to start the conversation he dreaded. "I want you to know I won't hurt her. She's everything to me."

Derek didn't look at his friend while he took a moment before responding. "I know that. I knew that when we were in junior high. You were never subtle about how you felt."

Kyle gripped the wheel and sighed. "Well, I tried to hide it. I didn't want to lose you as my best friend, and you even told me to stay away from her. The only way I got to keep you both close was to honor your wishes."

"Please tell me that you didn't stay away from her all this time because of something I said when we were teenagers."

Kyle cringed. "At first, yeah, but once the time came close for me to go to college, I knew I needed to give us both space to grow up a little. I hoped that she wouldn't find someone else until the time was right for us."

"You have to know she would have moved to Philly for you."

"I know that she would have, but she would have been miserable there. She loves it here. She is a small-town girl. That city would have torn the sweet, amazing woman she is apart. It tore me apart. I accomplished what I wanted to do there. I wrote stories for a big paper, won some awards and was kind of a local celebrity, but I never felt so alone as I did out there. Once I made up my mind to come home, every day that I was still in the city was torture."

"And you will be happy just running a small-town paper?"

"Ridiculously happy. I thought my desire for journalism came from a need to tell the hard stories no one else was telling, but my drive comes from telling stories about people and I found that it had nothing to do with crime and drama. The best stories are the ones that show the heart and soul of each individual person. I couldn't do that only getting the chance to write about death, violence and scandals. While these things are important to the news, there is so much more out there, and there is so much life and individuality in our town, how could I not be happy sharing that with the world?"

Derek nodded and let the quiet settle for a moment before he smiled. "Man, you are a sap."

"Eh. I'm still not as bad as Tyler."

"That's for damn sure."

KYLE AND DEREK WERE pulling into their last stop from Ariel's shopping trip. Kyle silently read the store sign as he parked. Pleasure Principles. She did this on purpose. He hesitated as he turned off the engine and looked back up at the sign again.

"Kyle, why are we at a porn store?"

Kyle looked down at his phone and shook his head. "I didn't know we were going to a porn store. Ariel just programmed all the stops in my GPS. I didn't ask for specifics."

Derek abruptly opened the door. "Next time ask for specifics. These women are evil."

"Even your sister?"

"Especially my sister. They are all bad influences on each other."

They walked into the store and hesitantly walked up to the counter that was pretty busy for a small shop. Kyle at least felt a little more at ease after looking around. This wasn't one of those seedy porn stores he had seen in Philadelphia. This was clean, bright and tastefully set up with sections of books, lingerie, toys and what looked like trinkets and decorations for parties.

While they were standing in line, Derek leaned over and whispered to Kyle. "Am I really looking at metal balls with a silicone wrap that costs three thousand dollars?"

Kyle felt his throat swell and had to give a slight cough. He looked over to the object Derek was referring to and sure enough there they were two gold balls with silicone bands wrapped around them. They must have been staring at the offending object when the woman behind the counter called for them to approach for their turn.

"Hello, gentlemen. Are you interested in buying the Kegal exercise balls today?"

Kyle shook his head both in confirmation that he wasn't buying the overpriced balls and in disbelief. "Uh. Why are they three grand?"

The woman smiled pleasantly at him. "They are from an exclusive luxury brand. The balls vibrate for her pleasure. The silicone around the balls helps to eliminate noise, and these are twenty-karat gold."

Derek shook his head. "If I am giving a woman three thousand dollars' worth of gold, it sure isn't going somewhere that no one can see it."

Kyle gave a small snort. "Just out of curiosity, is that the most expensive thing you carry?"

The woman smiled proudly. "No. Actually, it is the vibrator over here." She pointed to the other side of the cabinet. "This model is coated in twenty-four-karat gold and is fifteen thousand."

Derek rubbed the back of his neck. "I am totally in the wrong business."

The woman gave a small nod. "The sex toy industry in the US alone is almost a thirty-four-billion-dollar industry. Women are claiming their sexuality and want to explore with their partners." She looked between Kyle and Derek and redirected their conversation after seeing their obvious discomfort. "Is there something I can help you find?" she asked looking at their obviously empty hands.

Kyle sighed in relief. "Yes. Ariel McKenna called and requested for some items to be put on hold."

The woman's face paled a bit, and she looked at a few papers on her counter. Finally, she found a paper under a couple binders. "I am so sorry. My part timer took her request, but then left for the day. I can gather the items for you if you wish."

Kyle looked around to see a few customers behind them along with several already on the floor. He extended his hand for the paper. "We can grab them. You're busy. If we need help finding something we can ask."

Taking the list, they walked over to the edge of the store. Derek slapped Kyle's shoulder and shook his head. "Fantastic. Just a couple of guys shopping for porn."

Kyle looked at the list and frowned. "Want to split the list?"

Derek swiped the paper and tore it in half. He slapped one half back into Kyle's hand and laughed. "Good luck."

"Gee, thanks."

Kyle wandered over to a section that looked like supplies for bachelorette parties. There were feather boas with penises, penis shaped straws and penis topped tiaras. He never understood the appeal for women to wear penis draped items when they celebrate their last night as a single woman. It isn't like the men go out wearing a bunch of vaginas. He grabbed the bride to be sash, penis-shaped straws, and a penis-shaped ice mold. He looked around the store to see if anyone was staring at him, but nope, everyone seemed to be in their own little worlds and didn't care what others were looking at. Thank god.

Kyle had managed to grab all the items on his list when he went to find Derek. Once he found him, Derek was talking to a girl who was writing something on his hand. Kyle only assumed it was her phone number. The man was constantly drawing attention from women. It soon became obvious that Derek was going to be a few more minutes after watching him brace his arm on the wall and lean in closer to the starry-eyed woman. Not wanting to watch the show, Kyle's attention was drawn over to a mannequin that was wearing a pink lace cut out teddy. It was so incredibly feminine and perfect. He started looking at the ones on the table beside it for the right size and struggled holding each one up and trying to compare.

Finally, a soft voice came from behind him rescuing him from his thoughts. "You looking for something for your girlfriend?"

Kyle gave a sheepish grin. "Yeah, but I can't tell which one is the right size."

The woman nodded. "Okay, well let's start with her dress size. Do you know what that is?"

"Uh. Nope." Even when he bought that dress for Ariel from a Stitch Above, the owner had known Ariel very well and knew her size already.

The woman's smile didn't fade. She probably dealt with this all the time. "Okay do you see someone around here that would be similar."

Kyle looked around and shook his head. "No, but her waist is about the same as yours, but she is much shorter. She is about this tall." Kyle held his hand up to his chest. "And she has kind of a big... um..."

The saleswoman's grin widened. "She has a larger chest size."

"Yeah."

The woman looked around the store and pointed out a package with a woman modeling a bra on the label. "How about like that?"

Kyle nodded his head slightly embarrassed. Next time he took off her clothes he was going to take note of her size.

"Okay, so she has a classic Marilyn Monroe figure." She quickly found the garment she was looking for and held it out to Kyle. "I believe this will work out well for you both."

Kyle provided his thanks to the cheerful woman and made his way back to Derek who was now staring at the DVDs and down at his torn paper. Kyle looked over his shoulder at the list. "Can't find something from the list?"

Derek grimaced. "Oh, I found it, but I am trying to wrap my head around my sister and my best friend watching porn together. Usually, the idea of two women watching porn together would be hot, but this is freaking me out, and I don't want to be an accomplice."

"At least it is better than them getting a stripper." Because then Kyle would have to throw Ariel over his shoulder and drag her back to his place like a neanderthal. The thought of Ariel putting her hands on another man was driving his mind in all kinds of unwanted places.

"You think that Tyler is okay with this?" Derek asked nodding to the DVDs.

Kyle thought about it for a minute and shrugged. "How about we make an executive decision and not get the video?"

"That's the best idea you have had all day."

With their mission accomplished they were now back on their way to Blossom Hills. Derek had been very quiet since they made their way out of the store. "Hey, are you okay?"

Derek was quietly pounding his fist on his leg, that showed he was thinking about something he didn't like. "I am trying to decide if I am going to punch you or not."

"Me why?"

Derek turned to him with an are-you-fucking-kidding-me look on his face, but Kyle still seemed a bit lost. "Did you seriously just buy a teddy for my sister in front of me?"

Kyle let out a nervous laugh. "Uh, well... yeah."

Derek gave a low growl in obvious annoyance.

Trying to ease the tension Kyle finally said, "If you are going to punch me, could you at least do it in the stomach? Tyler would kill me if I still had a black eye for the wedding."

"Yes, especially since Zoey would probably kill me for giving it to you."

It was about half an hour later when they stopped for gas and drink when Derek finally had a smile on his face as he went in to buy the drinks while Kyle filled up. When he returned, he handed Kyle's drink to him and Kyle felt a pain coming from his stomach. He bent over trying to breathe and replace the air that had been suddenly escaped his body. It took just a few seconds to realize that Derek kept his promise to punch him in the stomach. Derek's voice cleared his fog. "Jackass."

Kyle nodded. "Yup. Feel better now?"

Kyle felt Derek's eyes on him as he was beginning to recover. "Yeah. I do, thanks."

Straightening, Kyle croaked. "Fantastic."

IT WAS THE DAY OF THE shower/bachelorette party for Zoey and Ariel was putting the finishing touches on the decorations. They were having it at Chase and Dixie's since they had the biggest house. Zoey had been stressing out the past couple of days because her mom and stepdad arrived into town and would be staying until the wedding. At one point she found Zoey in the back of the bakery stress eating. She was trying to mix icing while eating a brownie. Her eyes were bloodshot, and her nose was red. Ariel hated how stressed-out Zoey's mom made her, but in the end, it was only Tyler or Zoey's brother Xander who could talk her down. Derek tried but he could only take a few hours with Zoey's mom before his filter stopped working and he would say something a bit too honest and well... mean.

Dixie and Josie were in the other room giggling about something as they put together the photo wall. Dixie had been doing several of these for weddings and the guests loved playing dress up and being silly for pictures to post on their social media. The backgrounds that Dixie created were always amazing and unique to the couple. This one played on the bakery and Tyler's nickname for Zoey of Sweetness. The backdrop was blue skies with giant, fluffy clouds, and it had hanging oversized candies and cooking utensils.

Ariel walked into the other room and smiled. "You guys almost done?"

Dixie hopped off the ladder and winced a little when she landed on her bad leg. Ariel had to restrain herself from rushing over to hover and help her, but Dixie was fiercely independent and didn't want anyone to fuss over her when she had flare-ups. She quickly seemed to shake it off and smiled. "I think we're all ready."

"Good. Derek texted and said he is on the way with the food and Zoey. He said it took a few minutes to pull the spider monkey off of Tyler."

Josie laughed. "You should have heard the weird little monkey sex noises they were making last night."

"Tyler said that he was going to keep her sexed up this week to keep her mind off her mom driving her crazy."

Ariel internally laughed at the image of Josie hearing them have sex through their shared walls of the apartments. "I thought you bought those noise cancelling headphones?"

"Oh, I did, but I ran out of batteries. This town really needs a twenty-four-hour store. Life does happen after midnight."

"There is that pharmacy about thirty minutes outside of town that is open all day," Dixie chimed in helpfully.

Josie rolled her eyes. "Yes, how convenient, all your needs just an hour round trip away. Talk about a mood killer if you need condoms. 'Hang on honey, I'll be back in an hour.'"

Dixie smiled. "That is the great thing about being in a committed relationship with birth control. No condoms."

Ariel's face flushed as she thought about the jumbo box that Kyle had bought so he could have condoms in every room of the house. They hadn't been together very long, but they had been breaking in every inch of Kyle's house. They both had made appointments to get tested next week. She was already on birth control, and they were looking forward to making love without having to stop for a condom.

Josie and Dixie were now looking at Ariel with matching smirks. "What?" Ariel asked indignantly.

"Did you even hear what we asked you?" Josie asked.

Crap. She wasn't listening again. "We asked if you were all stocked up with Kyle."

"Oh, yes. We have a stash of about ten in every room of Kyle's house. He can't seem to keep his hands off me."

"Oh, God. I didn't need to hear that."

Ariel turned around to see Derek holding two large aluminum pans, looking a bit green, with Zoey biting her lips together trying not to laugh at her friend's discomfort. Ariel walked over and grabbed the pans from her brother. "Thank you, brother dear. Perfect timing as always."

"Yeah. Happy to help," Derek said hesitantly. "Do you need me to stay and help with anything else?"

"No. You brought the food and the guest of honor, so we are all set. Unless you would like to stay, the penises won't be brought out until later tonight."

Derek gave a small shudder. "Nope. I'm going to get some rest before we celebrate with Tyler tonight."

"Was Xander able to get some time off to come down?"

Derek looked over at Zoey who was now sitting with Dixie and Josie in the kitchen and gave a small shake of his head. "No. He wanted to come down for the bachelor party but with the short notice and the fact that he will be here for the wedding later, he couldn't get the time off work."

"That's a shame. I know his dad was hoping he would be here since they don't get to see him often."

"Yeah, but I think he is enjoying getting to know Tyler too. He has always been such a nice man and always seems to know how to keep Cassie in check."

"Where is Cassie?"

"She said she would be a few minutes behind us, so make sure Zoey gets in a glass of wine before she gets here."

They both looked over at the kitchen and laughed. Zoey was already taking a big gulp of wine and gave a shiver as she slammed the now empty glass on the counter.

Modifying his earlier statement Derek said, "Okay, just make sure she's still conscious by the time Cassie gets here."

ARIEL WAS SAYING GOODBYE at the door to the last guest who was not staying for the bachelorette portion of the night. She was relieved that for the most part everything went off without a hitch. Zoey and Tyler had quite the haul of gifts that they had registered for, and many that they didn't. The guests enjoyed the photo wall and the games that Dixie and Ariel had organized. Even Cassie had eased off Zoey a bit and let her daughter have a good time. While they all had fun, Ariel was ready to really blow off some steam.

When Ariel came back into the living room, she saw that the moms, Cassie, Hannah and Amanda had retreated to the kitchen to enjoy more of the overpriced wine that Josie had brought. Dana, Zoey's part- time assistant at the bakery, was draping the feather penis boa around Zoey's neck. By now Zoey had been cut off from the alcohol until she could sober back up a little, but the pink flush to her face still showed just how tipsy she was.

Dixie was over by the far wall taping up a poster of a nearly naked man holding a football with a blank space where his penis would be. Ariel walked over to the coffee table and held up a blindfold and small gift bag. "Okay ladies, let's have some real fun now. We are going to play pin the cock on the jock, and the winner gets this mystery prize from Pleasure Principles."

Amanda popped her head through the door and asked, "Is that the sex toy shop?"

Slightly embarrassed Ariel looked at her mom. "Yes."

Amanda put down her wine glass and swiped the blindfold from Ariel's hand. "Thank god. I need a new vibrator."

Josie laughed. "I guess Amanda is going first."

Amanda put her hand on her hip. "I am the only one here not getting any sex. So, yes, I am going first. Now hand over that cock sticker."

"Jesus, Mom," Ariel whispered as she handed the phallic shaped sticker over to her mom.

"Ariel, darling, this is a bachelorette party, and I am going to talk about sex and have fun. So get used to it."

It was only a couple seconds later when Amanda was blindfolded and being spun by Hannah. Ariel watched as Dixie came over, wrapped an arm around her waist and leaned her head on Ariel's shoulder. "I love your mom."

With a slight smile Ariel replied, "Yeah, me too."

Cheers erupted as Amanda slapped the sticker right on the man's belly button. She proudly puffed out her chest. "That's pretty damned close."

Each woman took a turn, but no one was getting as close as Amanda. When it was Zoey's turn, she whispered to Ariel. "Don't spin me too much. I might puke on you."

Ariel giggled, gave Zoey the required five spins and watched in amazement as Zoey staggered and stumbled to the wall. At the last minute she took a sharp right turn and slapped her sticker on Josie's breast. Zoey seem to realize that she hit another human and ripped off her blindfold. Her mouth dropped open in horror and she whispered. "Oh, Josie, I'm sorry."

Josie gave a sly grin. "You manhandled them just like the last guy did. Hope you are more careful with Ty's junk."

Zoey gave a squeak of horror. Feeling sorry for Zoey, Ariel guided Zoey back to the couch. "Just ignore her. She loves to see us all squirm."

Josie shrugged. "Gotta get my entertainment from some-where."

Ariel looked over to where the other girls were standing as she heard loud bursts of laughter, and in the center of it all was her mom brandishing her new vibrator like a knight drawing his sword. Now there is an image that would take years to shake off.

With a devilish look in her eye Josie turned off the music and asked, "Let's have some real fun now. Where's the movie you ordered?"

Dixie plopped on the couch on the other side of Ariel and asked, "What movie?"

"The porn of course."

Zoey's eyes widened. "We got porn?"

Josie narrowed her eyes. "Oh please, don't even try that little innocent girl crap with us. I saw that book you had on your counter. That book is way dirtier than the movie we picked out."

Ariel finally interrupted. "Yeah... about that. Derek and Kyle decided we didn't need the movie and decided not to pick it up."

Josie frowned. "Those little bastards. Who do they think they are?"

Dixie quickly stood up and said, "I'll be right back."

They watched as she went back to her bedroom and returned with a DVD case.

Ariel looked at her friend and then to the DVD. "You have porn?"

"Sure. Chase and I watch it together. It's great for building sexual tension, but some of it is just funny. Sometimes we watch it and end up just laughing at the ridiculousness of it all. This one has a good mix."

Josie snatched the movie and loaded it into the player. "I am so damn proud of you right now; I can't even begin to tell you how much."

The movie started and grabbed the attention of the rest of the women who all joined them in the living room and began to watch and pass around the wine. They all laughed and giggled as each scene passed, and they soon began a game of never have I ever. Surprisingly, they only had to explain the rules to Hannah and Dana. Ariel poured a glass for Dana and began the rules. "We take turns saying something that we have never done. If you ever have done what was said you take a drink, and we may or may not interrogate you for more details. We are going to start with the bride."

Zoey perked up. "Okay, never have I ever gone skinny-dipping."

Ariel lifted her glass and took a drink and quickly noticed everyone else did as well.

Zoey frowned. "Really? I am the only one?"

Ariel placed her hand on Zoey's arm. "Sweetie, everyone goes skinny dipping in the lake at the orchard. It's like a rite of passage here in town."

"Huh. Okay, who's next?"

Dixie lifted her glass. "Never have I ever had a one-night stand."

Josie, Zoey, Dana, Ariel and Amanda all took a drink. Ariel tried not to look at her mom so she could avoid seeing her reaction at her precious daughter having a one-night stand.

Cassie was next. "Never have I ever kissed a girl."

Ariel looked around the room and saw that no one was drinking until a groan escaped Dana's lips. "Fine." She picked up the glass took a sip and Ariel watched as she realized that everyone was staring at her. "What? It was a party, and I was dared to do it. It's not like I had sex with the girl."

"Now that would have been a great story to tell if you had."

The questions all made their rounds and as they continued, they just got dirtier and dirtier. Ariel couldn't believe how at ease their moms were about talking about all of this, and how adventurous they really were. While she could have gone without some of the details she learned about her mom, she was happy to see that she was still open to new things, even if she was on what she called a "never-ending dry spell."

All the women were pretty intoxicated, and they were only about halfway through their evening. Zoey was drunk texting Tyler and blushing with each ping that came back in reply. "I miss Tyler. Can we go to McKenna's and see the boys?"

Ariel shook her head. "This is their bachelor party too. They should get their guy time."

Zoey swayed a bit and held out her phone. "But see... he said he misses me and wished I was there. I wanna go." Now she was pouting like a toddler who was just told they couldn't have dessert.

Ariel looked at Dixie. "I don't know."

Dixie smiled. "Let's go. I want to see Chase too. Maybe he will cuff me for being a bad girl and crashing the party. Besides don't you want to see Kyle?"

She did. She really did, but they were all way too drunk to drive over there, and it was too far to walk. "How would we get there?"

Dana must have been listening, because she said a little too loudly. "Roger can take us."

"Sweetie, we can't all fit in your hubby's car."

Dana pouted her lips out. "Doesn't your dad still have that big van?"

Ariel thought for a moment. If Dana, her mom and Hannah rode with Roger, then the rest of them could fit in her dad's van. She looked over at her mom. She didn't want there to be trouble with the two of them seeing each other, but she couldn't think of anyone else who could help. "Give me a minute and let me call Dad."

It was all too easy to get her dad to agree to pick them up. He actually sounded eager to see her. She told the girls the plan and Dana had already made the arrangements with Roger. Ariel was relieved to know that Roger would be there quicker than she thought since the kids were with their grandparents. At least this meant that her mom would be gone by the time her dad showed up.

About fifteen minutes later Zoey, Dixie, Cassie, Ariel and Josie piled into the van. Ariel's dad gave a warm smile and hug for each of the women who were all more affectionate than normal. The women all interrogated him on the drive with questions about his new girlfriend. Ariel felt a warmth in her stomach as he answered each one with clear adoration of his new love. She really hoped that he was serious about wanting to change his ways and treat this new woman with the respect and faithfulness she most likely deserved.

Her dad's voice suddenly changed tone as he asked, "Sweetheart, were you expecting company tonight?"

Ariel shook her head and looked out the window just down the street to her house. "No, why can you see someone there?"

He leaned forward on the wheel trying to get a better look as they passed. "Maybe not. I thought I saw someone in your yard, but I don't see them now."

Ariel waved it off. "Probably one of Derek's conquests looking for him. No biggie."

Her dad nodded and leaned back in his seat. "Okay then."

It only took a few more minutes for him to pull up to the front door of the pub, and he rounded the van and opened the door for the women like a true gentleman. "Okay, ladies. Have fun and stay safe."

Ariel hugged him and gave him a kiss on his cheek. "Thanks, Daddy. I really appreciate this."

"Anytime, sweetheart. I would do anything for you."

Ariel looked into his eyes and knew that he meant every word of that and sent her thanks to the heavens that she had been given a father who may have had his faults but would always love and look out for her.

Chapter 13

Kyle was losing at poker again. Seriously what was wrong with him? He was always losing to his brother or Derek... or even worse Zoey, if she was around. He knew how to play but it seemed like every time he would get decent cards no one would stay in the pot. He thought that if Tyler would get drunk enough tonight, he would stand a chance, but then Derek invited Tiny to play since the kitchen was closed. Of course, the overgrown muscle meathead was kicking all their asses.

Just as he was looking at his pathetic hand and was thinking about calling it a night the girls burst open the doors to the private room and made their loud entrance. It only took a few seconds for Ariel to enter the doorway and find his gaze. She looked amazing, and he was trying to hold himself back from picking her up and leaving the bar.

Zoey quickly but clumsily made her way to Tyler and sat on his lap only to look at his cards and everyone around the table. She was still studying the chip stacks when Ariel found her way to Kyle and sat on his lap. He nuzzled his nose into her neck and whispered, "Did you girls have a good time?"

Ariel wiggled on his lap and giggled. "Yup, and I won the glow-in-the-dark condoms."

Kyle shook his head. "That's just wrong on so many levels."

"Do you think if we put it on and you wiggled your hips you could make it look like a complete circle like they do with sparklers?"

Kyle nearly choked. "Is this what you girls talk about when we aren't around?"

"Believe me, you don't want to know everything. I learned way more about our moms than I ever wanted to know."

Kyle crashed his lips to hers and felt her body relax against his and she leaned into his chest. Once he released her, she looked up at his with wide lust-filled eyes. "What was that for?"

"To stop you from sharing the details."

"Details?"

Kyle gave her a light kiss. "See it worked."

Derek's voice interrupted them from resuming their kiss. "Hey, jackass. Stop mauling my sister and finish the game."

Kyle looked at his horrible hand and then at Ariel. Yeah, he was done. "All in." Then with a dramatic shove he pushed his chips into the pile and kept his eyes on Ariel as both Derek and Tiny called his bet.

"A pair of threes? Seriously?"

Kyle gave a shrug while still keeping his eyes locked with Ariel's. "Guess I'm out for the night."

Kyle stood and looked around at everyone. Dixie was in a chair next to Chase leaning on his arm, Zoey was in Tyler's lap shuffling his chips like a pro, Dana and Roger were out in the main room dancing, while the moms were getting drinks at the bar. Finally, he walked over to Tyler and put his hand on Tyler's shoulder. "Ariel and I are going to head home. You good?"

Tyler grinned back at Kyle with amusement. "Yeah, man. Go on home."

With a nod Kyle led Ariel out of the bar and to his truck. She paused before getting in the truck and tilted her head. "You really okay to drive?"

Kyle leaned down and kissed her on her forehead. "Yes, I promise. I had two beers early on in the night but that was a couple hours ago."

After a moment to consider what he said she climbed into the front seat and fastened her seat belt. Kyle got in the truck and started the engine. Reaching out his hand he grazed his thumb along her cheek. "My place or yours tonight?"

Ariel sighed. "Mine. I want the fluffy bed tonight. Yours is like laying on a piece of plywood."

Kyle chuckled. "Okay. Your place it is."

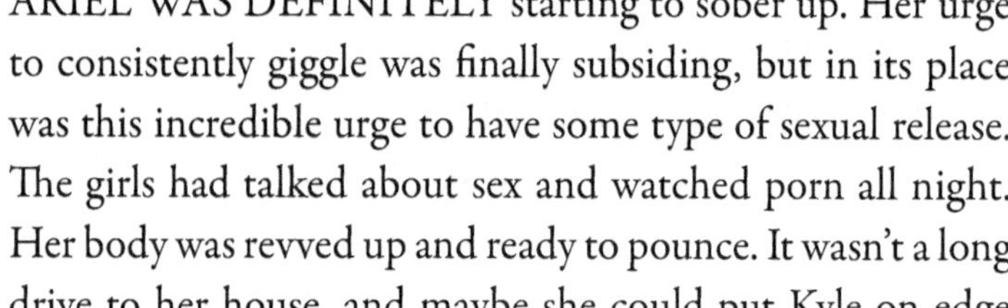

ARIEL WAS DEFINITELY starting to sober up. Her urge to consistently giggle was finally subsiding, but in its place was this incredible urge to have some type of sexual release. The girls had talked about sex and watched porn all night. Her body was revved up and ready to pounce. It wasn't a long drive to her house, and maybe she could put Kyle on edge just as much as she was.

She tenderly put her hand on Kyle's leg and began slowly moving it up and down. At first there was no reaction from him, or at least it seemed that way to her. Feeling a little bolder she moved her hand further up his leg and gently glided her fingers over his crotch and felt that he was definitely affected.

"Ariel," he growled.

"Hmmm..." She didn't stop. She was having too much fun torturing him.

"As much as I am enjoying this," he sucked in a breath as she squeezed him harder, "Shit. You need to wait until we get home."

Ariel pouted her lower lip. "But I am having so much fun. Aren't you having fun too?"

Ariel's hand lowered and applied pressure to his balls. Kyle groaned in response. "You have no idea what you are asking for."

Ariel leaned in and whispered, "I know exactly what I am asking for, so bring it on."

It was only a few minutes later when they pulled into her driveway and Kyle threw open her car door. She smirked at him as his wild lust-filled eyes took her in. She deliberately took her time taking off her seatbelt as she heard his breathing increase. She had just started to turn to get out of the truck when she heard a deep growl coming from Kyle and she felt his arms wrap around her and picked her up from the truck over his shoulder.

Hanging upside down Ariel tried to sound annoyed. "This again?"

"Someone was taking their sweet little time and I'm done with that."

Ariel laughed and gave a slap to Kyle's butt as he walked her up the stairs. He didn't respond. Instead, he just kept walking with purpose to her door.

"Keys?"

Still hanging upside down Ariel replied, "Well if you would have given me a minute, I would have grabbed my purse... you know... where the keys are."

Kyle grumbled as he set her back down on her feet. "Stay."

Truly amused now Ariel smiled. "Okay."

She watched as Kyle nearly ran back to the truck to get her purse. By the time he got to the door he was already rummaging around to find the keys.

"What ever happened to a women's purse being off limits."

Kyle pulled out the keys in triumph and shook his head. "I have licked and kissed every inch of your body. Nothing you have is off limits."

"Does that go both ways then?"

With the door now open Kyle wrapped an arm around her waist and nuzzled into her ear. "Absolutely."

Ariel's feet lifted off the floor as he pulled her in and slammed the door shut. With a quickness she didn't know that he possessed he had her up against the door with his body flush against hers. His lips crashed down upon her with fierce ownership. He wasn't holding back. She felt every taught muscle tightening against hers. His frenzy only escalated her need too.

Ariel shakily started to unbutton his shirt. She wanted to feel his chest and rigid hard lines of his abs. She only got two buttons undone before she was getting frustrated. She tried to pull each side of the shirt to rip it open but it wouldn't give. She felt Kyle smiling against her lips as he realized what she was trying to do.

"Let me help you."

She moved her hands away and watched with unabashed lust as he pulled at each side and ripped off his shirt sending the buttons flying to her floor. He dropped the shirt to the floor and leaned his head back in to kiss along her neck.

"Holy crap that was hot," she whispered.

His fingers found the zipper in the back of her dress and he slowly pulled it down while his lips followed down to her collarbone. She felt his hands lightly slide the shoulders of her dress down and felt it drop to the floor.

He lifted his head only long enough to gaze at her wearing her matching black lace and panty set. His hand traced down the edge of the bra as he said, "No, this is fucking hot."

Ariel shuddered out a breath and leaned her head back as he relieved her of her last garments. Their lips met again, and she felt the electric jolt of desire she always felt when he touched her like this. Deciding she wanted to take some control she slowly kissed her way down his cheek and stopped only when she reached just below his navel. Kyle sucked in a breath as she undid his pants and lowered his boxer briefs. He stepped out of his pants and she watched in wonder as his cock bounced in invitation. She finished lowering to her knees and wrapped her hand around his shaft.

Kyle put his hand in her hair, and said in a low tone, "You don't have to—"

Before he could finish his sentence, she had her lips wrapped around him. She loved the smooth feel of him in her mouth. She wanted this, craved it. She wanted the power of controlling his pleasure. She had only done this a few other times, and really hadn't found any enjoyment in the act, but this... this was completely different. She slowly moved her head closer to his body feeling him deeper in her mouth.

She felt Kyle's hands grip her hair tighter, and she moaned in pleasure as he took obvious pleasure in her eagerness. She began rocking her mouth back and forth moving him almost completely out and then back to the edge of her throat. She occasionally released him only to stroke him a few times and circle her tongue around his head. Kyle's hips began thrusting to meet her movements, and she knew that he was close. She wanted all of him.

"Ariel, you need to stop if you don't want..."

She only slightly shook her head in response and began to suck harder and dug her nails into his ass. It only took a few seconds after she dug in that she felt the pulsing release coming from him and tasted the salty essence of him.

After she had swallowed his last release, she looked up at him with a wry smile. Ariel thought that he might be shy kissing her after she just swallowed, but he immediately helped her up and pressed his lips to hers and his tongue sought out hers.

Kyle removed her bra and panties, and she felt his mouth lathing her nipple while he lowered his hand, tracing the seam of her lips and then up to her clit. She quickly realized that he was moving his hand in the matching pattern of his tongue on her breast. Heat crept up her spine as he continued his movements, and she knew it wouldn't be long before she would reach her climax.

He finally entered two fingers inside of her and brought his thumb to her clit, rubbing against it with each motion. That fluttering feeling began, and she felt the overwhelming sensation of weightlessness as she lost herself to him.

"That's my girl," he cooed.

She was blinking her eyes in a daze when she heard him rummage around on the ground. "What are you..."

He rose back up and kissed her. "I can't wait for the bedroom."

She slightly shook her head still partially coming down from her orgasm. It was the tearing sound from the condom that made her refocus her eyes on him. His cock was fully erect again and nearly touching his stomach. She giggled. "Nice recovery time."

He lifted her from under her legs and braced her back on the door. "He is always ready for you."

Wrapping her arms around his neck she started to give a smart reply, but it was stuck in her throat as she felt him quickly push into her. "Ohhh..."

She held on tighter as he began moving his hips faster and faster. She couldn't keep a coherent thought as she felt him glide in and out. This man was everything she ever wanted. He owned her entire heart. Her whole life, it was always him.

She allowed him to keep control as he continued making love to her. His lips moved and found that sensitive spot behind her ear and he whispered, "Are you mine?"

Ariel felt his desperation as he held her even tighter. Yes, she was his. How could she not be his? How could he not know just how much he was a part of her? She felt him slow his movement and watched as he brought his eyes to hers seeking an answer. She leaned her forehead against his and breathed. "Yes. I have always been yours."

This seemed to ignite a spark in Kyle as he took her lips once again and quickened his movements until they both reached their climax.

Chapter 14

"Tell me again why Derek isn't riding with us?"

Ariel flipped the visor up on after giving a final glance at her hair. "Because he said the only way he would go to Dad's for dinner was if he could drive himself, so if he needed a quick escape he could leave on his own."

Kyle nodded his head. He knew that Derek had a complicated relationship with his dad, and they hadn't talked about it much since Kyle returned to Blossom Hills. "So, he didn't want to come to dinner?"

Ariel gave a slight huff of annoyance. "No. He only caved because when I told him about it, I was having a really bad day and I may have threatened him."

"May have?"

Ariel shrugged one shoulder. "He needs to get over this thing with Dad. I've had enough of going to dinners without him. Did you know that at Thanksgiving Mom was nice enough to have an early dinner so that Derek and I could go to Dad's too? Our grandparents came in from Connecticut to be with all of us. Derek left Mom's acting like he was going to the dinner, but he dropped me off at Dad's and said he would pick me up when I was done."

"I can't believe he didn't at least go to see your grandparents."

"Oh, he spent time with them, but he just refused to do it when Dad was around."

"How did your dad take it?"

"He did his usual act of pretending like it doesn't bother him. He doesn't want to see me upset, but I can read him better than he thinks."

"Do you think it was a good idea to force Derek to come to meet your dad's girlfriend the first time he is spending time with your dad in years?"

"He promised to behave for me. He does not want my wrath. I could make his life a living hell."

"Yeah? How is that?"

"I will make sure he gets cock blocked until I forgive him."

"Do you think that is even possible? I mean, you can't be everywhere all the time."

"I have connections with people who owe me favors. This is why I love small-town life. I can make just about anything happen."

"Remind me not to piss you off."

Kyle pulled into Jeremy's driveway with Derek parking behind him.

Kyle could see the hesitancy in his friend. Derek was standing with his hands in his pockets staring at the front door. "Standing out here isn't going to help. Come on, before your sister drags you in by your ear."

Kyle and Derek both looked over at Ariel who was standing by the first step of the front porch with her arms crossed and eyes narrowed. Derek cleared his throat. "Yup. That is her move-your-butt-now look."

Once they entered, Jeremy greeted his daughter with a big hug and kiss on the top of her head. He extended his hand to Kyle and shook his hand a little too strongly for a simple friendly greeting. Once Jeremy met his gaze to his son, Kyle could see him struggling with his emotions. It was obvious it meant the world to him to see his son in his home, but he was holding back and just gave a polite greeting with a word of thanks for coming to dinner.

As the awkward moment between Derek and his dad ended, Miranda walked in carrying a plate of stuffed mushrooms. She was a woman who showed her happiness to everyone. Her smile was genuine and warm. She was slightly curvy with brown hair pulled back with small clips, so it was away from her face.

Kyle felt Ariel reach for his hand, and he wrapped his fingers around hers. They were still a room away from Miranda, but he felt Ariel tense as she got her first look at her dad's new love. He watched as Jeremy took the plate from Miranda and set it on the dining table. He placed his hand on her back and led her into the living room to meet them.

"Miranda, these are my kids. Ariel and Derek. And this is Ariel's boyfriend, Kyle."

Kyle's mind tripped over the word boyfriend. Was that all he was to her? She meant so much more to him than just a boyfriend. It was too small a word to describe how much he loved her. His thoughts were quickly interrupted as everyone greeted Miranda politely and then followed into the dining room.

"I hope you are all hungry. We have the mushrooms, but I also made a pork tenderloin with macaroni and cheese and asparagus."

Ariel brightened. "That sounds amazing. Is there anything I can help you with?"

Jeremy stood beside Miranda. "Not at all. We have it. Just sit and relax, and we will bring it right out."

Jeremy left the room for the kitchen and Kyle saw Ariel mouth the words, "Be nice," to Derek.

Derek made a halo shape with his hands around his top of his head and Kyle tried to hold back a laugh.

They all were finally sitting and settling into conversation when Miranda turned her focus on Kyle. "Jeremy tells me that you run Blossom Hills Press."

"Yes. Only for a little while now. I used to work for a major paper in Philadelphia, but I always wanted to come back home."

Miranda's eyes lit up with interest. "Philadelphia. That must have had some exciting stories to report on up there."

Kyle set his fork down and reached for Ariel's hand under the table. "Yeah, they were exciting, but you can only report on so much tragedy before it starts to eat at your soul. At times it felt like we were a part of the problem. People would commit these horrific crimes but then smile for the cameras as they were being arrested or being led into the courtrooms."

The table had grown quiet, and he felt Ariel squeeze his hand in support. He really needed to tell her everything. She deserved to know what happened and why he had kept them apart for so long. But could she handle the truth? He knew what an incredibly strong woman she was, but if she knew his role in Gianna's death would that loving look in her eyes fade?

Derek was the first one to speak. "Well, I'm glad you came back. Could you imagine me trying to drag Zoey on our hikes?"

Kyle gave a grateful smile to his friend. "No. She would have fallen down the hills and broken some bones. Then Ty would have had to kill you."

Derek shook his head. "Or he would have sent her with me wrapped in bubble wrap."

Miranda looked a little confused. "Isn't Zoey the owner of the bakery?"

Derek nodded. "She is also my best friend from college and is engaged to Kyle's older brother."

A warm smile appeared on Miranda's lips. "Must be something in the water in this town."

Kyle immediately saw Jeremy straighten his posture like he was getting ready for an attack. Then Kyle looked at Miranda who was obviously confused at how the room suddenly got quiet, and then he saw it. A small vintage diamond ring on her left hand.

Derek clanked his fork down loudly. Shit, this was going to go to hell quickly. Kyle placed his hand on the small of Ariel's back and began rubbing in a soothing up and down motion.

Ariel was now staring at Miranda's hand and asked in barely a whisper, "Daddy?"

Jeremy cleared his throat and threaded his hand into Miranda's now shaking one. Kyle could see the fear of rejection in Miranda's eyes. She seemed like such a nice person and did not deserve what he knew was about to go down.

"Miranda and I are engaged, and we are going to get married in November."

"You have got to be fucking kidding me," Derek exclaimed. "I mean you can't be serious. You will just do what you always do and break this poor woman's heart." Derek turned to Miranda and continued, "I'm sorry, you appear to be a nice person but do yourself a favor and run now. Don't let this guy give you the same bullshit promises he gave to Mom. You want to date the man, by all means knock yourself out, but don't trap yourself with him. You will only regret it."

Jeremy stood up and looked at his son with fire in his eyes. "That's enough! You're angry and I understand that, but I will not have you upsetting Miranda and your sister."

Derek, who was now standing too, stopped and looked down at his sister, who was now letting silent tears fall down her face. "Shit. Ariel, I'm sorry. I tried."

Ariel didn't respond. She only sat in her chair looking down at her hands that were now gripped together, white-knuckled, in her lap.

Kyle scooted his chair closer to Ariel's and wrapped his arm around her so she could lean against him.

With a loud exhale Derek bent down, leaned his head to hers, and whispered, "I've gotta go."

Ariel gave a small acknowledgment through her tears as Kyle nodded at Derek in a quiet understanding that he would take care of her.

After Derek's exit, Miranda said in a shaky voice. "Ariel, I'm so sorry. I thought all of you already knew." She turned her head to Jeremy who now was starting to lose some of the redness in his face. "Jeremy said he was going to tell you both before dinner, so I just assumed...."

Ariel lifted her head and wiped away a tear. "No, it's okay. I'm not upset that you guys are getting married. I want Dad to be happy, and if that is with you, I support you both."

Jeremy's tension visibly eased. "Thank you, sweetheart."

Ariel picked up her glass and took a sip before finally saying, "But, you definitely should have told me and Derek before we came. Geez Daddy, you can be such a moron sometimes."

Finally looking a bit more relaxed, Miranda said, "You were right dear, I am going to love this girl."

ARIEL WALKED INTO KYLE'S bedroom and was just exhausted from the dinner at her dad's house. After Derek left things were a little better. She got to know Miranda a bit more and felt at peace with the fact that her dad had found someone who would keep him in line. She was no pushover. Miranda had no problem telling him how disappointed she was that he let all of them find out about the engagement this way. She also made him promise to reach out to Derek and try to make things better between them. Yeah, good luck with that. Ariel didn't even object when Kyle pulled into his driveway. She didn't want to go home and risk seeing Derek. She was afraid she might say something she'd regret later.

She realized that she dazed out when she felt Kyle's arms wrapped from behind her. "You doing okay?"

"Mmmm. Yeah. I need to talk to Derek, but just not tonight. I think we both need some time."

"I figured. How about a nice soak in my ridiculously overpriced bathtub?"

Ariel grinned at the thought of his bathtub. It was big enough for two people and had massage jets. When Kyle first moved in the house had six bedrooms, but he expanded the bathroom and master bedroom making it now a five-bedroom house. He also created this spacious walk-in closet that wasn't even being half used.

Feeling Kyle's hands graze down to her thighs she relaxed into him. "Are you going to join me?"

"If you will have me. Think you could share the tub? I'll even put in one of those girly bath bombs you love so much."

Ariel spun around and wrapped her arms around his neck. "You bought me bath bombs?"

"Yup. I had Dixie help me pick out the right flavor."

Ariel patted his cheek. "Flavors are for food. Fragrances are for scents."

Kyle gave her a quick pinch on her side where he knew she was ticklish. "Uh-huh. Keep it up and I will just pour man soap in there."

Ariel gasped. "You wouldn't dare."

Kyle took a slow nip at her ear. "Oh Princess, I would dare to do many things."

About ten minutes later, Ariel was leaning back on Kyle's chest as he slowly washed her arms when she pensively asked, "Do you think Derek will ever get over his issues with Dad? I mean I thought he would, but it has been so long now, and if he doesn't sort it all out, I am afraid he will never let himself be happy."

Kyle stopped for a moment and didn't immediately respond. Ariel looked back at him wanting to see his face. "I don't really know. I always thought he would find someone eventually, but I really thought it would be before now. He seems to have this messed up idea that he is just like his dad, and he doesn't want to hurt anyone like he saw with his mom. He once told me that his dad was great with friendships, but was terrible at relationships."

"I know he struggles with it, but I don't know how to help him anymore."

Kyle laced his fingers with hers and said, "I think for this, you are just going to have to let him figure it out on his own. He is happy for now. He has you, me and Zoey. And maybe watching each of us find love will help him realize that he can have it too."

Ariel sucked in a breath. Did he just imply that he was in love with her? Did she dare ask? Before she could stop herself, she asked, "Love?"

"Shit."

Before she knew what was happening Kyle slipped from behind her and got out of the tub, without saying another word. Did she do something wrong? Was he mad that she brought up love? Ariel felt her heart plummet to the floor. She brought It up too soon. He was going to break up with her. Now Kyle was standing over the tub holding a towel and extending his other hand to help her out.

Tentatively, she stepped out of the tub. She must not have been moving fast enough, because he wrapped her in the warm towel, picked her up and carried her onto the bed where he settled her on his lap. He lifted her chin to meet his eyes before he spoke. "This was not how I planned on telling you, but I want you in my arms and looking at me while I do." Kyle grazed his thumb across her cheek before he continued, "I had this big plan of trying to make it the perfect moment, but you just made me realize that moments are made better by life's imperfections. Ariel, you have been my life and my heart since I found you under that tree. Our fairy tale began in those woods. I have always known that I loved you. When I pictured falling in love and creating a life with someone it was always you. So, this is the imperfect me in this imperfect moment telling you... I... love you."

Ariel's heart was just about to burst out of her chest. He loved her. He was sitting there with his heart in his hands and giving her everything she ever wanted. She couldn't imagine ever being happier than she was right now being held in his arms and knowing that he loved her. She reached up to his face and gave him a gentle kiss.

Once she released him from the kiss, she ran her fingers through his hair. "You may be imperfect, but you have always been perfect for me. I love you too."

They continued for long minutes kissing and exploring each other, and she drifted way into the bliss she found in Kyle's arms as he made love to her.

Chapter 15

Ariel was losing her mind. She was searching the office at her shop for the spare trinket box key that she normally had hanging on a magnetic hook on the mini fridge. A customer had called and asked if she could gift wrap it for pick up later that afternoon and that key was nowhere to be found. She was going to have to ask Lana or Myrna later if they moved it and she could mail the extra key later if they found it. She heard a knock on her back door and walked over stopping for a minute before asking, "Who is it?"

Zoey's voice came through a little muffled. "Ariel, it's Zoey. I brought breakfast."

Ariel thrust the door open and greeted her friend with a wide smile, and found that she was also not alone. Dixie followed in behind her. Ariel shook her head. "What, no Josie too?"

Dixie shook her head. "She was making some poor IT guy cry on a conference call. I can't believe she gets away with scaring the other employees like that."

Zoey handed over a donut to Ariel and said, "Yeah, but she is amazing to watch in action. She keeps that company running like a well-oiled machine. You should see the number of spreadsheets she has and how many emails she sends.

Whenever we are slow, I sometimes just watch her in action. I wish I had just a fraction of her drive and organizational skills."

Ariel giggled. "Yeah, we have all seen your accounting system. You're a mess."

Zoey lifted her cup of hot chocolate. "Not for long. Phil is taking an accounting class at school and said that he would get extra credit for helping me build a better, easier system. He said he would show me how to use it, but I think I want him to do it all and just have me review it."

Ariel looked at her files and sighed. "I need a Phil."

"Sorry you can't have him. I may have to beg him not to ever leave me. He can do construction, accounting, muscles for delivering heavy cakes, and he is quickly learning how to decorate some more elaborate designs."

"Greedy bitch."

Zoey just shrugged and took a bite of her donut.

"Hey, Chase said that Derek was at your guys' place this morning when he went to get Tyler for his run," Dixie said with a look of concern.

Zoey nodded. "Yeah. He came over last night and looked terrible. He just said that he had a really bad day and didn't want to go home and asked if he could crash on our couch."

Ariel winced. "That's because he knew I was... well... I don't know if mad is the right word for it. Frustrated maybe?"

"Why? He wouldn't tell us anything."

Ariel sighed and put down her food. "Me, Derek and Kyle had dinner last night at Dad's with Miranda. It was our first time meeting her. Everything was going well, but then Dad told us that he was engaged. Actually, it was more like she accidentally told us and then we saw the ring."

Both girls looked at Ariel with wide eyes not saying a word.

"Anyway, Derek lost his mind, and basically told Miranda to run away for her own good. Dad finally put his foot down and Derek stormed out of the house."

Dixie gave her friend a soft look. "Are you okay?"

"Yeah. I mean it was horrible at the time, but the rest of the night was good, amazing actually."

"Kyle make it all better for you?"

Ariel felt her face flush as she remembered the previous night's events. "Yes, he did. He made us a bath in that amazing tub of his and then he told me that he loved me."

Both girls smiled.

"I remember when Tyler first told me that he loved me. Actually, we were having a fight, because he thought Xander was some guy hooking up with me when he surprised me and came home early. I got mad at him, told him who Xander was and said that he was being an idiot because I loved him. Then he told me that he loved me too."

"Chase told me that he loved me while we were playing a kind of newlywed game at my family reunion. He just gave this amazing story about when he knew that he was in love with me, and I knew that I would be his forever."

Ariel proceeded to tell them about the events that led up to Kyle's confession of love and how he made her feel loved and safe in his arms all night. Ariel scraped some icing off her donut with her finger and studied it before saying, "Do you think we could work some magic and get Josie a nice romantic story like ours?"

Dixie shook her head. "I think that Josie will need someone to completely take control and basically sex her to death until she lets her walls down. It is going to take some serious alpha male to conquer her."

Ariel thought for a moment. "Maybe we should hook her up with Tiny."

Zoey shook her head. "No way. He is all muscle-bound yumminess, but he is a giant teddy bear with women. He would treat her like glass and that would just piss her off."

"Good point."

A small knock interrupted their talk and Ariel opened the door to let Myrna in. Myrna greeted everyone and went to the cabinet to put her purse in the drawer. Ariel suddenly remembered about the missing key. "Hey Myrna, do you know what happened to the spare key that was on the hook on the fridge?"

Myrna frowned and looked down at the now empty hook. "No. I saw it there just the other day."

"Okay, well if you find it lying around can you let me know?"

"Sure. Want me to go unlock the door? It's almost time to open."

"Yeah, go ahead, and grab a donut for yourself too."

Myrna looked around at the girl, with a grateful smile. "You girls sure are hell on my waistline." She grabbed a glazed donut and raised it in a cheers motion to the girls before walking out the door to the front of the store.

"I love that old woman," Zoey said as she gazed at the door.

Ariel smiled as she watched Myrna greet the first customer who was already waiting to be let in. "Me too. She only works here for fun. She told me that she just got bored sitting at home watching tv all day. She said that we give her something to talk about when she plays bridge with her friends."

Ariel looked at Dixie who was gazing at the empty hook. "I can't believe you lost the key. You are normally so good about things like that."

Ariel rubbed her forehead almost as if she was trying to rub away a headache. "I have been going a little crazy lately. I think Kyle is keeping me up too late. I have been forgetting all kinds of things lately."

"Like what?"

"Well... last week I forgot to shut my jewelry case lid down. I came home, and it was wide open. At first I thought someone broke in, but everything was there. Then the next day I forgot to lock the car. I'm just a hot mess."

Zoey gave a devilish grin. "Tell Kyle to keep his dick in his pants so you can get some sleep tonight."

Dixie's smile was much weaker, and she paused before finally saying, "Chase is rubbing off on me. I don't like it. Please just be careful, okay?"

Ariel looked at her worried friend and began to wonder if she should be more concerned. "Okay, I promise."

KYLE'S WAS FINISHING up an article about the upcoming school fundraiser when a Styrofoam box landed in front of him. He looked up to see Derek holding another container and seating himself in the chair across from him. Kyle slowly lifted the lid and scrutinized the hamburger and fries. "Did you poison this?"

Derek was already biting into his sandwich and shook his head. After swallowing the bite, he finally said, "Why would I poison you?"

"Because I am having sex with your sister?"

"I wouldn't poison you, just punch you, but I got over that a long time ago. Even before you guys..." Derek shuddered. "Anyway, we're cool."

Kyle smiled and picked up the sandwich. "Don't you ever work anymore?"

Derek shrugged. "I went in early and did inventory and caught up some paperwork. This is my lunch hour."

"Wow. You chose me over doing some random chick. I feel honored."

"You're an ass."

"Speaking of asses have you called Ariel to apologize yet?"

Derek set down his food on the table and groaned. "Thought you would let me eat first before you made me talk about this crap."

"Hey, I would have but you said you only had an hour, so no easing into it."

"I admit that I could have handled that better, but shit, this is the first time we meet the woman, and he is already going to marry her?"

"From what I understand they have been dating a little while now. If you talked to him more, you would have known that."

"Not helping."

"Look, your dad isn't the same person he used to be. Ariel has talked to me a lot about this, even before we got together. She wanted to talk to you about it, but every time she brings up your dad, you shut down and turn into Mr. Grumpy Pants."

Derek raised an eyebrow. "Mr. Grumpy Pants?"

"Her words, not mine."

"Great."

"Look. Your dad is not some supervillain out to destroy your world. He made mistakes and I hope that he learned from them. He wants what everyone wants. He wants to be happy and be with someone who understands and loves him."

"Yeah, but look what he did to Mom."

Kyle leaned forward and put his elbows on his desk. "Do you secretly want them to get back together?"

"Do I look like a dumb five-year-old?"

Kyle smirked but didn't answer.

"Don't answer that jackass. I know that they are better apart. She deserves someone who hasn't broken her heart. How can I look up to him like I used to, knowing what he did?"

"You broke off completely with him for years. Don't you think you have punished him enough?" Neither man spoke for a moment and then Kyle continued, "I can't even begin to imagine how my life would be if my parents split like yours did, but it could be worse. Think about Zoey. All she wanted was to be loved by her dad, and from what I understand wasn't even upset about the divorce that much, but he just gave her up. He walked away from a sweet girl and just decided he didn't want anything to do with her. Your dad has been trying for years to keep that connection with you. You are the one who has kept that great divide between you both. Get over your shit, be a grown up and appreciate what you do have."

"You're not my best friend anymore. I thought you were supposed to be on my side."

"I am on your side. I don't want you to wake up one day and realize it is too late. Now, are you going to call Ariel?"

"I will make her dinner. Would I sound like a jerk if I asked if it could be just us tonight so we can talk?"

Kyle shook his head. "No, not at all. Just tell her to call me if she wants me to come over after."

"Right. Like I am going to tell my sister to call you so she can get laid."

"We do more than just have amazing sex you know."

"And we're back to me wanting to punch you."

LATER THAT NIGHT KYLE was taking out the trash when he was stopped by his elderly neighbor Lenny. The old man was shuffling his feet and doing his best to quickly walk over to him. Feeling sorry for the man, Kyle set down the garbage and walked over to him. "Hey, Lenny. How are you doing?"

Lenny smiled and looked back at his house. "Oh good. The Mrs. is making me chocolate chip cookies for helping clean the bathroom. Word of advice. Always help the woman with the housework, the rewards far outweigh the cost. Plus, she will brag to all her friends what an amazing husband she has."

Kyle laughed. "Good to know."

Then Lenny's smile disappeared. "I don't want to upset you, but could you tell your friend not to block our driveway with their car? We couldn't get out the other day to go to the store, because their car was in the way."

Kyle looked confused. That doesn't sound like something Ariel would do. She was always careful where she parked if she doesn't park in his driveway. "Ariel blocked you in?"

Lenny's eyes widened. "Ariel? Oh goodness no. That sweet girl wouldn't do that. No, I am talking about a balding man, maybe in his fifties?"

Kyle was confused. He hadn't had anyone over at the house except Ariel lately. "He said he was a friend of mine?"

"Oh, I didn't get to talk to him. I just saw him come out from your backyard and go to his car. I wasn't able to get out the door fast enough to talk to him."

Kyle rubbed the back of his head in confusion. "Well, I haven't had anyone over in a while except Ariel. You sure it wasn't my dad?"

Lenny nodded. "Yes. I've met your dad a few times. Such a nice man. Good head of hair too. No, this wasn't him."

"Hmm. Sorry about that. If I figure out who it was, I will certainly talk to them."

Both men then heard Lenny's wife call for him with a plate of cookies in her hands. Lenny smiled and said, "Well, I'm off for my treat. Would you like to join us?"

"Nah. You go ahead. Enjoy your cookies, and your wife."

Lenny turned and waved as he said in a low tone, "I always do."

Kyle watched as Lenny made his way to the door with his wife and she leaned in to kiss him on the cheek. He knew that they were very happy together and hoped that him and Ariel could grow old together and be just as content and happy in their lives.

He pulled out his phone and was going to call Chase about the man in his yard, when it pinged with a text message.

Ariel: Done with dinner with Derek. Want to come over?

Thinking about Lenny and his cookies, he typed out his reply.

Kyle: Do I get to have some dessert?

Ariel: Oh, I have dessert in mind.... And it's sugar free.

Kyle: Damn woman... I will be right there.

Running back in the house to grab his keys he forgot all about the mystery man and calling Chase.

ARIEL WAS LYING IN bed wrapped in Kyle's arm when he started nuzzling closer into her neck. She felt a grin come across her lips as he kissed her shoulder. "Give a girl a break. Round three sounds like fun, but you might just kill me."

"Well, we can't have that, can we?"

"No, we can't."

"Okay, so tell me how dinner was with Derek."

"It was good. He apologized to me, but I told him he needed to also apologize to Dad and Miranda. Honestly, I was kind of surprised how quick he was to agree to that. We didn't talk about Dad too much. He promised he would make a better effort to connect with Dad."

"Do you believe him?"

Ariel traced her fingers along Kyle's arm. "Yeah, I do. It wasn't me pushing him this time. He looked like he truly regretted how he acted. Anyway, he said he would visit Dad and Miranda in a couple days to take that first step. I offered to go with him, but he refused saying that this was something he needed to do on his own and I shouldn't have to suffer the awkward conversation."

"Wow, that is progress. Did he say anything else?"

"Some stuff about the bar, we talked about my shop a little too and of course Zoey's wedding."

"Oh, about that. I promised Tyler we would make the wedding favors this week."

"We?"

"Yes, we, little Miss Maid of Honor."

Ariel laughed. "I knew I would be helping, but I am just trying to picture you tying pretty little bows and up to your neck in lace and ribbons."

"I seem to tie you up in knots just fine."

"My yoga helps make me be all flexible for you to tie me in those knots."

Kyle growled. "Thank God for your yoga."

"Yeah, without it, that muscle I pulled when you flipped me over would be much worse."

Kyle frowned and leaned over her. "I hurt you? Why didn't you say something?"

Ariel palmed his face. "Because the pleasure you gave me taking charge like that far outweighed the pain."

"Where does it hurt?"

"It's just a little stiff in my shoulder, I'll be fine."

Kyle kissed her on her nose and rose from the bed. He heard Ariel protest on his way out, but he promised he would be right back to make it all better. Entering the bathroom, he pulled out his shaving kit bag that had all his overnight necessities that he kept at Ariel's. Opening it up, he found that everything was not in its place where he had left it from the night before. He moved around a few items, found what he was looking for and made his way back to the bed.

"I have a surprise for you. Lay on your stomach and close your eyes."

Smiling Ariel did as he asked and beautifully laid across the bed allowing the sheet to fall away. He gently covered her naked ass and left her back exposed.

"What? You don't like my butt?"

"Princess I love your ass, but if I don't cover it, I will get distracted." He quickly opened the bottle he grabbed from the bathroom and drizzled the clear liquid across her upper back.

"That smells good, what is that?"

"This is a lavender scented massage oil I picked up from the porn store you made me go to."

Ariel let out of huff of annoyance. "It's not a porn store. It is an adult boutique."

"There were naked boobs and penis pictures all over the place in there. Call it what you want, but it's a porn store."

He could almost feel her eyes roll as she decided that she wasn't going to win this conversation with him. He let hands smoothly glide across her shoulders and he kneaded the muscles. Ariel hissed out a breath when he hit the tender area. "Just breathe. It will be better in just a few minutes." He watched as she relaxed into the bed letting out small, satisfied moans. Wanting to let her body have some recovery time he decided to divert his attention down to her legs where he rubbed in more oil and worked at her calf muscles. They were so smooth and toned he smiled as he thought about her sitting in her tub readying herself for him. That reminded him about his travel bag. He dug his thumbs into her thighs and asked, "Did you get in my bag to borrow my razor?"

Ariel popped up her head and turned to look at him. "God no. Your awful man razor would tear my legs up. What do you pay for those things like three dollars a pack?"

Kyle huffed out an indignant puff from his chest. "There is nothing wrong with my razors. They work just as well as your overpriced pink razors."

"Yeah, for like half of your face, then you have to grab a new one."

Not able to help himself Kyle smiled. "I think that is a bit over exaggerated."

Ariel shrugged her shoulder and put her head back down on the pillow as he continued his massage. "What made you think that I stole your crappy razor?"

"All the stuff in my bag was moved around. That was the only thing I could think of that you would have needed."

"Believe me, I need a lot of things from you, but definitely nothing that is in that bag."

Kyle flipped Ariel on her back and hovered over her. "You need things from me hmm?"

Ariel's face flushed as she drew her arms around his neck. "Yes, so many things."

Kyle kissed gently and said in a low tone, "Well, who am I to deny you your needs?"

Kyles lips trailed down her neck and his hands wandered down her body as he proceeded to show her exactly how he always intended to fulfill her needs.

Chapter 16

It was finally the day of Zoey and Tyler's wedding and Ariel was exhausted. The days leading up to the wedding she had been spending all her free time wrapped up in Kyle's arms and helping Zoey with last- minute details. Kyle had also been helping Tyler with preparations and a surprise for Zoey that both men were being tight lipped about.

Ariel was placing some finishing touches on Zoey's hair when Zoey's stepdad, David, gently knocked and entered the room. Dixie was taking some photographs and David blinked in surprise. "You don't give any warning when you point that thing do you?"

Dixie gave a small quirk of a smile. "Sorry, but Zoey said you hide from the camera whenever possible, so I wanted to get some candid shots when you weren't expecting it."

"I promise I will behave today. This is my little girl's day, and she deserves the best."

Ariel saw in the mirror as Zoey's eyes welled with tears. "Your little girl?"

"Of course, you're my little girl. You have been my daughter ever since those wide eyes looked at me as if I could always make everything better." David crouched down beside Zoey and took his hand in hers. "You may not be my biological daughter, but what we have is more special. You let me into your heart and called me dad, not because you had to, but because you wanted me to be the one to provide and protect you. I wish I could have protected you more, so that you didn't have to go through so much at an early age, but you have turned into an amazing woman and I am so proud of you. But now I have to step aside and let someone else protect you, and I can't imagine a better man than Tyler."

David reached into his jacket pocket and pulled out a small rectangular velvet box. "This was my mom's and I want you to have it now."

Zoey accepted the box and opened it to find an art deco bracelet with a single diamond surrounded by filigree and small fillagree squares linking at each side of the centerpiece. After bringing her fingers to her lips, Zoey leaned forward and gave him a big hug and mumbled. "Thanks, Dad. I love you so much."

"I love you too, honey."

After a moment Zoey released her hold on David and smiled as she tried to wipe tears away before they messed up her makeup. "Josie is going to kill me if I destroy her makeup job."

David looked at Ariel. "Is that the scary one?"

Ariel nodded and was amused that he already had a healthy fear of their friend.

Looking at Zoey, David asked, "Should I tell you one of my jokes to get you to stop crying?"

Zoey laughed. "No. Your dad jokes are the worst."

David frowned. "You always thought they were funny."

"Yeah, when I was eight. I only laugh now because you don't realize just how bad they really are."

David looked at Ariel. "Are my jokes really that bad?"

Ariel shoved the last flower in Zoey's hair and pulled out her phone. "Oh, would you look at that? Derek needs me to help with something at the gazebo. Gotta go."

Ariel grabbed her bouquet and made a quick exit as she heard Dixie mutter, "Chicken." That may be true, but she did not want to hurt David's feelings, and she was a horrible liar.

After a few minutes of checking on the reception decorations, Ariel made her way over to the gazebo where she saw Derek and Kyle leaning on the railing in their tuxedos. "Hey, everything all set for you guys?"

Derek nodded. "I've got the license ready and the vows all right here," he said as he patted his jacket.

Kyle then patted his pants pocket and smiled. "And I've got Zoey's ring here. How is she doing?"

"She is good. Her dad and Dixie were still with her when I left. David really is a nice man."

"Yes, he is," Derek agreed. "He was always pretty quiet around me at first. I think he was trying to figure out if I was trying to take Zoey away from Trevor or if I was really just a friend."

Kyle gave a soft kick to the railing and then wrapped his arm around Ariel. "I've gotta admit I wondered the same thing, but once I got to know her the more I understood."

Derek gave a small laugh. "I blame *When Harry met Sally*."

Ariel gave a small gasp. "I love that movie."

"You would," Derek retorted with an eye roll.

Kyle took a quick look at his watch and said to Derek, "Only about half an hour left before the ceremony. If you still want some time with Zoey before it starts you better get a move on it."

"Yeah. I still need to give her the last chance offer to run away and find someone not quite so nerdy."

Ariel gasped. "That's horrible! Don't you dare."

"That's me. The horrible best friend. See you guys later."

Ariel watched as Derek made his way to the back room of the event center where Zoey was still hiding. She felt Kyle nuzzle her neck from behind and whispered, "You did an incredible job. Everything looks amazing."

Ariel tilted her head to give him better access. "Mmm. Thanks, but Josie is a miracle worker. She had this whole thing planned down to the last microscopic detail."

Kyle started gently swaying back and forth and Ariel melted into him and followed his movements. "I think we should get married here."

Ariel stopped and turned to look in his eyes. "Are you asking me to marry you?"

Kyle gave an arrogant smile. "No, Princess. When I ask you will definitely know I am asking you. I am just having a conversation about the inevitable."

"Saying that it is inevitable doesn't sound very romantic."

Kyle framed her face with his hands and started to rub his thumbs along her cheekbone. "Okay, you want romance? Princess we are meant to be. I messed up our beginning, but I promise to make our future worth the wait, and your marriage proposal, when it happens will also be worth the wait."

Ariel sighed and tilted her head into his palm. "I don't need some elaborate gesture. I just want you, and your honest words promising our life together."

Kyle leaned down and gave her a gentle kiss with all the tenderness and affection he was promising her future. Ariel's spine tingled as she wanted more. She wanted to wrap her legs around his waist and find a quiet area to continue what he was starting, but then she heard a throat clear behind her.

Josie was standing in her bridesmaid dress next to Zoey's brother, Xander. "Okay, Pip Squeak. Time to go get the bride, let go of the poor boy."

Resigned, Ariel said, "We need to find you a man to loosen you up. Hey, Xander, you up to taming the beast."

With his mouth dropping open, Xander looked at Josie and back to Ariel, "Uh... no. I have a girlfriend remember?"

Yeah, Ariel remembered. She also remembered how Zoey complained about the woman all the time. Xander's girlfriend never joined him for important family get togethers, and didn't want to make any real effort to get to know Zoey. "Hmph. You mean that woman who couldn't bother to come to the wedding?"

Xander looked a bit ashamed. Ariel knew he already felt bad about her not coming for the wedding, or even that she had never been to Blossom Hills yet during his other trips. "She had to work. She couldn't get the time off."

Stepping down from the gazebo she walked over and straightened his lapels on his jacket. "You deserve better, sweetie."

He started to open his mouth, but she was quick to cover it with her hand. "Don't bother. You are just going to dig yourself into a bigger hole. Get your shit together in your personal life for everyone's sake. Got it?"

With his mouth still covered all he could do was nod his head.

Ariel looked at Josie who nodded in approval. "Well said, Pip Squeak."

Ariel rolled her eyes. "Come on, Josie, let's go before we mess up your precious schedule."

KYLE CLINKED HIS GLASS to get everyone's attention. It was finally time for his best man speech. The wedding was perfect. He had never seen his brother so happy and Zoey looked stunning. He didn't even think that Zoey saw anyone else during the wedding. Once she made her way to the aisle her eyes were locked with Tyler's and they didn't break their gaze from each other nearly until the ceremony was over. Now he looked around at all the guests and felt his heart full as his eyes stopped on Ariel. He cleared his throat and began.

"Attention, everyone. I know we are all enjoying this amazing food, but it is time for me to say a few words about the bride and groom. I may be the best man, but Tyler has always been the better man. While I was causing some trouble in school, he kept his head down, studied hard and did what he was supposed to do. He wasn't always this pretty either. My dear brother was a nerd. His body was too small, his glasses too thick, and he was best friends with the hall monitor."

Everyone laughed as Chase gave a scowl at the reminder of his hall monitor days. Kyle gave a devilish grin before continuing, "But here is the thing about Tyler, he is the best man I know. He always looked out for me, helped me when I asked and was also there to kick me in the ass when I needed it. I followed him to Philly because I needed my brother. There was just something about knowing he would be close by if I wanted to see him or needed his advice. Then we both moved back home, and I watched as he built his company from nothing and fall in love with the woman who broke into his apartment."

He looked at Zoey who shook her head. "I didn't break in. I had the key."

Kyle laughed along with everyone else and continued, "Anyway, it was clear from day one that my big nerdy brother was going to fall hard and fast for our new town baker. I think anyone of you here can agree that watching the two of them fall in love was like watching all the pieces of a puzzle finally fit together. When they're together, you can see the whole picture of what love is supposed to be. May you both always find happiness and stay on the sweet side of life. To the bride and groom."

There was a chorus of toasting to the newlyweds and Kyle went to hug his brother and new sister-in-law. He then made his way to Ariel who eyes glistened with tears that he knew she was holding back. She stood up and wrapped her arms around his neck and kissed him. "Very impressive Mr. Ashford. I didn't know you had it in you."

Kyle sat in Ariel's chair and sat her on his lap. "I'm a writer remember? I am good with words when I can write them first."

"Good point."

Later when Kyle and Ariel were dancing in slow movements across the dancefloor Kyle imagined it was their wedding and Ariel was wearing a white glistening ball gown and his ring. He wanted that. He wanted it more than anything else he wanted in his life. And to think he almost threw it all away for his ambition to be a journalist in a big city. There was nothing better than holding her in his arms and knowing that they had their whole lives in front of them. But that nagging little voice in the back of his head reminded him that before they could move on and have that life together, he needed to come clean about what kept them apart for so long once he came back. She had said something to him at the gazebo that pulled at his gut and he hadn't been able to shake it since. "I just want you, and your honest words promising our life together."

Honest words. He needed to give her all his honesty before they started their life together. He had been putting it off for too long and he needed to man up. She had told him that she wanted to know what kept him from her for so long. She had graciously accepted his request to talk about it later, but he kept putting it off, and now the guilt was gnawing away at him.

He felt Ariel run her hands through his hair as she pulled him down and whispered, "Are you ready to go home and have some quiet alone time?"

Kyle took her hand into his and quickly walked back to their table to grab her bouquet and purse. "Let's go. I have been dying to get you out of that sexy dress all night."

Ariel giggled. "Good to know I can still torture you."

Chapter 17

It was the morning after the wedding and Ariel was sore in all the most delicious places. Kyle had made good on his promise to make her scream his name and yet still beg for more. He had left to cover a story about a woman who was nearly beaten to death by her husband and told Ariel to make herself at home until he got back. She looked over at the door to the bathroom and saw his tuxedo hanging up ready to go back to the rental shop. Thinking she would help out, she decided to get a shower and deliver the tux for him.

After getting ready she pulled out her overnight bag that also needed a fresh change of clothes. She packed up her dirty laundry and saw the gift she bought for Kyle earlier in the week. It was a leather- bound journal embossed with his initials in gold. Wanting to surprise him, she wrapped it in tissue paper and went to his desk to find tape and a piece of paper to write a note.

He was such a mess when it came to his office space. There were random Post-it Notes everywhere with incoherent scribbles and printouts of articles and other research he needed for certain stories. He might be a small-town reporter now, but he still took it very seriously. With a smile she opened the top drawer and found a pen but didn't see any tape. When she pulled open the last side drawer her eyes were immediately drawn to a picture of her with a giant red X across her face.

Ariel fell into the chair, no longer trusting her legs to keep her standing. Why would he do this to a picture of her? She felt the blood drain from her face as she stared at the picture. She finally tore her eyes away and saw a folder with what looked like more pictures falling out of the side. Gently pulling it from the drawer, she felt bile rising up from her throat. After opening the folder, she found more pictures of her with similar red markings and threatening notes. Kyle didn't create these pictures. Someone else had and sent them to him.

Ariel's chest tightened and found that she could barely breathe as she studied each image and read each article. One article wrote about a young woman who had died, and the picture included Kyle standing by the body. Why wouldn't he tell her about all of this? He told her that he loved her, but obviously he didn't love her enough to respect her and tell her the truth. Her tears were flowing freely now, and she couldn't stop the sudden rise of panic. How could they ever have a future now? Could she ever look him in the eye and trust him when he could hide something this big?

Feeling the new wave of nausea, she knocked the file over to the floor and ran for the bathroom. It took a few minutes, but she finally picked up her phone and called Derek. He greeted with his usual cheer and Ariel had trouble taking in enough air to talk. "Derek. I..."

"Ariel? What's wrong?"

"I need you."

"Where are you?"

After desperately trying to take a breath she whispered, "Kyle's."

"I'll be there in ten minutes."

Ariel hung up the phone and grabbed her bag. She glanced at the folder filled with pictures and articles now sprawled on the floor and decided to leave it there. Let him find out the same way she had, with the evidence laid out ready to destroy his world.

Derek's squealing tires could be heard coming around the corner as Ariel sat on the porch waiting for him. She supposed she should have told him that she wasn't dying, but with the way she could barely get oxygen into her lungs, who knows? Maybe she was. Derek sprinted out of his car, took one look at her face and muttered a curse.

Pulling herself up to her full height she wrapped her arms around his neck and began to cry. "Take me home."

"Okay. Get in the car, I'll grab your stuff."

The ride home was thankfully quiet. She knew Derek wanted to ask a million questions, but she barely had any answers herself. She just wanted to curl up on her bed and quiet her thoughts. While waiting for Derek she had managed to put together some puzzle pieces. Kyle had gotten involved with a story about gang violence. He came home shortly after the story about the woman who died where Kyle was in the picture from the news clipping. Trouble seemed to follow him home since there were threats made to her, but why didn't he tell her? Why keep all of this a secret and risk her life and the lives of her friends and family? How could they ever have a life together when it was so full of secrets?

When they finally pulled into their driveway, Derek slowly turned off the engine and grabbed her hand. "I am coming up with you and we are going to talk about what happened. Whatever this is you are not keeping it from me. Understand?"

Ariel nodded as a couple stray tears fell down her cheek. Derek needed to know.

Walking into the threshold of her entry Ariel dropped her travel bag and purse on the floor and walked like a zombie to the couch. She turned just in time to see Derek pick up her purse and put it on the table. He walked into the kitchen and filled the kettle with some water. They both remained silent as he finished making her some tea and he pulled the bourbon from the top of the refrigerator into a glass and sat down with her on the couch.

After he gulped down his bourbon, he wrapped his arm around her and gave a gentle squeeze. It was that final gesture of support that broke the dam holding back her emotions. A sob ripped from her chest and it felt as if she was going to break a rib from trying to get enough oxygen. Derek didn't move, and he didn't demand more of her. She was so grateful that he was letting her purge all this built-up pain and fear before answering his questions.

When she finally felt empty of her emotions, she said in a barely whisper. "He lied to me... to us."

"What did he lie about? Did he cheat on you?"

"No, I wish it was that simple."

"Okay, tell me what happened."

"I don't know where to start."

"Start with when you woke up this morning and we will go from there."

Still laying her head in his shoulder she told him everything, from the good morning she had, to finding the file in Kyle's desk and finally ending with her waiting for him on the porch to go home.

She felt Derek tense with each piece of the story that she told him. He was already protective by nature, but with her life possibly still in danger she knew he was going to lose it completely. "I can't face Kyle right now. I need some time to process everything, and if I see him, I won't think clearly."

"I am going to fucking kill him."

Ariel sat up straight and looked her brother in his eyes. "You can't kill him. He is still your best friend, and as broken as I am right now, I still love him."

"You are not going to see him. I will make sure of that."

Ariel sighed. "I don't want to see him... for now. I just need to process all of this."

She felt Derek clinching his fists on her back. "You are going to forgive him, aren't you?"

Ariel desperately searched the back of her mind for an honest answer and just didn't have one. "I just don't know. I have loved him all my life. I can't turn it off or ignore it."

Derek let out a low growl of frustration in response. After a long pause he said, "I am going to call Chase and see if he will drive me to get your car. Where are your keys?"

Ariel sagged in his arms. "On the key hook at Kyle's by the front door. I didn't think to grab them before I left."

"Did you lock Kyle's house?"

Ariel shook her head. "I didn't think..."

"Shh... it's okay. We'll take care of it."

"Okay. Thanks. I am going to go lay down for a bit, okay?"

"Of course. I will check on you when I get back."

Ariel stood and gave a weak smile of appreciation to her brother. She tried to take comfort in the fact that she would always be able to count on him to take care of her.

KYLE PULLED UP TO HIS house to find Chase's cruiser parked in front. His heart plummeted into his chest as he saw the front door open as well. Had something happened to Ariel while he was gone? He was only gone for a few hours. Why did he trust Pablo that it was really over? With shaking hands, he ripped open his car door and sprinted up to his house. He stopped dead in his tracks when he saw Chase and Derek holding the threatening pictures of Ariel and other items from his file. "Derek, what are you—"

Before he could finish his sentence, Derek had dropped the pictures and ran straight for Kyle. He felt the first blow to his jaw and then another to his stomach. He was doubled over in pain when he heard Derek say, "Get.. the... fuck... up."

Kyle inhaled a breath to replace the air that he lost with that last blow and rose to his full height. He looked Derek in the eyes and fear gutted him as he asked, "Where's Ariel? Is she okay?"

Derek's frown deepened and Kyle again suffered another punch to the gut. "You don't get to ask about her. You lost your right to be anywhere near my sister, or me."

Kyle only slightly raised his head only to see Chase casually leaning against the wall with his arms crossed holding the damning evidence of his betrayal. "Are you really going to let him keep hitting me like this?"

Chase looked at the picture that was not only of Ariel but also of Dixie who was in the background. He slowly turned the picture for Kyle to get a better look at it and said in a low menacing tone. "You should count your damn blessings that it is Derek throwing the punches instead of me. My wife is in this picture. You knew that anyone around you was in danger, and it didn't occur to you to talk to me or any one of your friends who would have stood by you and helped. Instead of taking responsibility for your mistakes and asking for help, you risked Ariel's life, my wife's life and from what I can see your new sister-in-law and brother's lives too."

"There isn't anything you could have done to help." By now Kyle was standing upright again and worriedly looking at his two friends. The friends who he failed. Chase wasn't wrong, but Kyle had done what he thought was right.

"Do you think I am some dumb hick cop?"

Kyle ran his hand through his hair. "No! They told me as long as I never allowed myself to be happy with Ariel, they would leave all of us alone. They kept an eye on me. Any time I got too close they would send me a friendly reminder to keep my distance."

Derek looked like he was going to lose his temper again. "Then why come home? Why bring all of this on our doorsteps? You could have just left and protected everyone."

Kyle slowly shook his head. "They wanted me to suffer. They wanted me to be here, to be close enough to see what I couldn't have. They told me that if I moved out of town, they would kill her anyway. When I came back home, this whole mess with the threats hadn't started yet. I was already back home when I got the first visit."

Chase sat down and took out his notepad and pen and gave Kyle a tired look. "Okay, you are going to have to start from the beginning. Make me and Derek not want to rip the lungs from your chest."

It was about an hour discussion with Kyle explaining how it all started with the story about Sangres Nobles, the death of Gianna, how they kept an eye on him in town and finally with the story about how they all died, and everyone should be safe now.

Chase closed his notepad and shook his head. "You really are some special kind of stupid."

Feeling as if a boulder had been lifted off his chest, he looked at Derek and asked, "Is she okay?"

"What do you think? She's heart broken. She had to find out about all of this because she was looking for some god damned tape in your desk. Why did you still hang on to all of this shit if it was all over?"

"I was going to tell her. I didn't want to have this over our heads for the rest of our lives, but it never seemed like the right time. Derek, you have to know that I love her so much, I would never do anything to hurt her."

"No, you would just let someone else do it."

Hanging his head down he shook it. "I thought I was doing everything I could to protect her... to protect everyone."

"You should have come to me. We could have figured something out together." Chase said in a resigned tone. "But instead, here we are. All of us knowing what happened anyway, and you losing the trust of your friends."

"I... I'm so sorry." Kyle looked at Derek. "Please don't call Tyler and Zoey on their honeymoon about this. I don't want to ruin this time for them."

Derek nodded his head in agreement. "I won't, but I'm not doing it for you. It's for them. They deserve some quiet happy time this weekend. But you need to understand that I won't hide this from them. Zoey deserves to know, and Tyler deserves to hear it from you, so you better act quick when they get home."

Kyle nodded in understanding and watched as his friends left. After closing the front door, he felt the quiet and loneliness of his house and feared that it might stay that way for the rest of his life.

Chapter 18

It had been four days since Ariel found the file in Kyle's desk. She spent the first three days locked away in her old bedroom at her mom's house. She didn't want the interference of the girls and needed some space. Her mom was good about giving her the space she needed to figure things out, and she didn't hover like the others would. She had only told Derek where she was, and Lana and Myrna were thankfully stepping in for the shop. Now she wanted to go back to the shop and take back control of her life, but Derek insisted for her to take another day and that Josie was helping out today.

She sent a quick text to Josie.

Ariel: Don't threaten my customers and scare them off.

Josie: SHE LIVES!

Ariel: Funny

Josie: Seriously though, are you okay?

Ariel: I will be.

Josie: You should know that Kyle has been sitting in the park across from the shop every day like a lost puppy dog.

Ariel: I know. Dixie told me.

Josie: Do we still hate him and want to kick his balls into this throat? I taught you how to bring a man to his knees without breaking a nail.

Ariel laughed. After Zoey's attack from her ex-boyfriend, Josie had taught all the girls self-defense. They were all surprised to find out that she had the certification to teach but hadn't been doing anything with it. Josie had simply shrugged and said she used to help out with the classes in Atlanta and it wasn't something she really was interested in doing anymore.

Ariel: We don't hate him, but I still don't know what to do yet.

Josie: Take your time, Pip Squeak, and just know that we all would understand if you forgive him too.

Ariel: Thanks

She was close to forgiving him too. Kyle had been sending her text messages full of apologies and voicemails that nearly brought her to her knees hearing the pain in his voice, but she was trying to reconcile his lack of faith in her to know every piece of him, including the ugly parts.

She pulled her little car into the driveway and saw Kyle sitting on her porch with a brown file box. She stopped in the driveway and considered going back inside of her car and turning around. Kyle immediately stood up and walked towards her but stopped when she put her hand up. "Don't. I am still not ready to talk to you yet."

Kyle put up his hands in a placating motion. "I understand. Just give me two minutes and I will go."

Ariel exhaled and closed her eyes. "Two minutes."

"Okay. I fucked up."

Ariel quirked an eyebrow.

"I really fucked up, but please know that I never intended to hurt you. I was trying to do the opposite, actually. I thought by keeping all of this to myself I was protecting you and everyone we care about."

"I understand that, but you didn't have enough faith in me... in us... to tell me everything. I can't live with a man who hides things from me."

"I know, and that is why I am here. No more hiding. I will be a complete open book, literally," he said while nodding to the box. "I have something for you. I want you to take your time with it, and if you still think that I am not what is best for you, I will walk away, but I am begging you to give me this last chance to show you that I mean it when I say I won't hide anything from you again."

In a slightly quivering voice she replied, "Okay."

She walked past him and opened the front door to let him follow her in with the box. She pointed to the coffee table when he asked where to put it. After gently setting it down, he walked back to the front door and gave her a sad smile. "Be kind, some of what you might see in there comes from a moronic teenager."

Ariel gave him a look of confusion as he gave her a tentative smile. "I love you, Princess. That hasn't changed since we were kids, and it never will. I just hope your amazing heart can find some way to forgive a prince with a broken crown."

It was twenty minutes after Kyle left and she was still staring at the unopened file box. It seemed like a twisted version of Pandora's box. If she opened it, she was told that there would no longer be any secrets between them. Is that really a good thing? Should there still be some mystery? But she needed to know some things to make her final decision. Holding her breath and squeezing her eyes shut, she ripped open the lid. When nothing jumped out and attacked her, she slowly opened her eyes.

She really smelled the contents before she saw them. It was that warm familiar scent of books, like standing in the back forgotten section of some grand library. Her eyes focused on the contents. There were stacks of leather-bound journals and some notebooks. Each was bound by a rubber band with a small note with a handwritten number and years that they must have been written. She laid them all out in sequential order on the table and traced her fingers along each one. The highest number journal she recognized as the gift she was leaving him that day she found the file.

The book with the written number one also said "Read me, first." Unable to resist any longer she pulled off the rubber band and opened to the first page and began to read.

August 6th

Last week I told Mom I wanted to be a reporter when I grow up. Today she gave me this notebook and told me that if I wanted to be a reporter, I needed to learn how to write better and I need to practice. I still don't know how having a diary like some dumb girl is going to help me be a reporter, but Dad says that Mom knows everything, and I should listen to her. They promised me that they won't read it or tell Ty about it. Yeah, right.

August 10th

Dad says we are moving to somewhere called Blossom Hills. Mom and Dad seem really happy. Ty doesn't seem to care, but I have to leave all my friends. Ty doesn't have friends, so of course he doesn't care. Dad says they have a good football and baseball program that I will like. It better be good.

Ariel continued reading the next several passages that were all similar. They were short, talking about the upcoming move and his first few days in Blossom Hills. She noticed with each entry he got a little more detailed and careful with his writing. She smiled as she found that first entry that mentioned her and Derek.

Sept 28th

Derek invited me to his house today. He has nice parents like mine. His mom made us a pizza and didn't treat me like a five-year-old, like other parents do. Derek is way better than me at sports, but he isn't a jerk about it like other guys were at my old school. He has a younger sister named Ariel too. She has pretty hair and the best laugh. She told me that she thinks I'm funny.

At first, I thought she was going to be mean, since she's so pretty. All the girls at my old school who were pretty were so mean to everyone, but not Ariel. She is friendly and I like having her around. Derek tried to ditch her a few times, but I told him it was okay to have her around. I like having her around. I hope he doesn't get mad at me for that.

The next several entries were much of the same. Kyle spending time with Derek, school functions and several mentions about how much he liked Ariel. She couldn't believe that he had these feelings for her for so long and didn't do anything about it. Her heart stopped when she read about the day he rescued her.

October 20th

I have never been so scared in my life. Ariel got lost today. She got into a fight with Derek and ran off on her bike. She was gone so long, and we couldn't find her. She told me once that she loved to play in the woods and pretend that it is a magical forest. Everyone was searching for her on the streets, but I found her in the woods. She fell and broke her arm and had blood all over her. I wanted to carry her home and rescue her like they do in those movies, but I knew I couldn't carry her all the way. I had to go home to get the wagon and my dad helped me get her home. I wish I was bigger and stronger so I could have done it without his help. I called her Princess today. I just hope that someday she will see me as her Prince.

Ariel smiled and hugged the journal to her chest. She spent the rest of the day going over the first journal. It chronicled their childhood like replaying a movie and saw everything through Kyle's eyes. She looked at the other books and was torn about whether or not she wanted to read them all. Did she really want to read about his college days, or about the times he was with other women? Not really. She didn't need to know every detail about his life. No matter what happened, he deserved some privacy, but she needed to know about the events that led up to Kyle moving back home and the threats that were made against her.

Ariel pulled the second to last journal and held her breath as she opened it. It started well before he moved home and still worked at the paper. Entry after entry it was filled with the words of anguish and exhaustion at everything he saw each day. One day he would be reporting on a murder, another a gang rape, two days later the murder of two children committed by their mother. It was just horror story after horror story until she came upon one entry.

January 13th

I can't do this anymore. Ariel, I'm coming home. No more wasted time.

She looked at the date and thought back to when he came back home. It wasn't until late February when he finally returned. She went and got some tea and cozied up in her chair where she continued to read the important passages.

January 14th

I told Alan today that I was quitting, and he begged me to do one more story for him. I don't want to do it, but he has done so much for me. How can I refuse him? He said if I could do this last investigative piece it would give him time to find a replacement and I could go with no more guilt trips. I just want to go home and start the life with Ariel that I should have done years ago. I hope that she will forgive me for my ambition and idiocy that has kept us apart.

The next days were several notes of failed leads and doors slamming in his face when he tried to research the gang. Ariel could read his frustration and anger at not being able to wrap up this story quickly and move back home.

February 7th

I finally got a source. This amazing brave girl is coming forward to not only help me but help herself and her family out of a bad situation. If she is right about everything and is able to deliver on her promises, this really could bring down Sangres Nobles, and I can go home with a clear conscience. She wants the same thing that I do. She wants to leave this broken city and find a better life. I want to be near my family and finally start one of my own with Ariel.

February 9th

I gave Alan the evidence to give his police contact, and the first half of the story. We just need to watch it all go down, complete my story and then it is over. Finally. It won't be long now. I can leave and go back home.

February 11th

Gianna is dead. That beautiful, amazing, sweet, brave girl is dead. She didn't deserve this. All she wanted was a normal quiet life, and it's all gone, because I screwed up somewhere. They used her as a message to others to keep their mouth shut and to not talk to police or the press. I can't sleep. All I can see is her body sprawled on the sidewalk and left out on display. Make no mistake that is exactly what it was. A display, a giant fucking billboard saying to follow the rules of the street or suffer the consequences. I don't know how the leaders found out about her betrayal, but her death is on me. I told her that I would be careful and that she would be able to leave just as she planned. As soon as the police are done with my part for the investigation, I am leaving. Alan can shove it up his ass. I am done. I can't even sleep without seeing that poor girl with blood surrounding her and her cold, lifeless eyes staring at me in judgment. I just can't anymore.

The next several entries were just Kyle expressing his regrets, his feelings of helplessness and self-loathing. With each line Ariel's heart broke for him. There was no reprieve in his voice until she found the entry when they first saw each other again.

March 1st

I finally saw her. She looked amazing, but when doesn't she? I was picking up lunch at Daisy's when she glided through the door. She was light and air and sunshine wrapped up in a temptress's body. My hands itched to touch her, but I can't let them. There is blood on these hands and bourbon on my breath. I can't start our life while I still have to drink away the nightmares. She can't love this broken version of me. She deserves so much more. I need to conquer these demons, so they don't pull the light away from her.

For several weeks after this, the journal showed the struggle Kyle was going through trying to become the man he thought she deserved. If only he had come to her, they could have chased the demons away together. Didn't he know that all that light he saw in her was always for him? How could he not know that they could have been stronger together?

May 28th

It has taken some time, but I am finally going to make her mine. I haven't woken up in a cold sweat for nearly two weeks now. I know that Gianna's death will always haunt me, but I won't let it control my every action anymore. If something would have happened to me instead of her, I would have still wanted her to move on with her life and chase that happy peaceful life she always wanted. I have to believe she would want the same for me. I can't wake up to this empty feeling anymore. Tonight, I am taking Ariel as my date to the senior center prom, and I will do what I should have done the minute I moved back home.

Ariel remembered that night and how she was initially excited. Kyle had seemed friendly but had withdrawn compared to the flirty banter they had the night before. Noticing that the next entry was the following day she continued to read.

May 29th

My world has been destroyed... again. Gianna's boyfriend, Zeke, who was supposed to run away with her is now the leader of Sangres Nobles. He found me. I don't know how, but he found me, and now my life, my love... my happiness is fading into blackness. No more light. No more air to breathe life into my soul. Zeke gave the declaration that if he can't have Gianna, I can't have Ariel. Gianna must have told him all about me. It never occurred to me at the time to ask her not to tell him about me. Now, he wants me to suffer. He promised he won't hurt Ariel as long as I never take that step to be with her. He wants me to stand by and watch her build a life with someone else. To watch her fall in love and be so close and never getting to have what I want. I can't even move out of town to make it easier, or he will kill her. How am I supposed to do this? How can I be so close and not allow us both the happiness we were supposed to have? Losing her like this is going to destroy me, but at least it will only destroy me, and she will be safe. I just hope that if she ever finds out about all of this, she can forgive me.

The remainder of the entries up until recently were mostly filled with work notations, things about Tyler and their parents with occasional moments when he had come close to violating Zeke's demands and nearly told Chase about what was going on, or when he would almost cave into his desires for her. Not once did she see anything about finding temporary comfort in another woman's arms. Each entry about desire was always linked to her. The struggles with his conscience and broken pieces of his life were laid bare for her to see. It was almost as if all these journals were love letters written for her. When she finally finished the last entry and knew everything up to that day when he was waiting for her on her porch she was completely spent.

Ariel now knew that Kyle thought that he was always doing right by her and never intended to hurt her. She loved this man with every piece of her soul. She was about to pick up the phone when Derek popped his head into the door.

"Geez, don't you knock?"

Derek frowned. "Why would I do that? I have a key."

"Oh, I don't know. Maybe to respect your sister's privacy."

"Eh. I never let you have that before, so why start now?"

"Butthead."

Derek walked over and gave a kiss on her temple. "Awesome. You're feeling better."

"Because I called you Butthead?"

"If you were still sad, you would have been way nicer to me."

"You are so weird."

Derek shrugged and grabbed an apple from the counter. After taking a large bite he nodded to the table of journals. "I see Kyle gave you all his journals."

Ariel turned around to the table and sighed. "Yeah." She paused and narrowed her eyes. "How did you know they were his journals?"

"I have known about them since we were kids. He used them for all kinds of things, from just writing his own thoughts to taking notes for an article for the school paper. He tried to hide it from me at first, but I was always around, and he just gave up after a while. How far up do those go?"

Ariel sighed as she sat on the kitchen barstool. "All the way up to two days ago."

"Did you read all of them?"

"No. I don't need to know everything. I read the first one and skipped the middle and then picked up when this whole mess started back in Philly."

"And?"

"And, I understand now how things got so completely out of control, and what he was thinking when he didn't tell any of us what was going on."

"Guess I should tell you that Kyle and I had a long talk about everything."

"Yeah, I saw the aftermath of your *talk*."

"Those were just love taps, and I mean we had a talk after that. He's been through a lot, and I can't say that I know what I would have done if I was in his position."

"Honestly, I don't know what I would have done either. He has entry after entry about how the cops failed all these innocent people time after time and he had to tell their stories. How much of that can you see without losing faith in the system? Then I think about Zoey too. The police were involved, and that asshole still found his way to her and nearly killed her. Would you want to take that chance when all you had to do was keep your mouth shut and everything would be fine?"

"I don't know. We've never had to make those kinds of life-altering decisions before. We haven't been through what he has. I can already see it in your eyes that you are going to forgive him, but to what extent. Will you forgive him enough to build a life together or enough to just remain friends who could have been more?"

Ariel tried to envision each life. She saw a life where she was happy and building a family with Kyle surrounded by family and friends. Then she saw her life where he would always be there just on the outside, both of them just a little broken and lost. "Will you be upset if I choose to be with him?" Not that she would let that stop her, but for some reason she just needed to know.

"I'm not going to lie. I'm still angry. And I told him as much, but he will always be my friend. I told him we would eventually be okay, but that it would take some time. I also told him that you are my first priority. I would follow your lead and let you make your own choices."

"How shockingly mature of you."

"Yeah, well I used up my maturity for the week so don't get used to it."

"God forbid."

Derek stood up and gave her a hug. "Take your time. You don't have to make a decision today. He will wait forever for you."

"Thanks."

Derek walked to the door and started to leave but groaned as he looked up to the sky. "I almost forgot why I was up here. Can I take your little clown car today? My battery died and I need to swing by Tank's to get a new one."

"Sure. Just grab the keys off the table. I'm not going anywhere today."

With his all too smooth, charming grin he grabbed the keys and said, "Love you, sis."

With a smile, Ariel replied, "Love you too."

IT WAS A COUPLE HOURS later when Ariel finally decided to send a message to Kyle.

Ariel: Can you talk today?

Kyle's response was immediate.

Kyle: Yes. Where and when?

Ariel glanced down at her yoga pants and baggy shirt.

Ariel: How about my place in twenty minutes? Derek has my car, so I'm stuck here.

Kyle: Okay. Do you want me to bring anything?

Ariel: No.

Kyle: See you soon.

Ariel felt her heart flutter. She had been overthinking everything all day, but in the end, she just kept going back to that image of having a full life with Kyle. He would never cheat on her or disrespect her. Even when he failed to tell her about the threats, he was still doing it out of what he felt was protecting her. She certainly wished that he would have been open with her from the beginning, and told her what happened, but they had been living in this incredible bubble wrapped up in each other. She couldn't blame him for wanting some time to enjoy what had been denied to them for years.

In an optimistic mood that things were going to go well she went into her bedroom, closed the door and decided to quickly put on some makeup and change her clothes. She heard the front door open and close, and she smiled as she looked at the clock. That was quick. It had only been ten minutes. She smiled as she quickly changed into a pale pink dress and opened the bedroom door.

"I can't believe you got—"

She froze in her tracks. There was a man sitting at the coffee table reading Kyle's journals. Startled the man jumped up, grabbed a gun from the coffee table and pointed it at her. The two quietly stared at each other waiting for someone to move first. Ariel held her breath as recognition finally began to settle in. "You're that man from the shop. Max."

The man's hand was shaking terribly, and Ariel was afraid that too much more movement would cause him to accidentally set off the trigger. He frantically looked from the pile of journals and back to Ariel. "You weren't supposed to be here. Your car was gone."

Ariel's eyes grew wide as she realized this man had been following her, watching her and probably Kyle too if his interest in the journals was anything to go by. She didn't respond to his statement only watched his trembling hand holding the gun that was still pointed at her.

With his free hand the man pointed to the pile of journals and asked, "Have you read all of these?"

Ariel shook her head. "No. Just a few of them."

"Well, Princess, now you are going to help me."

With her hands held up and shaky legs, she began to move out of the small hall and into the main area. She glanced over at the clock only to see that Kyle would be here soon. Would this man kill him, if he walked in on them? She couldn't let that happen. They were going to finally have their chance, and she didn't want to lose him now. "Okay, I will help you, but I need to know what you are looking for."

The man's voice wavered as he seemed to be grasping at his last thread of determination. "I am looking for a thumb drive. I have looked all over your damned shop, his office and your houses, only to find nothing! Zeke told his man that he hid the drive where fairy tales begin in the land of happily ever after. Christ, at first I thought he was talking about fucking Disneyland until I found out about one of Zeke's trips to visit Kyle."

Ariel's face grew pale. "Are you part of Sangres Nobles?"

The man tilted his face and readjusted his grip on the gun. "He told you about that, huh?"

"Yes."

"I guess he also told you it was all my fault too."

Ariel quickly shook her head. "He never blamed anyone for that except himself." Her mind was racing trying to remember everything that she had read. Zeke was the leader of the gang. Gianna was his girlfriend who was killed over the story that.... the story that Kyle's editor had given him as his last assignment. The same man who was reported missing. "You're Alan, aren't you?"

The man's face fell, and he nodded, giving Ariel the confirmation she needed. "Sangres Nobles had stuff on me that would destroy my family. I thought Kyle could investigate them, and they would be brought down so I could be free of it all. It all started out because I just needed some money to pay for my wife's cancer treatments. I couldn't let her down. She deserved to live. I couldn't just let her..." His mind started to drift, and he stretched out his arm with the gun.

"Of course, you couldn't let her die. You did what you had to do."

"It was just supposed to be a couple times, but they kept on pushing and I didn't have a choice. When the leader was killed, I thought I was free, but then Zeke stepped up and it just continued where the other one had left off. Zeke always told me that he had a man on the outside who would turn in the evidence if anything ever happened to him. When I finally got one of his men to tell me what he knew, all I got was this god damned riddle."

"Maybe I can help." Ariel just wanted to keep him calm. He wasn't steady with the gun and maybe if she could get close enough, she could get the gun away from him.

"I've been all over this damned town and there's nothing! The answer has to be in these journals."

Ariel shook her head. "I read all about Sangres Nobles, and there isn't anything about handing over a thumb drive with stuff about you. It has to be one of the men who was sent down here to spy on us all the time." She took another step closer. "Tell me the riddle again. Maybe we can figure it out together."

"He said he hid the drive where fairy tales begin in the land of happily ever after. Kyle always called you Princess. I listened to him pining away for you for years. It has to be here somewhere."

Kyle. Ariel looked frantically at the clock again. She was torn between wanting him to come and rescue her and not wanting him to come and possibly get hurt. Was this how it was for him willing to sacrifice himself for her? She now knew with complete certainty she would do the same for him. Her hand mindlessly went down to rub the tree from her charm bracelet and then gave a small gasp. "I know where it is."

Alan's eyes widened and his body seemed to vibrate with anticipation. "Where? Show me."

Ariel looked at the clock again. She needed to get him out of there and warn Kyle somehow. "I can show you, but you have to let me text Kyle to cancel our plans tonight or he will be here soon. I will take you there and then you can let me go."

"I don't know."

"Look, you're never going to figure out where this is on your own. You can keep hiding in the shadows trying to find it by yourself or we can do this my way." Ariel's heart was beating out of her chest. The man was desperate and looked like he hadn't slept in days. He had to be tired. She was pretty certain she knew where the drive was, and she was going to do her best to lead Kyle there somehow, but at least with a warning.

"You can read the text as I type it. I won't even hit send until you approve it."

She watched as he struggled with his decision. "Okay. One message then you turn off the phone and we leave it here."

Well, there goes the idea of turning on the find my phone feature that Derek insisted on installing so he could help her find her phone when she would inevitably lose it somewhere. Ariel picked up the phone and pulled up the messages and began to pray that Kyle would understand.

Ariel: Sorry, I have to cancel our plans for tonight. Summer called, and she needs me to come over. I'll see you tomorrow.

She handed the phone over to Alan who read the text and seemed to approve the message then hit send.

He turned off the phone and put it on the hall table. Standing back, he motioned for her to open the door. She turned the lock and glanced back. "I am going to need shoes where we're going."

"Go, get them then."

She walked over to the edge of the couch where she kept a pair of sneakers and walked back to the entry table. He continued to hold the gun at her standing a bit of distance away. She cautiously bent over and put the first shoe on then quickly unclasped her charm bracelet. After putting on her second shoe she stood upright hiding the bracelet in the palm of her hand. With slow movements she moved her hand over next to the phone and gently let it go. As they finally walked away, she prayed he would keep his promise and always find her. Hopefully this time with a little extra manpower with him.

Chapter 19

Kyle looked down at his phone and recognized the number that was now coming in was from Philadelphia. He gave an apologetic look to Chase. Kyle had stopped by Chase's office to get a press release statement about a suspicious fire at an abandoned house just on the edge of town and was just getting ready to leave for Ariel's house. "Sorry, I think I need to take this."

Chase nodded, gave a small wave of his hand and turned his attention back to his computer.

Not seeing an immediate private place to take the call he simply swiped and accepted the call. "Hello?"

"Hi, is this Kyle?"

"Yes. Who is this?"

"This is Nancy, Alan's wife."

"Of course, Nancy. Have you heard anything from Alan?" He still hadn't heard any updates and he knew that she was frantically reaching out on social media in hopes of finding him.

"Actually, that's why I'm calling. We had someone reach out to us that they thought they saw him in North Carolina of all places. You are the only person we know out there, so I thought you might know something."

Kyle turned to grab Chase's attention. "Nancy, I am actually at the police station right now with my friend who is the Sheriff. Can I put you on speaker phone?"

"Oh... uh... Yes."

"Alright, hang on just one second."

Kyle covered the mouthpiece quickly and tried to give the short version on what was going on. "Alan is my old editor. He's been missing a while. Nobody knows what happened, and he just isn't that guy who would walk away from his wife. She just called saying someone saw him in North Carolina."

Chases nodded quickly and grabbed a piece of paper while Kyle put her on speaker. "Nancy are you still with me?"

"Yes."

"Okay, can you give us some details?"

"As you know I have been putting his picture all over social media hoping to find out something. Someone made a comment on the post that he looked like a guy someone saw at a card shop in North Carolina."

Kyles eyes widened as he looked at Chase. He mouthed Ariel's name and watched as Chase nodded his agreement. "Did the person say the name of the shop or even the town?"

"No. I tried to reach out to the person who made the comment, but they haven't replied yet. Alan told me you left the paper to move back home, so I was hoping if he was in trouble, maybe he went to see you."

"I'm sorry, but I haven't seen him."

"Nancy, this is Chase Montgomery, Kyle's friend. Can you send me the link on the post where the person commented about seeing Alan? I might be able to do some digging around and find out more.”

“Of course. Can I just text it to Kyle?”

“Yes, ma'am. We'll call you right away if we find anything that will help you.”

Nancy gave her thanks in a shaky voice, and the message came through within seconds after the call. Kyle handed the phone over to Chase who made a couple of quick movements on the screen and he had the profile pulled up from the person who posted the comment.

“Look, she took a selfie in front of the gazebo. They had to have seen him here.”

“Shit. If he was here to see me, why hasn't he reached out to me by now?”

“I don't think he wants to be found.”

Their discussion was interrupted by another ping from a text message. Chase handed the phone back to Kyle. “It's Ariel.”

Kyle opened the message and felt his heart drop. “Something's wrong. I have to get to her.”

As he was turning to leave, he felt a strong grip on his arm stopping him from leaving. “What the fuck is going on?”

“Ariel said that she was cancelling tonight and has to go see Summer.”

Chase's lips drew into a small line at the mention of his deceased sister's name. Before long he seemed to process the message, and with a growl he said, “Fuck. I'm driving.”

The men raced out to Chase's car where he requested back up on his radio to Ariel's house. As they started to speed to her house, Kyle was trying to calm his racing heart but felt like he was two steps behind. His fingers were frantically dialing Ariel's number over and over again only to be sent to voicemail each time. Finally, he looked at Chase. "What do you know that I don't?"

"Doesn't Ariel ever tell you about the books that she reads with the girls?"

"Um... no?"

"Well Dixie does. They all just read a book where a woman got kidnapped and she was allowed to send one text message to supposedly prevent them from being interrupted. Only the girl mentioned going to a dead friend's house in the message to let her boyfriend know there was something wrong."

Kyle's world just dropped from beneath him and he pounded his fist on the roof of the car. "Shit! Drive fucking faster."

Chase was already speeding through the street with lights passing everything in a blur, but Kyle's panic level was rising with the pass of each house that still wasn't hers. What would he find when he got there? Is she hurt? Was this Alan, or one of Zeke's men who got away?

The car was barely at a complete stop before Kyle was jumping out and sprinting to the door. Chase was trying to get him to stop, but it was just all white noise as blood was rushing through his veins. He burst through the door with Chase right on his heels.

Kyle called out Ariel's name was he went through all the rooms. The unanswered silence was deafening to him. How could she not be there? Where is she? Is she okay? The questions kept running through his head and he felt his stomach churning at the thought of losing her.

Chase holstered his weapon and took a look around the main area. Kyle looked too but wasn't sure what he was looking for. "What are you thinking?"

"Just looking for something else to give us a clue. If she managed one clue, she might have left us something else."

Kyle heard the backup arrive that Chase requested, but his mind was flooding with dread. Where would she leave a clue? He kept circling the room until his eyes landed on the entry table. There was her phone and laying on top of it was her charm bracelet. The bracelet that she never took off. The bracelet that he gave her to remind her of the enchanted tree and that he would always find her. In a whispered tone he said, "Just rub the tree and know if you need me, I will find you."

Chase was now standing beside him looking at the charm that Kyle held in his hand. "Isn't that the bracelet she always wears?"

"Yeah. She never takes it off." Kyle gripped it in his hand even harder. "I think I know where she is. Let's go."

ARIEL GAZED UPON THE maze of trails that led to the place she hoped held what Alan was looking for. Kyle and Ariel's fairy tale began at that tree where he found her helpless, hurt and crying. He was her rescuer, and she knew that he was supposed to be hers.

Alan's sharp voice broke her away from her thoughts. "Wait! Where are we going?"

Frustrated Ariel turned around and narrowed her eyes. "You said where the fairy tale began. Well, this is it. It began here in the woods."

Alan shook his head. "You want me to believe that Zeke took a thumb drive out here?"

"I don't know, but obviously you haven't found it yet. I assume you are the one who has been moving everything around in my shop and home. This is where Kyle rescued me and started calling me Princess. I had fallen off my bike, broke my arm, scraped up my legs and he found me sitting under a tree alone and cold. If this isn't what Zeke was talking about, I don't know where else it could be."

"How would he have known which tree it was?"

Ariel thought about that on the walk to the woods and had come to the conclusion that he must have followed them there one of the times they met when she was having a bad day. If either of them wanted to talk about something bothering them, they would meet there. "Both of you had this creepy stalker thing going, he probably followed us one time we went there. You've tried everywhere else and haven't found it, so let's go and get this over with." She just hoped that when it was over, she would still be alive.

After a couple minutes of walking Alan finally said, "I can see why Kyle is so fond of you. You're soft but still fierce... like my wife."

Ariel paused for a second before stepping over a downed log. "Does your wife know what you are doing?"

"No."

"Have you even called her since you left home?"

At first, she didn't think he was going to answer, but she finally heard his whispered, "I can't."

They continued on, with him keeping close enough to be a threat, but not close enough to touch. Ariel was careful enough to take him the long way to the tree, but not so off course where he would notice they were going in a circle. She knew these woods... each trail, each slope of the hill and where animals tended to hide.

Just as Alan seemed to be losing his patience, they came upon the tree. She saw the clear flat ground where her and Kyle would sit and talk and a new small patch of wildflowers just off to the right. "Here. This one right here," she said pointing to the tree.

Alan frantically started looking around and finally said, "You are going to have to dig."

Ariel looked around and then back to him. "With what? I didn't bring a shovel, did you?"

"Find something to break up the ground or use your hands."

He had to be kidding. Who knows how far down Zeke would have buried the thing, that's even it if it was here? She found a short thick branch and picked it up. Wishing she wasn't wearing a dress; she knelt down and began dragging at the dirt hoping to find a soft area that would have been recently dug up.

She scraped and scrounged desperate to find something but it was probably ten minutes from when she started, and she was still coming up empty. She sat back and set the stick down getting frustrated. When she started to wipe a section of hair that fell in her face, she felt the hard metal of the gun pressed against her head.

"Keep digging."

Hearing the change in his tone and knowing that he was losing the grip on his control she whispered, "Okay."

A few minutes later she heard twigs snapping to the right of her. She dared a glance at Alan who hadn't noticed the sound and she went back to work trying to make more noise to cover the sounds of someone approaching. Just as she moved to start a new section of dirt, she heard Kyle's voice. "Alan!"

Ariel's head jolted back as she felt the hair being pulled from her scalp. He was pulling so hard she was nearly being lifted off the ground.

Ariel stumbled when he pulled and was partially dragging her away from Kyle. "Back off, Kyle. I just need to find something. Then I will let her go."

Kyle walked forward with his hands up in the air. "What are you looking for? Maybe I can help."

"No. I don't think you even knew that Zeke left anything here."

"Let Ariel go, and we will figure this out."

Ariel was still being held by her hair and was looking at Kyle with a deep fear tearing away at her heart. She needed him to let go of her hair, get his attention and get the gun pointed away from Kyle. Realizing that she may never see him again, she said in a low frightened voice, "I love you."

Kyle's face crumpled. "I love you too. It's going to be okay. I promise."

With those words Alan loosened his grip on Ariel's hair and gave a frustrated growl. "You can't promise her that. I promised that to Nancy. I was supposed to protect her, but I forgot to protect her from me. She is going to suffer because of the choices I made."

Kyle took a tentative step forward. "She's looking for you, you know. She is spending every day making calls, posting on social media, asking everyone she knows to search for you. Nancy won't care about what you did. The only thing she will want, is to have you back home."

Alan finally released Ariel's hair and firmly extended his arm holding the gun in Kyle's direction. "Don't talk to her again. Let her think that I died, she can live with that. She wouldn't be able to live with the things I've done."

"I think you would be surprised by what she could live with," Kyle said with caution as he took another step forward.

Now free of his hold, Ariel watched as Alan struggled with his emotions and his need to control the situation. Hearing footsteps of more people, she knew this would end horribly if Alan saw people surround him. Taking a fortifying breath, she stepped in front of Alan blocking his aim at Kyle.

"Ariel! Get of out the way!" She heard Kyle's desperate plea but ignored him.

Ariel took a small step towards Alan's trembling arm. "Alan? I know about everything. I can make her understand how things went wrong. Kyle made his mistakes, but I know that he did everything out of love for me. I can explain that to her in a way that would make her understand too."

She watched as his face softened and his arm relaxed either from letting his guard down or exhaustion. She wasn't sure which. Once his eyes seemed to lose focus, she whispered, "Finally."

With lighting quick movements Ariel grabbed the muzzle of the gun and pulled it away from her body while taking her other free hand and slamming hard against his wrist which caused it to bend awkwardly and for him to lose his grip on the gun. She was able to grab firm control of the firearm and quickly took several steps back and pointed it at Alan.

Ariel took an additional step back and still held the gun firmly pointed at Alan. "Chase, is that you behind me?"

She heard a small grunt from behind and more footsteps. "Yeah. Ariel, put the gun down. I've got him."

Ariel turned around to see Chase walking forward with his gun drawn and holding cuffs in his other hand. Risking a look at Kyle, she saw him standing a few feet away with a dumbfounded look on his face. She gave him a smirk. "What?"

"Holy fuck that was hot. Where did you learn to do that?"

"Josie." Ariel looked at the gun and released the clip and then went to empty the chamber. When no bullet was released, she looked at the magazine again. She turned back to Alan and gave him a confused look. "It wasn't loaded?"

Now completely restrained and being held by Chase he responded, "No. I never wanted to hurt anyone; I just wanted the files. I just..."

"Wanted to protect the people you love."

There was no reply from Alan, only a slumping of his shoulders. It seemed as if Chase had heard enough, and he gave a slight push to Alan and told him to move. As they, Chase, and Alan climbed the hill Ariel noticed a few other officers who had been surrounding their position.

Ariel's eyes found Kyle who was visibly shaken. He finally shook off his daze and made quick strides over to her. He wrapped her in his arms and spoke into her hair as he kissed the top of her head. "I am so sorry. God, I was so scared."

She squeezed him harder and let her tears flow. "I know. It's okay. I'm okay."

Chase's voice broke the tender moment. "Great. Everyone's sorry; could you guys kiss and make up now so I can get started on all this damn paperwork?"

Kyle placed his hands on her face and looked down at her. "Can I?"

"Can you what?"

"Kiss and make up?"

"God yes."

Ariel saw the visible relief in Kyle's eyes that was quickly replaced by desire as he crashed his mouth onto hers. She melted into his arms and took comfort in knowing that this is where she always belonged.

IT WAS A FEW HOURS later when Kyle and Ariel finally went home from the Sheriff's station. Kyle was relieved when she asked to go to his house instead of hers. He just wanted to wrap his arms around her and hold her tight for at least a week. He doubted she would let him hover over her that long, but he sure would try.

He kissed her neck as she stepped out of her shoes. "How about I draw you a nice hot bath?"

Ariel nodded and went into the bedroom.

It only took a few minutes to prepare her bath and add the salts that she loved so much. She gently stepped in and gave him a questioning look.

"I will join you in a few, I need to call Mom and Dad, so they don't find out through the grapevine."

Ariel nodded. "Good idea. Just hurry back."

Kyle bent down to kiss her and promised to return soon. He didn't make it far when he got a call from Chase. "Hey, what's up?"

"I just wanted to let you know we found the drive. It was buried by the tree like Ariel thought, but it was actually under the small patch of flowers next to it."

"How did you figure that out so quickly?"

"Metal detector."

"Ah."

"Anyway, I am pulling up the files now, but they are all password protected, so that will take some time. And I just wanted to say thanks for calling Alan's wife. At least she will get some peace knowing he is still alive."

Kyle sighed as he remembered that call. He called her on speaker phone with Ariel, who insisted that she talk to the woman to let her understand everything that happened. She said that telling her everything would need a gentle woman's touch and that Kyle would have the finesse of an elephant. That was probably true. He was so angry with Alan and felt violated and betrayed, but Ariel wasn't even mad anymore. Mostly, she was just sad for someone who once was a good man who lost his way. Once they reached Nancy, she was originally relieved that he was found alive, but as they had finished their story, they could feel her broken heart just as clearly as if she were in the room with them. Ariel had calmed her down, tried to explain that she thought Alan still loved his wife and just made the mistake of trying to handle everything on his own instead of sharing the burden with the person he loved the most. She had given a direct look at Kyle as she told her that, as Kyle wished that he had done things differently.

Refocusing on the call with Chase, Kyle thought about the thumb drive. "Didn't Alan say that Zeke made these files?"

"Yeah."

"Try Gianna, or Queen."

"Okay." Kyle heard the keyboard click as Chase entered the attempts.

"Nope."

"Damn. I thought for sure he would have used her info for the password." Then like a lightning bolt he remembered after the Ides of March party when Zeke told him it was Gianna's birthday. "Try Gianna315."

Kyle listened as Chase entered the information and said, "Huh. Damn impressive, Ashford."

"Thanks."

"It looks like I am going to be getting home late tonight. I need to go and call Dixie."

Kyle said his goodbyes with Chase and then called his dad who picked up on the first ring. It was a long and uncomfortable call. He hated explaining how he let everyone down and had kept everything from his family who he knew would always support him. Thankfully, his dad was reassuring and accepting of Kyle's explanations and apologies. "As long as you understand where you went wrong and learn from it, that is all I care about. Well, that and that everyone is safe."

"We are, and thanks Dad."

"Of course. Now go take care of your girl. I am sure she needs you."

Kyle agreed and went back to check on Ariel. Instead of her still sitting in the tub he found her lying in his bed wearing only his old college t-shirt. He climbed in behind her and pulled her close. She stirred and gave a little smile.

"I gave up on you. I was turning into a prune."

Kyle grazed his thumb on her stomach and groaned. "Well, we can't have you turning into a prune. I happen to love your soft smooth skin."

Ariel turned to face him and let her fingers trail down his biceps. "And I happen to love your firm toned body."

He leaned over her and brushed her blonde hair away from her cheek. "Do you want to talk more about everything? I mean we never got to the talk you wanted earlier."

Ariel's eyes searched his. "No. I think we have told this story so many times to so many people we understand each other perfectly, and you will never try to solve big problems without me anymore, right?"

"Right. I promise from now on I will always be an open book."

Ariel bit her lip. "About those journals. I want you to know I only read a few. I read the first one, which was so sweet by the way, and then picked up where you decided to move back home. I don't need to know every little detail about your life, just the important things that affect us and whatever else you decide to share. Okay?"

Kyle nodded. "Okay."

Seeing the warmth and love returning to her eyes Kyle kissed Ariel and full of hope and promise for their future to-gether.

Epilogue

Ariel looked at her full little car and gave an exhausted sigh. It has been four months since the night everything had happened with Alan. Ultimately, Alan had been able to give a plea deal to prevent having to serve time with a home arrest instead of in a prison. As it turned out he had information on several corrupt police officers, city elected officials and other dealers in the surrounding area. The files that Zeke had kept was an insurance policy on just about everyone he was connected with. Alan's wife had reached out to Kyle to thank him and Ariel on their help for her husband. Her cancer had returned but Alan was at least able to help her as needed at home.

Today, Ariel was starting a new chapter in her life. She was moving in with Kyle. He was still everything she ever wanted. He was attentive, supportive, funny, and it didn't hurt that the sex was amazing. She watched as Derek came down the stairs with the last small box. He quirked a smile at her and said, "Hey, I think you forgot something in there."

"No, I didn't. The place is empty."

"I think you better take another look at the second bedroom."

That was odd. She had emptied that room a week ago. She didn't even open that door since she cleared it out. Deciding to humor her brother she went back inside and opened the door.

She gasped as she was greeted by the warm glow coming from what must have been at least fifty candles. Her gaze moved to the center of the room where she saw a little red wagon covered in flowers and a small pedestal holding a little black velvet box. Then she felt her hand being held by another. She turned to see Kyle smiling at her, looking a bit nervous. He led her further into the room and picked up the velvet box.

Her eyes filled with tears as she watched him drop to one knee. Looking as vulnerable as she had ever seen him, he finally began to speak. "Ariel, years ago I asked you to be my princess. I was enchanted by you, and I used this wagon to rescue you from the woods. I told you then that I would always find you, but what I didn't tell you was that I also made a silent promise that I would always love you. I thought that I was supposed to wait for the right time and for things to be perfect, but what I realized is that it will always be perfect as long as you are standing beside me. So, as your prince with a broken crown, these are my honest words... I will always be true, always put you above all others and be the luckiest man alive if you would agree to be my wife."

Ariel couldn't speak. This man was giving her everything, and he already had her heart and soul. Since words seemed to be stuck in her throat, all she could do was nod her head enthusiastically. Kyle beamed as he placed the ring on her finger and then picked her up in a circle and kissed her with a fierce passion she could feel to her core.

One he put her down he gave her another small gentle kiss. "Are you ready to go live in your new castle?"

Feeling light and filled with love for him she smiled and said, "Absolutely."

A Blossom Hills Romance

Don't miss these other great titles in A Blossom Hills Romance Series

Book 1

A Taste of Sweetness

http://mybook.to/ATasteofSweetness

Book 2

Images of Devotion

http://mybook.to/ImagesofDevotion

About the Author

Kate grew up in the suburbs of Cincinnati, Ohio. While attending school, she participated in writing competitions and workshops for young adults. After college, she stayed in Cincinnati and chased her passion of helping others with her work in social services and volunteering in the community.

Shortly after marrying her husband, Tom, they moved to Phoenix, Arizona where she again found a love for reading and writing romance books. When she isn't writing new stories she can be found out with her husband taking in a movie, playing mini golf, shopping or cuddling with their dog Sally.

Read more at https://www.katealexanderauthor.com/.